"Awesome, action-packed right from the very beginning."

—*BookLoons.com*

"OMG, this book was so freaking good. So GOOD! I loved the world! I loved the characters! I loved everything about this book and cannot wait for the next in the series to come out."

—*Smitten with Reading*

"I have found a new series to drool over..."

—*Confessions of a Toxic Friend*

"A heart-warming romance, kick-ass powers, a tender-hearted brooding vampire, and so many other yummy characters..."

—*The ParaRomance Club*

"It's the gray areas between good and evil that become the focus of this well-plotted and exciting paranormal romance."

—*Debbie's Book Bag*

Praise for *Deliver Me from Temptation*

"Intriguing paranormal creatures and torment abound... The sex is great, and the ending is fun."

—*Booklist*

PRINCE OF SHADOWS

TES HILAIRE

sourcebooks
casablanca

To my wonderful street team, Hilaire's Hellions.
Imagination is just the beginning of the
journey to completing a book. Your help and
encouragement dispels the darkness along the way.

Prologue

Four months before…

VALIN FOUGHT TO BREATHE THROUGH THE LAYERS OF dust shifting through the stale air of the cave. One aftershock tremor after another rumbled through the cavern.

He blinked, striving to make out anything in the darkness. Nothing could have possibly survived that blast. Even Valin's skin felt singed, and as a Paladin he was supposedly immune from the burn of heavenly light. Unlike the vamps and demons they'd been battling in this godforsaken place.

He shuddered, dread settling in his core. Gritting his teeth, he pushed out with his senses, striving for any signs of a living, breathing essence. Nothing. Absolutely fucking nothing.

Because you're too late. Just like you were with Angeline. Too late to protect her. Too late to save your unborn child. And now your little vampire is dead too.

He clenched his jaw. He would not believe Gabriella was dead. She might have been a vampire, but she was *his* vampire.

"Fuck." He raked his hands down over his face. "What the hell am I thinking?" He'd just met the pint-sized pain in the ass. He knew nothing about her other than that she was stubborn, annoying, and…brave. So fucking brave. Brave enough to face down *him*, her

natural enemy, while chained to a wall. Brave enough
to stand against her master. Brave enough to run toward
death in some vain hope that she might save the lives of
two others. Stupid, impossible brat.

Swearing, he pushed off the clammy wall, stumbling
along, randomly picking tunnels whenever he came to
a split. Maybe she made it far enough. She was fast and
determined. Maybe…

His boot kicked into something soft, causing a pile of
ash to billow up around him, clogging his lungs.

He ground to a halt, breath trapped tight behind his
ribs as he sifted his hand through the cloud of ash. So
soft, so light, and all that was left of a life. His hand
began to shake, pain radiating from behind his ribs,
even though he knew, *knew* it could just as likely be
some random bloodsucker who'd decided to take their
chances in these caves rather than facing the Paladin
who'd come to eradicate them.

This wasn't her. He'd prove it. He clenched his hand
into a fist, taking another step into the darkness. He just
had to find her first.

Chapter 1

IT'S NOT HER BLOOD. NOT GABBY.

Valin's hand shook as he splayed his palm across the splotch marring the pavement. The slick fluid masqueraded as nothing more than the leftovers of a long-sitting vehicle, though it wasn't. Black, oily blood. Blood from a creature so inherently malicious that its dark essence had leached into the blacktop upon its death, leaving a pall of evil.

Definitely not Gabby's blood. Sitting back on his heels, he dragged his hands down over his face, half-surprised to feel the stubble on his jaw. Endless nights of searching, sleepless days of worrying. How long could he keep this up? Four months of nothing, then last week he'd seen her. It had been from a distance on a dark street and she'd been wearing a wig, but something deep in his gut had screamed that it was her.

He had to find her—alive and well, and most importantly, before any of his brothers did. Every time one of his Paladin brethren claimed another kill, his gut tightened into knots, his fear that this time one of his seemingly offhand inquiries would yield a tale of a redheaded vampire's demise and he would completely lose it.

Like you did when Angeline died?

He swore, closing his eyes. It would be worse than when he'd lost Angeline. She'd been his best friend, their unborn child his heart and hope, but Gabby…*She's my mate. My very soul.* He hadn't even claimed her yet and it seemed the universe was conniving with friend and foe alike to take her from him too.

"What is it, Valin?" a voice rose from behind him. "Can you tell what happened?"

Valin tensed and twisted, quickly closing in on his shields as he glared up at the blond Paladin who'd snuck up behind him. And wasn't that just great? Caught having a "moment" by Bennett, the one Paladin who had a shit's chance in hell of reading him. Luckily the empathic warrior didn't seem to be attributing Valin's case of nerves with his spiraling grasp on his sanity, his focus solely on the stain at Valin's feet.

"I can say pretty definitively that someone killed a merker here."

"Dead?" Bennett's brow winged up. "How, though?"

Valin shrugged. It wasn't that he didn't want to answer the question, more that he wished he knew what the answer was. It wasn't easy killing a merker. Slice 'em up, fry the heart and gray matter in His light, and serve was the only tried-and-true recipe he knew of, but given the potency of the residual stain, it was just as obvious that someone had found another way.

"Bloody hell." Bennett took a deep breath, running his hand back and forth across his short, spiky hair. "It's one of them, isn't it?"

Valin's brow shot up. As in one of the gifted humans who'd managed to send the council all in a tizzy after their little surprise break-in last week? Not only had the group's actions compromised the safety of the Paladin sanctuary Haven, but the misguided band had just enough power to be dangerous—to themselves, to others, and to the random merker, it would seem.

"You think?" he replied, sarcasm dripping heavily in his tone. Not like there were many other options.

Bennett didn't rise to Valin's sarcasm. His face was solemn as he met Valin's gaze. "No Paladin has reported a kill in this area, so yes, I do think so."

Valin sucked in a breath, acid churning in a stomach already raw with nerves at the mention of the daily kill reports the council had taken to posting. Eleven vampires and three succubi in the last week and a half alone.

But none of them were Gabby. She's tough. Smart.

A memory surfaced, Gabriella's lips curling to reveal her pretty little fangs as she jerked at the manacles. *"Do I look like the fucking enemy?"* she'd demanded, her sinful red locks sticking to the trails of salty tears coating her cheeks. The truth was she hadn't—which was his reason for not immediately staking her. Chained in that dilapidated coalhouse, a cloud-break away from extinction, attitude had poured off the pint-sized vamp, exposing a backbone that may well have been bent, but never broken. He'd known instinctively that she, like his brother Roland, had had no choice in her turning, and the IV bag lying on the floor beside her proved she fought her nature tooth and nail.

Unfortunately, it wouldn't matter to a Paladin that she'd been turned against her will. Didn't matter that she was free now, her maker Christos having fallen to Roland's blade. Nor did it matter that Gabby had always seemed to bat for the good guys. Nope, the only thing that would matter to his brothers if they were to come face to face with her was her heritage. Part succubus and all vamp—not exactly the credentials to put on an application for the angel-blood-only club.

"Hey, mate…you in there?"

Valin blinked, taking in Bennett's pinched face, the suspicion burgeoning in his eyes. Not cool. He didn't need his Paladin brothers watching him too closely. Play along, go with the flow…find her. The rest of the shit he could figure out later.

"I'll be fine," Valin replied, tugging up his hoodie's zipper. "Just cold and cranky."

"Right then." Bennett blew out a deep breath as he searched the less than lively street around them. "So, any ideas how we're going to track down who did this?"

"Yeah, I got one," Valin replied, carefully stepping around the stain.

"What's that?"

"Find the prey and you'll find the hunter." He curved his lips up in a semblance of a smile. "Let's go find some bad guys."

"Really, Aaron, you don't have to stay," Gabriella said, emphasizing the words with a full-on stare down. It was the umpteenth time she'd told him to leave, and the umpteenth method she'd tried, but she'd yet to have any success convincing her self-assigned tagalong to leave her side. His lack of compliance was really beginning to put a chip in her ego of badass-extraordinaire, not to mention a throb in her fangs.

"I'll stay. Unless you want to try and make me leave." He flashed a grin, showing off the chip he'd gotten in his front tooth last week when she'd attempted to do just that. Gabby ground her fangs against her lower eyeteeth. Tempting, but then she'd have to explain to Jacob why she couldn't seem to keep his little brother in one piece.

Sighing, she turned her attention back to the almost deserted street. From here, in this fenced-off playground, she had a great view in both directions, including the old restaurant-turned-club down the way. In another time, or perhaps just another lifetime, she might've raised an eyebrow at having a playground so close to a club that catered to the depraved, but with the things she'd lived through and seen, it came nowhere near a WTF on her radar screen. Besides, it really was the perfect location to scope out the club. A good hoodie, some torn jeans, and boots, and as long as she didn't get close enough for a face-to-face, she could still pass for a high school delinquent looking to score some on the teeter-totter.

Too bad Aaron in his camo pants and clean-cut crop of brown hair ruined the image.

Maybe she should just bite him and get it over with. It would be one way of deterring him from following her everywhere.

She swallowed, jerking her gaze away when she realized she'd focused on his neck. Not that it helped. Short of cutting off her ears, there was no way to ignore the pounding heartbeat still throbbing against her eardrums.

"Eats garlic. Probably tastes bad. And who would fix the base's computer?"

Aaron twisted his head, forehead bunched. "What are you muttering on about?"

"All the reasons I shouldn't eat you for dinner."

His brown eyes widened, but then he laughed, Adam's apple bobbing. "Good one. But I'm still not leaving."

She shrugged. "It's your jugular."

And okay, even saying that as a joke was bad, because as he shook his head, chuckling, she noticed she was running her tongue over her fangs.

Goddamn. Would a vampire just show up already? She was getting really sick of scoping out club after club looking for action. This one had all the traits of being prime pickings for the prey she hunted. Its patrons certainly bought into the vamp culture. Hell, some even filed their teeth. It was the type of place she hated—she had no respect for anyone who craved the life she'd been forced to live—and she would have walked away in a heartbeat but for one thing: She needed a replacement. Her last unwitting spy in the coven had gone blip and fallen off the radar, which meant the blood bond had been destroyed and the vamp was dead. Ergo she had no fucking idea what the vamps' newest leader, Stephan, planned to do next. Which was not cool, given his ultimate goal appeared to be capturing and turning as much of the gifted population of the city as possible, presumably to make his own little army of super-powered vampires.

Gabby couldn't let that happen. Ganelon, with his army of demons and merkers, was bad enough. Though maybe if she were lucky, *really* lucky, Lucifer's right-hand man and general would catch wind of Stephan's delusions of grandeur, take offense, and wipe him out before he could complete his recruitment plan.

And why don't you wish for hell to freeze over while you're at it, Gabby?

Aaron shifted, arching his back. "Tell me again why we don't wait inside? Maybe get a drink?"

"That's just it. I'd want a drink."

He narrowed his eyes, for the first time looking at all concerned. "You *are* looking a little peaked. Have you…you know…lately?"

She glared at him. Really? For three months she'd worked with the small militia of gifted humans that Jacob had enlisted, turning them from a hodgepodge bunch of wannabe warriors into the well-oiled fighting machines they were now. And yeah, perhaps they weren't quite ready to step into their Paladin cousins' shoes and take on Ganelon's army yet, but they could at least hold their own in the smaller skirmishes against the fangy recruiters out there. Which was a far cry from when Gabby had rescued Jacob and a handful of his groupies from shit creek back at the end of the summer.

Jacob, ever the opportunist, had immediately tried to convert Gabby to his cause. The idea of leaving a legacy behind when she died—something more than her former stepdaddy and mommy dearest had planned for her—had sounded appealing. So Gabby agreed to some part-time help. The only condition being that no one ever, ever, ever pry into her personal life—past or present—and that included the who, what, where, when, or how she took care of her…needs. So far no one had broken that rule. Until now.

"Because, if you…you know…if you needed to…" Aaron swallowed.

"I don't feed from humans," she snarled, then pretty much ruined it by flashing her fangs as she did. *Way to go, Gabby.*

His mouth cracked, turning up into a boyish grin. "No

problem then. Considering I'm not one hundred percent human, right?"

She gave him a penetrating look...and fell into his thoughts. An image of her, riding him, then bending down to sink her teeth into his neck...

"Oh, God, Aaron, stop!" She clamped down on her shields, cutting off her accidental intrusion into his mind.

"What? What did I do? Am I doing it again?" He glanced around, his brow puzzling up at the unchanged landscape.

"Don't. Don't even think it, much less say it."

He snapped his mouth closed, color flooding his cheeks as he finally clued in to what had happened. He turned away, doing his best to at least pretend he was focused on the street on the other side of the chain-link fence as he attempted to shore up his shields.

Gabby squirmed, trying to ease the prickling sensation riding through her limbs that urged her to get up and run from the graphic images that still coated the inside of her skull after that little mind bump. But that wasn't going to help, not when she'd have to face him again later. And it wasn't like this was the first time it had happened, either.

"Listen. I'm sorry. I really am. But *a*, it wouldn't be safe and *b*, you'd regret it after."

"Isn't that my concern, not yours?" he asked softly, his voice filled with the longing she'd been valiantly trying to ignore and couldn't now that he'd said something.

Damn him. She didn't want to do this. She normally didn't give a crap what people thought of her, but she wasn't cruel. Even so, short of the timelessly detested *I'm just not interested*, what could be said? Not to take it personally, that she didn't think she could ever feel that way about anyone? And even if she could scrape up some feelings for him, that any sort of intimacy they shared would be a one-way street? Both succubus and vampire sex, at their core, were about power and control. Even before she'd been turned she'd been taught that.

She rolled her shoulders, fending off memories as she prepped herself for the heartbreak ahead when something tickled her senses. Twisting, she pushed back the edge of her hoodie, scoping out the dimly lit sidewalk. Sure enough there came a vampire, dressed to party in bicep-clinging black silk and snugly fit trousers. And what do you know? He'd brought a few buddies with him. One of which she knew…intimately.

"Lawrence…" she hissed, already imagining the hot warmth of his blood trickling down her throat before she stuffed her knife up under his ribs.

One of the others would have to do for her new puppet.

She smiled, and something of her eagerness must have slipped through her shields because Lawrence drew up short, causing one of his buddies to bump into him. The lead vampire took another couple steps before he, too, noticed something was wrong, his head lifting, tongue flicking out as if he could taste her on the air.

Not likely. The only thing in the air was the standard mix of human sweat, desperation, and the vices they used to drown the latter out with…oh, that and death. Death was definitely in the air tonight.

"Lawrence? You know one of them?" Aaron whispered, reminding her that she wasn't alone on this hunt. She flicked a glance at him, annoyance spiking again before she tamped it back down. *Eats garlic, computer whiz*…and she had other prey in mind.

"Yeah, but I think it's past time to end the relationship." She stood. "Either get ready or get lost. Just don't get in my way." And with that she whistled, raising her hand for a gleeful wave at the scowling group of vamps.

Chapter 2

"PAY DIRT. LOOKS LIKE WE AREN'T THE ONLY ONES hunting tonight," Valin said, nodding to the skirmish going on near the back edge of the playground. It was one hell of a fight, an opinion validated by a staggering couple who exited a nearby club, took one glance at the violent encounter, then sobered up enough to scurry down the street in the opposite direction.

"Should we help out or wait until they're done and follow?" Bennett asked, stopping beside Valin.

Valin considered the fight. Six against two. It would have been staggering odds but for the fact that the two fighting were obviously not your average humans. The air around the man wearing the camouflage pants practically sizzled with power, overshadowing any power signature that the petite blonde might have. Not that she seemed to need to resort to any sort of magic given how she wielded her knife and axe like a vengeful Valkyrie. Not a big axe, granted, just one that could be clipped on to a tool belt, but the thing must have been seriously sharp for how she cut through the vamps as if they were butter. And just watching her seductively lethal dance had him buzzing with adrenaline.

"I don't see why they should have all the fun," he finally said.

Bennett nodded, then reached under the back of his jacket. There was a snap, and he pulled out his curved blade.

Valin blinked, rocking back on his heels. "Hey, where'd you get that?"

Last he knew all the Paladin weapons were being kept in a shielded trunk down in one of Senior Calhoun's off-limits storage rooms. His paranoia about the blades falling into the wrong hands (or being exposed to the general public or other such blah blah blah) was beginning to eclipse logic.

"Think I'm going to go hunting without my knife?" Bennett shook his head, disgust plainly written on his face. "Not bloody likely."

"And you didn't bring me mine?"

Bennett shrugged. "I figured you wouldn't want to lose it if you had to ghost."

There was that point. He lost his clothes and anything on him any time he entered the shade, but still…"You wouldn't have offered to carry it for me?"

"What am I? Your valet?" Bennett called as he dashed across the street.

Valin swore and jogged after him, still in shock that easygoing, it's-all-good, sure-thing boss Bennett had gone against council edict and stolen back his knife.

"And where are your *cojones*?" Valin muttered to himself as he scanned for something to use other than his bare hands.

There were a few ways to kill a vamp—sunlight, stabbing it in the heart, lopping off its head, snapping the neck, and severing the spinal cord—but using a Paladin blade was certainly the easiest. One good plunge with that sucker, heart or not, and there was a better than good chance that the vampire would be dust.

A mangled pallet sat half under a pile of broken

bricks nearby, left over from an attempt at re-facing the building it sat beside. Valin jogged over, grabbed a prime piece of the splintered wood, and yanked it free. A couple nails came with it, but he pounded those in quickly with a brick. And look at that, a stake.

He cursed the time it took him to run down the street, climb over the chain-link, and join the fray, but he didn't want to ghost—not when he'd lose his perfectly good weapon, and not when he hoped to talk a little business after. Birthday suits were fine and dandy for the right occasion, but not when trying to make friends and influence people.

By the time he arrived, Bennett had already taken care of one vamp and was helping the tall, camo-clad guy take on three more. That left one for the axe-wielding Valkyrie and one for himself.

He whistled, drawing the attention of the vampire currently circling the woman and her dancing partner. The vampire—a big motherfucker—glared, then chuckled at Valin, who probably didn't look all that imposing to the behemoth, even with the splintered piece of wood.

Valin smiled back.

The vampire hissed and charged. Easy enough to dodge, and Valin even got in a good kick to the vampire's kidneys. The vampire roared and charged again, this time coming away with a busted knee and a nice gash across its ribs from Valin's rough-edged stake.

His opponent hesitated, his eyes gleaming a wary crimson.

"It's all in how you use it, big guy," Valin jibed. The vamp made a low, back-of-the-throat growl and came at Valin again. They danced, Valin settling into a dodge and attack pace that was guaranteed to wear his partner down, eventually allowing for a final strike with the makeshift stake into his opponent's chest cavity.

Through the cloud of ash, Valin saw the blonde go down, her boots losing purchase in the thick puddle of blood she'd made with that handy axe of hers. Her partner yelled from the other side of the playground, power pulsing and the lights in the street flickering as he threw his knife at the vampire standing over her. At the same time she rolled, slicing at the vamp's ankle. The vampire screamed, crumbling as the knife sailed harmlessly over it where it dinged into the nearby building. Unfortunately for her, the vampire fell *on* her, its anger overcoming the pain. A hand snaked out, grabbing her axe arm and twisting it into an unnatural position. A quick flash and its other hand had latched on to her side, dragging her further under him.

She swore, kicking and punching as the vampire snapped at her throat.

Yeah, not going to let that happen. No dinner for tall, dark, and deadly. Valin ran to the struggling pair on the cement. A quick plunge of his stake and right-o, disappear-o. Ignoring the lingering cloud of dust, he reached down to offer a hand, but the blonde was already up, her axe ready as she eyed him warily.

Whoa…and that was a whole lot of blood pouring out of a gash at the crux of her neck. "Are you okay?"

"Never better," she ground out from between clenched teeth, even as she tossed her hair. Ignoring the bloody mess on her shoulder, she struck a stubborn hand-on-hip pose.

Valin sucked in a breath. Holy friggen fuck. Gabby.

Never would he forget that pose—or the bite of attitude that came with it. And those eyes...well, he might as well lie down, roll over, and play dead because all she had to do was look at him with those emerald greens and he was her slave.

Even as his heart pounded against the confines of his rib cage, Valin forced himself not to show any reaction. Not with Bennett here. And not when Gabby had obviously gone out of her way to disguise herself. It wasn't just the wig or the stage makeup she must have used to add a good decade or more to her physical age, but holy crap, were those socks in that bra or had she invested in some enhancements?

Why was she in disguise? Her shields were what were important for flying low under the radar around any supernatural being, and if she were worried about being recognized, then she shouldn't be going after vampires in the first place. That left, what? Hiding from the Paladin? Maybe, but none of them, other than Logan, Roland, and himself, knew who and what she was. Roland wouldn't hurt her, and Logan, who probably wouldn't either, wasn't exactly up to doing much of anything these days anyway. That left...crap. Him. That left him.

The protein bar he ate earlier curdled in his stomach before he realized he was overreacting. She probably just wanted her new friends to treat her with respect. Must be hard being over a half-century old and stuck looking so young.

"Fuck me," he muttered, dragging his gaze from her newfound assets and back to the struggle that had drawn dangerously close once more.

"What?"

He jerked his chin. "Behind you."

She started to pivot, but he grabbed her quicker, shoving her aside as he stepped in to engage the vamp. This one must have grabbed camo's thrown weapon, and as cool as Valin's stake was, it didn't hold up against the jagged knife. The wood splintered further. Rather than keeping a useless weapon, Valin let it go, twirling under the attack and…

"Since you boys seem to have this covered…" Gabby called, slipping away from the edge of the fight.

"Shit…" He ducked the next attack that had come because of his distraction. "G— Wait!"

He barely managed to grab the vampire's knife arm as it plunged down toward his chest. A struggle ensued, mainly Valin trying to keep hold of the lethal knife arm as he simultaneously tried to avoid his throat being ripped out. A blast of pain erupted in his side from the vampire's balled fist. Valin pushed away, distancing himself from the knife as he struck out with a quick kick to the vampire's knee. The vampire swore, taking a stumbling step to the side. Enough time for Valin to scoot out of the immediate strike zone and make a quick scan of the street. Empty.

<<Bennett?!>>

<<Need help?>> He felt the other Paladin hesitate.
<<No, damn it. But I can't get away to track them.>>
<<Already on it.>>

Satisfied that Bennett would keep them in his sights until Valin could catch up, Valin settled into the fight. A seemingly endless three minutes later, using the same strategy of dodge and attack, he finally managed to rile the vampire into making his last mistake. Compensating for a leg that couldn't heal fast enough from Valin's continued kicks, the vampire lunged too fast and too far. Valin easily dodged, following through with a reverse roundhouse kick, taking the vamp down. Valin was on him before he could get his hands under himself to push up. One hand on the jaw, back of the head, twist, and…*snap!*

"Goddamn it!" he choked on the ash, trying to fan it out of his face. *<<Please tell me you're still tailing them,>>* he cast to Bennett.

<<Sorry, mate.>> There was a pause as if Bennett were distracted, then, *<<They slipped into the subway.>>*

<<And you didn't follow them?>>

<<No. Bloody chit screamed for security. I had to dodge out real fast. I'm camping in a pub as we speak.>>

Valin sagged down onto the pavement, the adrenaline crash hitting him like a freight train. Gabby had been here. Less than five feet from him. And he'd lost her, again.

<<Valin? What do you want to do, mate?>>

Valin stared at the puddle of sticky blood, thinking of how not all of it was the vamps. Some of that had been Gabby's too. A lot of it, actually.

She's okay. Okay enough to run away, at least.

<<Valin?>>

He rubbed his hands over his face, forcing his legs back under him as he stood. Looked like his plans for a reunion had been put on hold. *<<I'll meet you back at Haven.>>*

<<Calling it a night?>>

<<Yeah, we'll try again tomorrow.>> Only this time he'd be ready. There was no way Gabby would get a chance to run away from him again.

Gabby's heart hammered, her skin itching under the thin coating of sweat as she stared at the fifteen cement steps that might as well be Mount Everest for the Herculean effort it was going to take to climb them on her shaking legs. She couldn't decide if she was edgy or exhausted. Probably both.

Nothing had gone as planned. She hadn't been able to get away from Aaron to feed. Nor had she obtained a new recruit to spy on the coven with. On top of those failures had come the last straw: the run-in with the damn Paladin…or rather the *Paladins*. Not that she was going to think about him, no, *them*, right now. Not yet. Not until she was alone and could deal privately with her urge to scream. Or break something. Or damn it, curl up and cry.

First she had to climb those stairs.

She did it, though, as Aaron hovered beside her, his face pinched in concern, hand outstretched and ready to catch if need be. Good thing he didn't actually touch her. She might not have been able to control herself.

Blood seeped from the base of her throat, the sticky warmth forking over her breast to drip down her cleavage and run down the underside of her arm, coating her T-shirt in the process. The coppery stench filled her nostrils, turning her stomach even as it woke the beast within.

Eats garlic. And his trick with the flickering lights had come at just the right moment during their fight to distract the vampire.

"Hold on." Aaron raced ahead. Gabby dragged

herself up the last couple steps as he punched in the code, then yanked the rusted metal door open for her. The moment she was through he was back by her side, hovering again. *Garlic, garlic, garlic...*

"You should check in with Jacob," she told him, and when he opened his mouth to argue she said, "I think I can make it from here." She smiled, careful to make sure her elongated fangs stayed covered. It must've looked more like a grimace if the dubious look on his young face was any indication.

His jaw tightened. "I think I'll see you to Shae first."

Gabby started to shake her head, but thought better of it. Their resident doctor tended to hold to a very old-school form of medicine. Take two aspirin and call me in the morning if you're still alive. Gabby figured she could be in and out in under thirty seconds if she played her cards right. And given that Aaron would probably hound her until she had, it was better to just get it over with...so she could get on with her private temper tantrum. Damn, but the cocky bastard had looked good fighting. But conceited. Still so fucking conceited.

Don't think of him, Gabby. Not yet.

They started down the hall. With each step, Gabby forced herself to walk just a little bit straighter, even though it cost her even more of her reserves.

She didn't need a doctor, she needed a donor.

Trying not to think about the meals-on-legs beside her—or the man she really wanted to take a chunk out of—she concentrated on her surroundings, which, okay, were not all that inspiring. Built sometime in the mid-1900s, the old private school had either gone bankrupt or moved on to newer, better pastures. Grimy vinyl flooring, falling tile ceilings, rusted-out stairwells; either scenario was likely, but Gabby had never asked which had led to the building's abandonment. Didn't care. Only thing she cared about was after the mortgage, water, and electric bills were paid, Jacob always had enough funds left over to spring for her rather long list of equipment suggestions. Like cots—one of which was in her own private little room—that right now seemed entirely too far away.

It didn't take them long to reach Shae's domain; the old nurse's office was just a short jog off the main hall. Aaron pushed the door open, chivalrously holding it for her. She stepped in and frowned. No Shae. Just the sparse room with its neatly organized counters and cabinets.

"Huh…maybe on the training floor," he said, even as he scanned the room again, like Shae might be hiding in a cabinet or something and jump out at any moment. "Why don't you settle in and I'll go find her, okay?"

"Sounds good." Gabby plunked her butt down in the pint-sized chair that hadn't been replaced yet. "I'll just sit right here."

He gave her a narrow-eyed look, but when all she did was blink up at him innocently, he nodded and left the room.

She gave it a full ten seconds before she hefted herself out of the low seat and made her way to the cabinet. Wipes, gauze, tape. Check, check, check. At the door she took a moment to listen in case he'd been waiting to see if she stayed. No sounds nearby, no smells—well, other than the general combination of dust, dirt, mildew, and fresh, hard-earned sweat that permeated the air of the school.

Feeling like a convict making an escape, she slipped through the door and started back for the main hall. Her own slice of home was one of the old conference rooms back behind the main office. Most of the others who crashed here had taken the larger rooms: the old classrooms, the principal, vice principal, and guidance office, the teachers' lounge. The small conference room had been overlooked due to its distinct lack of windows. Gabby was okay with not having a window. In fact, she was more comfortable that way. Though she'd come to love the sun, there was something about waking with its rays beating down on her that still sent a wave of terror through her blood.

She made it to her room with only one other run-in, and that wasn't really a run-in, more a quick head nod as one of the women soldiers zipped by, obviously not at all inclined to stop and chat. There were still some people here who weren't comfortable around a vampire—even if that vampire fought on the "good guys'" side and could walk in the light now due to Karissa's blood running through her veins. However, when Gabby pushed open the door to her room, she found the one woman here who was most definitely *not* afraid of her, to Gabby's never-ending frustration: Annie. The tall redhead might not hover like Aaron did, but she was just as annoying. At least as of recently, though Gabby supposed she would've been too had she been in the same situation.

If Gabby played an escaped convict, then Annie was an actual inmate. A week before, after overhearing a conversation between Gabby and Jacob about the vampires' latest plans, Annie had enlisted some of the younger recruits to take their own countermeasures.

Together they made their way into Haven's sacred halls in an attempt to deliver the intel. Somehow Annie had taken an offhand comment from Gabby to Jacob of "if you see Logan tell him…" to "find Logan by breaking into the Paladin sanctuary and tell him…" Needless to say, Annie hadn't exactly gotten a warm reception at Haven. The Paladin leader, Logan Calhoun's father, had pretty much tried to take them prisoner.

Jacob, upon hearing about the near kidnapping, had decided the Paladin leader actually had a damn good idea and forbade his headstrong daughter from ever leaving the base again without permission. Which, if Gabby had to guess, would be when Annie was fifty maybe?

"Have fun tonight?" Annie asked from where she sat with arms folded on the bed.

"No, actually. Your uncle is a royal pain in the neck."

"Ah…" She leaned forward, cocking her head as she looked Gabby over. "He give you that nice hickey then?" She pointed to Gabby's bloody neck.

"Ha-ha."

Annie smiled, leaning back against the wall. "He get in the way?"

Gabby grunted a noncommittal answer as she un-buckled her belt and dropped it, the knife and her axe on the floor to be cleaned later. Despite the fact that Aaron had put a nix on her feeding plans, he'd also probably saved her ass. Six vamps to one might've been slightly heavy odds even for her, especially in her current depleted state.

"Huh. If I'd been there I bet we could have kicked some major ass."

"Maybe." Gabby glanced over her shoulder at Annie, wincing a little at the pull on her wound. "But we also ran into two Paladin. And they probably would have kicked ours, staked me, then dragged you back by your hair to their cave."

Annie curled her lip back in disgust. "Doubt that. We could have run if need be, and then they wouldn't have been able to find us."

"You think so?" Gabby unzipped the hoodie, frowned as she pulled one of the disinfecting swabs from her pants, tore it open, and dabbed at the wound. And hell's fire that hurt. Grimacing, she went on. "Then how is it that I can find you? How is it that I can always track you down, no matter where you are?"

"I don't know," Annie replied a bit uncertainly. "Do I have some sort of scent that you can smell because of…well…"

"My senses are good, but not *that* good. Smelling you only works if you're nearby and there aren't a lot of other masking scents." She tossed down the bloody swab—three of those weren't enough anyway—and turned to Annie. "But I know you're there from almost a full mile away."

"Fine." Annie folded her arms, taking on a distinctive pout. "I don't know then. You going to tell me how?"

Gabby tapped her head. "You're not on my radar. And neither is anyone around you. All I have to do is look for the black hole and I know where you are. Do you think I'm the only one who might notice that?"

Annie frowned, her brow drawing into a vee above her nose. Gabby watched as the new worry and concern warred with her frustration of being contained, her mouth finally thinning into a stubborn line. "Fine. I just won't pull at all."

Gabby gnawed the inside of her lip. Not "pulling," as Annie called it, was much easier said than done. A null, which is what Annie was, tended to naturally eliminate the magic energy around them no matter where they were or what they were doing. Even now, when she was obviously making a concentrated effort to choke it back, she couldn't fully tamp the instinct. To completely stop took extreme willpower. And besides, to not use her gift meant that any baddy who happened to clue into her little oddity would be at their full power, leaving Annie to fight with wits and weapons alone unless she pulled, which again might draw more enemies. Definitely a catch-22. "That would probably be better, but maybe you should talk to Jacob. He might have another solution."

Annie huffed, flopping across the cot. "Yeah, wrap me up in foam and assign people to stand behind me with catcher's mitts just in case I fall."

Despite herself, Gabby found her lips trying to creep up. Jacob *was* essentially doing that with his daughter. "Your dad cares about you, Annie. That's not a bad thing."

"If this is caring, I'd hate to see what happens when he doesn't," she said sullenly, waving her hand dramatically at the building around her.

Gabby's lips thinned as memories assailed her. If Annie wanted to compare notes on the unfairness of her life, then Gabby was almost willing to do so. Only Gabby had never been very good at all the sharing crap.

"Annie, I genuinely hope you never have to find out."

"Find out what?"

"What would happen if he didn't care."

Annie's eyes dimmed, a distinctive frown pulling on her lips. *Yeah, don't like to think of that, do you?* Gabby's satisfaction was short-lived when Annie huffed again, visibly shrugging off Gabby's words as she sat up, her feet plopping hard on the floor.

"Whatever." Annie stood, brushing by Gabby. When she was halfway out the door, she paused, her face a storm cloud as she glared over her shoulder. "You know, you're not as badass as you think," she said, then marched out the door.

"I'm well aware," Gabby mumbled, but the door was already closed.

She took a deep breath. A long calming one. She should probably say something to Jacob about his daughter's frustrations. They were petty, sure, but if left unchecked they could lead to trouble. Of course everything with Annie recently seemed like it brought trouble, so he was probably already well aware. His strategy, however, of wrapping her up in bubble wrap and stuffing her in this box of a base was probably not the way to instill cooperation.

Not my problem. Nope, Gabby had other issues.

Pulling her bloodstained hoodie off the rest of the way, she inspected her mangled shoulder. It was already healing despite the inflicted torture of the disinfecting swab. Still, it had been close. Couple more inches to the left and she'd be missing her throat, which was much harder to heal, maybe not even possible post her Karissa-blood transfusion.

A lot had changed after Roland's mate's blood had

been forced on her. Karissa's Paladin blood seemed to have negated a good number of Gabby's vampire characteristics. Being able to withstand the light was definitely a bonus and was something she'd been extremely grateful of when she hadn't fried to a crisp in that cave four months ago, but much to her continued frustration, she still couldn't handle real food. Her strength had also waned a bit, though it was better now that she was consistently training. All that training made her realize how much she'd relied on her vampire abilities before. Not that they were gone, just...dimmed.

Sighing, Gabby pulled off her blond wig and tossed it aside. Her red hair tumbled down in a curtain of lackluster waves. She rubbed the bridge of her nose, hoping to ease the stabbing headache that had gotten worse during the round with Annie.

When had she gotten so old? Four months ago that would have been her pouting and stomping around, but now all she ever felt was tired. Tired of the constant war. Tired of looking over her shoulder for enemies, some made by her own choices, but many made because of what she was as much as who. She was so damn tired. Tired of...everything.

She leaned in closer to the faded mirror that she'd hung on the wall, her hand jittering as she raised it to poke at the faint wrinkles that appeared when she squinted her eyes. Crow's-feet. She had goddamn crow's-feet now.

Too long since my last feeding. Not that it would help all that much. She could bathe in blood and it wouldn't erase the aging of her body. But it would, at least, give her more energy and keep her from biting the people she'd promised to help—even if some of them were annoying and deserved it.

"Hell's fire!" She spun around, hands on hips as she paced the small room. She was going to have to slip out while Aaron wasn't watching and go hunting again. Not that she dared go tonight, not with the Paladin sniffing around. And not just any Paladin. *Him.*

God, Valin.

She stopped, head tipped back as she took a long, deep breath. The uncovered bulb burned against her closed lids, but that wasn't what she saw. What she saw was Valin's face. That cocky devil-may-care grin, the dancing eyes that did nothing to conceal the wealth of pain he so obviously tried to hide. She'd never forget their first meeting and the moment when the disgust and disdain for what she was vanished from his bourbon gaze, his mask sloughing off as he peered further, the brief flare of surprise when he saw her for who she *could* be if not for her vampire heritage. That moment hadn't lasted nearly long enough. It had taken him less than a moment to start closing off the barriers. Slamming up the walls.

Not that their meeting mattered. There hadn't even been a flicker of recognition tonight. And it had nothing to do with the fact that she'd been wearing a wig.

Crow's-feet. Dead eyes. I'm the epitome of the walking dead. Only I'm not dead. Not since that night.

She turned back to the mirror, laying her hand upon the reflective surface, watched the steam that indicated the transfer of her own body heat to the cold glass. Still a surprise to her after all these months.

Fire pulsed through her veins.

A fire that was eating her from the inside out.

She leaned forward, tipping her head against the cool glass. "Nope, definitely not grave material yet, Gabby. But don't worry, you'll be there real soon."

Chapter 3

THEIR SECURITY SUCKED.

Valin looked around the dingy cafeteria turned mess hall of the old school he'd infiltrated, his lip curled back in disgust at the grime-covered flooring under his bare feet. Lax security and no maid service either.

A click of a gun brought his attention back to the crowd of wannabe warriors that had surrounded him the moment he'd fallen out of the shade. Okay, almost no security. That assortment of guns and knives would do a fine job at turning him to Swiss cheese if he wasn't careful. Thankfully the redheaded Amazon who first nulled his powers had been whisked out of the room within moments of his appearance and he could ghost again if needed. Not that he planned to, but if there were no other options he'd do so.

"It's okay. I'm not here to cause trouble. I only want to talk to Gabriella."

By the number of narrowed eyes he got and the way the tall, lean, brown-haired man's finger tensed over the trigger, Valin guessed mentioning Gabby's name hadn't been the right thing to say. Obviously they weren't about to buy into the whole I-come-in-peace, take-me-to-your-leader crap. Smart. He wouldn't have either. Though it wasn't like he had anything dangerous on him—couldn't exactly hide anything.

Pure dumb fucking luck. That's how he'd found

them. They'd been working in a radial search from their encounter in Williamsburg the other night when an overheard projective thought had allowed him to take a bead on the mind of one of their less experienced soldiers. He'd had to resort to ghosting to trail the two men coming off their patrol, but being without clothes or a weapon was a small price to pay for following them back to their base. Even if it did put him in kind of an awkward position now…being held naked at gunpoint and all.

Rather than digging himself into a bigger hole, he took his twiddle-his-thumbs time while waiting for something to happen—hopefully besides a firing squad—to tag Bennett. Not the easiest of tasks given the heavy shields on the place, but he managed, probably because he was inside reaching out rather than the other way around.

<<*Found 'em,*>> he told Bennett once the connection was established.

<<*Where are you?*>> Bennett's projected thought sounded distant and hollow, testament that the Paladin—who was almost as good as Logan and Calhoun Senior at projective thought—was having his own troubles circumventing their shields. Tough shields indeed.

<<*Old school, a few blocks over from Flatbush Avenue just off Flushing. Grab my stuff, would you?*>>

<<*On my way.*>>

<<*I'll tell them to roll out the welcome wagon.*>>

"My friend's coming over to say hi too," he told his band of gun-toting groupies. "Tall, blond, British accent. Don't shoot him when he shows up, 'kay? He has my clothes."

"What a shame," someone said from the back of the group. Valin was pretty sure it wasn't sarcasm, and similarly sure the husky voice was a woman's. Well, that was one out of a dozen or so who probably wouldn't go postal on him at least.

An awkward five minutes ensued. Valin figured it was a toss-up to see who got there first—Bennett, Gabby, or the person in charge of this shindig. Turned out it was the last, though he was followed almost immediately by a tightly packed group of men surrounding a familiar blond head. And yeah, Valin couldn't be sure this guy was the leader of this hodgepodge base of operations, but he was fairly certain. Tall, muscled, and bearing scars on every available bit of exposed skin, the older man oozed calm confidence. Of course, the fact that everyone's gaze at one point in time during his walk across the cafeteria met up with, checked in, then resumed their task of playing guard dog or dashed off to do something else if given a mere nod of his head was a real clue in too.

<<*All good?*>> He cast the thought into the room, not caring who overheard this conversation with Bennett. Besides, it was always good to know what you were up against and when at least a half-dozen other minds jumped into the stream he wasn't all that surprised.

Oh yeah, Senior was not going to be happy with the amount of power these less-than-pure-bloods had.

<<*Fine. Blokes took my cell and blade though.*>> The words were cast calmly, but Valin could sense the accompanying lash of annoyance.

<<*We'll get them back,*>> he assured him.

"As my men told you at the front doors, your weapon

will be returned when you leave," the man in front of
the group said over his shoulder to Bennett. What went
unsaid was *if* you leave. Wise, since saying things like
that tended to not invoke cooperation.

The man turned his hard stare on Valin. Valin suspected most men flinched under that brown gaze, so he
wasn't sure it was to his advantage or disadvantage that
he didn't. Another half-minute game of who will blink
first ensued before the man conceded a tie and spoke.

"I'm Jacob. My men said you wanted to speak with
someone?"

"Mind if I get dressed first?" Valin nodded at the
bundle of clothing Bennett was holding. Definitely some
major holes in security if they'd allowed Bennett to keep
them. Unless of course they'd already searched them and
found what was inside—Bennett wasn't the only one capable of pilfering his own blade from Senior's lockbox.

Jacob considered a moment, then nodded. The bundle was passed from Bennett through one of his guards
to Valin.

"Thanks." He took the clothes and started pulling them on. When he got to the knife that had been
wrapped in the center, he noted the immediate rise in
tension, including how the soldier who'd passed it to
him shuffled uncomfortably under Jacob's glaring look
and also how Valin's favorite fan shifted his grip on
his gun ever so slightly, as if he might either take the
shot…or maybe just forego the weapon and reach for
Valin's knife.

"Bennett's better natured than I. You try to take my
blade and I'll have to kill you," Valin said, injecting
what assurance he could with his calm tone.

Trigger Happy opened his mouth, but Jacob laid a hand on his shoulder, though his attention was all on Valin as he gave him a look that said he didn't appreciate being fucked with.

"Sorry. Just saying how it is." Valin quickly pulled on his T-shirt. And resisted smiling when the same soldier in the back—definitely a woman, a pretty little blonde, actually—sighed in disappointment.

Jacob flicked her a quelling glance before replying, "And I'm sorry, but you seemed to be under a misimpression when you came here."

"Oh? And what's that?"

"That we welcome visitors," Jacob said, his hand closing over the hilt of the K-bar on his belt. And though he was further away than at least three of those surrounding him, Valin thought it most likely that Jacob would be the first to connect if Valin did something threatening.

Valin flashed a grin instead. "Oh, I don't know. This kind of animosity makes me feel right at home. Right, Bennett?"

"You are a right bastard," Bennett replied, eliciting a brief glance from Jacob. "Valin's the black sheep," he explained.

"And he's the one you sent to say hello to your neighbors?" Jacob asked.

Bennett shrugged. "He's good at what he does."

"Ah. A spy then?"

"Hard to spy when you know I'm here, but yes, I do that too." Valin didn't expand. Scout, spy…assassin. Yup, he did it all. Not this time though. This time he was simply searching for lost treasure, and this old schoolhouse had a big ole *X* painted right on it. The

mental shield, the one he hadn't even sensed from outside the building, had the distinctive taste of Gabby all
over it. Not the Gabby he'd touched minds with back in
the mines though, but the one he remembered from the
street a couple weeks ago when he'd briefly skimmed
along a succubus's shields. She'd run from him that
night too, before he'd recognized her for who she was.
And though he knew now that she hadn't been part of
a trap, but rather leading them to one where a human,
Logan's mate to be precise, had been in danger, it still
didn't negate the fact that there had been a darkness to
her that set off every instinct of wrongness he had.

Something had happened to Gabby between now and
four months ago. Something that could account for the
taint of evil he sensed stamped upon her. A taint that
hadn't been there before, despite her maker's best efforts. Valin would be damned if he would go another
day without finding out what had caused it. And it
would be a cold day in hell before he let her leave again
before he could fix it.

"I'm afraid you also have another misimpression,"
Jacob said.

Valin tipped his head questioningly.

"We don't know who this Gabriella is that you're
talking about."

Behind him, Bennett raised his brow. Didn't need
projective thought to get that question across: *Who and
what the hell is he talking about?*

Yeah, yeah. He'd explain it all later. "Bullshit.
Amazon and her little group of buddies that broke into
Haven already gave away that you do."

"Haven?"

Valin sighed. "Are we really going to do this dance? You know exactly what I'm talking about and who I'm talking about, both the red-haired Amazon woman and Gabriella. I'll even guarantee you that I'm not here to bust your ass about sending troops into our sanctuary if you'll cut the crap and tell me where Gabby is."

"What about him?" Jacob jerked his head over his shoulder at Bennett. "You speaking for him too?"

"Bennett's pretty good at speaking for himself if you ask him."

Jacob twisted his head. Bennett lifted and dropped a shoulder. "Don't know anything about this Gabby my mate here's talking about. But I'm here to discuss what happened last week at Haven and to hopefully come up with a solution to the problem the null presents."

"The problem?" Jacob asked dangerously.

"Aye, namely the fact that she would be positively lethal to us if she were to be captured by Ganelon and subsequently used against us."

Jacob didn't even blink at the mention of Lucifer's right-hand man but met Bennett with a straight face as he said, "Annie would never allow herself to be used."

Valin felt his brow quirking and his lip turning up. Annie? As in little orphan Annie? Or perhaps she was named for Annie Oakley in *Annie Get Your Gun*. That image fit a bit better with the Amazonian null who'd been hustled out of the room.

Bennett shook his head. "She wouldn't have to allow it. If Ganelon got a hold of her, he'd find a way to force her compliance. Ganelon has…mastered the art of persuasion."

It was hard to miss the way Jacob's face paled, or

how it took him a moment to regain his composure. Either he took his troops' welfare very seriously or there was something personal here. Was he Amazon's older brother maybe? There was a bit of a resemblance, in height alone if nothing else. In fact, Trigger Happy looked a lot like him too. Way to keep it all in the family.

"Annie your sister?" Valin asked.

Jacob rounded back on Valin, his eyes narrowed dangerously. "Annie is off the table of discussion."

"Fine, but she needs training. And Bennett here is the best man we have for the job. Unless you have someone who's even better at shielding. Like, say, a certain vampire and succubus that you all seem to be acquainted with."

Bennett stiffened at the same time that Jacob choked out, "Succubus?" His gaze skirted briefly to Trigger Happy. Something in Valin's gut hardened, his blood pumping double-time. Why the fuck had Jacob looked at trigger-boy just then? As if Gabby being a succubus explained something. It better as hell not.

Trigger Happy's mouth thinned. "Get the hell out. We don't need you and your friend in here trying to scare us shitless by spouting lies."

"I'm not going anywhere without talking to Gabby."

"I don't know about that. Hell is a place, after all," Trigger Happy said, twisting his gun in true gangsta fashion. Was this guy for real?

Maybe yes, maybe no, but that gun is. So if you want to see her, you might want to play nicer.

"I'll talk with him," a voice cut through the tense silence. And there she was, standing just inside the doors at the far end of the cafeteria. Even from here the sight of her was like a brick to the jaw. The urge to plow through all obstacles or, hell, give up the clothes and knife he'd made such a big deal about and ghost over to her was intense. He wanted to touch her, push back the hefty hunk of hair that obscured half her face just to be sure it *was* her. Yes, he'd seen her twice now since the mines where he thought she'd died, but the first time he hadn't recognized her and the second he wasn't one hundred percent convinced. He was now though.

"Gabriella, you don't have to do anything for this ass-hole." Trigger Happy all but growled, his gun shaking in his hand.

"It's okay, Aaron. Valin just wants to talk." The corner of her full lips tipped up slightly on one side, not an amused smile, more a look of self-recrimination. "My fault, probably. Our good-byes were a bit rushed last time."

"Try nonexistent," Valin muttered. And he still wanted to throttle her for it. Not the lack of good-bye so much, but the fact that she'd taken off in the first place and put herself in danger. Whenever he thought of it he remembered the soul-clenching sense of panic that had consumed him as he'd searched those mines. It wasn't until he'd finally given up, returning to the surface, and gotten the shocker of his life when he'd seen both Karissa and Roland standing, unharmed, in the sun that he'd begun to believe it possible Gabby still lived. Gabby had been given Karissa's blood, and it seemed Karissa's blood was the cure-all for the whole vampire-to-ashes thing.

"You coming?" Gabby said over her shoulder by the

main doors of the cafeteria, pulling him from the chest-tightening memories.

Valin realized that a pathway had opened up before him. Well, almost; he still had to step around the gun-loving Aaron. Ignoring the itch in his shoulders that came with turning his back on potential danger, he did.

Gabby had already left by the time he made it to the other side of the cafeteria, the heavy doors swinging back and practically hitting him in the face.

Little chit. If he wasn't so happy to see her he'd want to wring her neck.

Despite the fact he'd been pretty convinced it was her the other day, he still couldn't believe he was here with her now. In a weird sort of surreal daze, he followed her as she turned off the main hall down a smaller side one, then stood drinking her in as she paused to open a door at the end. What he didn't like is what he saw. Those were no socks filling out that bra. These were the curves her younger body had promised. And though she was still petite, the lean muscles over the rest of her had similarly matured, firming at some point into textured hardness.

Gabby was aging. That was no makeup job the other night and not the harsh lighting that had chiseled the youth from her face. And those were actual lines — though faint — that fanned the corner of her eyes as she shut the door, flipped on the light, and turned her full-fledged glare on him.

"What the hell has happened to you?" he demanded, noticing how limp and flat her normally lustrous red hair looked in the light.

"And hello to you too. I'd say you look well, but

it might further inflate your ego and spin you off into the atmosphere."

And tired. Pale and tired. And were those dark circles under her eyes? God, what had she been doing? Or maybe the better question was what *hadn't* she been doing?

"Are you feeding enough?" he demanded.

She flashed her fangs, letting her eyes drift to his throat. "Every chance I get."

"Really?" He grabbed his shirt, stretching the neckline and exposing his throat. "Then go ahead, cookie."

She hissed, fear skittering in her eyes as she clamped her jaw tight and turned her head away, though not before Valin saw the flare of red in her black pupils.

Fuck, yeah, she was hungry. Hell, the air was so heavy with the pheromones she was putting off, he could practically taste her need. And what do you know, that was his second brain rising to attention. He tried telling it that it was simply a vampire's nature to equate feeding with sex, but the damn thing didn't give a shit. All it knew was that they'd been reunited with their mate, and that, holy hallelujah, their mate no longer lived in a body that could be considered jailbait. Far from it.

"Gabby…" He reached for her, wanting to soothe her obvious agitation, but she skirted away, dodging behind the metal desk butted against the wall in front of the cot, clenching the edge of it as if it were a lifeline…or like she might grab it up and toss it at him.

"I don't feed from humans…or Paladin," she quickly tagged on as if she expected him to toss out that argument.

"Where are you getting your blood from then?"

"None of your business."

"Gabby, everything with you is my business," he told her, rather proud of how he managed to keep the agitation out of his voice. Didn't she feel it too? Or, fuck, was he the only one suffering here with the need to claim his mate?

She looked at him straight on, her dark pupils that couldn't decide between black or crimson narrowed. "In your dreams."

"Exactly." He smiled, taking a step toward the desk.

She eyed him warily, but he couldn't miss how her pulse skittered at the base of her throat or how her breathing had sped up.

Not so indifferent to me, are you, cookie?

She cleared her throat. "What was so vital that you had to track me down here, anyway? Is Roland okay?"

"He's fine."

"Karissa?"

"She's fine too. They're all fine." Well, except perhaps Logan, but that was half the point of why he'd put so much effort into finding her now rather than waiting for another chance encounter. Logan's tragedy had been a real wake-up call for Valin. Not that he should've needed it. Not when he'd experienced for himself firsthand how fleeting life, love, and happiness could be.

"Then why are you here?" she asked, suspicion lacing her voice.

"To see you, of course." And to claim her. But that came later. Much later. First he was going to find out what the heck she'd been doing to make herself look so ill and then fix it. And he'd start with her most current need: blood.

"Did you ever think that maybe that desire wasn't reciprocated?" she asked snidely.

"I admit I've had my doubts. Especially when you keep treating me to the view of your lovely backside." He angled his head, leaning a bit to see around the desk and check out her luscious ass. When he looked back at her face he swore she was blushing. Hard to tell for sure with how pale she was. "Why is that, by the way? It's certainly not any way to treat a guy who went through so much trouble to see you safe."

"You…see me safe. How is that? Seems to me that you're putting me in danger by coming here. Putting us all in danger, if Logan's daddy finds out about this place."

"You don't remember the mines?" he asked, eating up another couple feet of distance between them.

"Of course I remember the mines."

"You left awfully quick after we rescued Karissa." And another step.

"Hello? Logan? Getting ready to let loose his little heavenly light bomb? Remember that too?"

"Exactly." He leaned forward over the desk and tipped his head close enough so that his breath caressed the side of her face as he spoke into her ear. "I searched for you. Practically tore those caves apart trying to find some sign of you. Four months I've wondered, hoped that you were out there. Prayed that you were safe."

She swallowed, shifting back from the desk closer to the cot. "You've come. You've seen that I'm all right. I want you to leave now."

"Leave? Like hell." There was no way he'd be leaving now that he'd found her. Nor was he going to let her escape again either. He made to step around the desk, determined to close up the distance once more. She leapt on the bed, hands splayed against the wall behind her. Her eyes had gone full crimson now, the green iris thinning to less than a sliver of a line. Her fangs had also elongated, the sharp tips slicing into her bottom lip as she strained to keep her mouth closed.

He took another step toward her, determined to ease her pain, when her voice in his mind brought him up short.

<<Don't! Just please... please leave.>>

The plea, powerful and filled with so much pain and desperation it made his knees threaten to buckle, had him fisting his hands so hard his knuckles ached. He couldn't leave her like this. It hurt his stomach just to look at her and see what she'd allowed to happen to herself. What must her own stomach feel like?

He pulled out his blade. She immediately recoiled, hissing as she dove for the set of knives neatly stashed on a shelf above her cot.

"What the fuck, Gabby. Do you really think I would use this on you?"

The look she gave him killed him. Yes, she did. It was a toss-up between what he felt more keenly—the anger that made his blood run hot or the hurt that put a vise around his heart.

He lifted the knife, balancing it at the point between hilt and blade so she could get a good look at it. Her eyes widened when she realized what it was, not just any knife but one of *His* knives. For a brief moment the fires banked enough that her pupils looked more like hot coals than fire, her mouth opening slightly in awe.

"This blade will never be used to harm you, only to

defend you. Even if I have to defend you from yourself."
With a sharp movement he snapped his hand back around
the hilt and drew the knife across the inside of his forearm, laying a shallow slice in the skin above his wrist.

She followed the movement, her tongue dipping out
to lick her lips as his blood welled up to bead along
his cut flesh. He held his breath, waiting for her hunger
to outweigh her reservations. It took less time than he
thought it might, but more than he hoped. Nearly a full
minute of his blood slowly welling, seeping down his
arm, and then dripping to the floor. He was afraid that
with his accelerated healing, he might have to slice his
arm again to reopen the cut, when she finally stepped off
the cot, her gaze locked on his slight wound.

He knew he took a chance. She was a vampire. And
he knew nothing of what might have formed the dark
taint on her soul after their meeting in the mine. It was
more than possible that she'd killed. That she'd starved
herself to the point of desperation and then lost control.
He could see it happening. The girl vamp who had felt
such shame over being force-fed blood through an IV
might be lost to darkness if she ever took and killed
a human.

But he wasn't human. And he could stop her if she
tried to take too much. He *would* stop her, and then he'd
do whatever it took to purify the darkness that had sunk
its slick teeth into her.

She took his arm, her hands gentle, tentative even as
she started to lift it to her mouth. Her touch was like a
punch to the gut. His dick, which still hadn't gotten the
message that it wasn't part of this reunion, kicked against
the front of his pants, liquid weeping from the tip.

Her head jerked up, nostrils flaring as she scented his arousal, and damn if he couldn't taste the air thickening with her own.

"Yes, Gabby. Take my blood." *And then take me. Let me be what you need. I need you to need me as I do you.*

He didn't project the thought, but somehow she must have heard. Either that or his spoken words had simply snapped her out of her bloodlust. She immediately dropped his hand, her fangs biting through her own lip as she took a step back, shaking her head.

"Shit. I'm screwing this up, aren't I?"

Her gaze darted to the door, and his own followed. No way, no way in hell was she running again.

"Fuck, Gabby, don't you dare…" But it was too late; fast as he was she was faster as she dodged around him to beat him to the door.

Chapter 4

WELL, THIS MISSION'S BOTCHED UP, BENNETT THOUGHT, warily eyeing the guards surrounding him. The orders from the council regarding the band of part-blood humans who'd broken into Haven last week had been crystal clear. Use any means necessary to track down the gifted humans to their base: check. Determine if there is enough untapped power in their group beyond the null that could make them a potential liability to the secrecy and safety of the Paladin mission: uh... potentially, yes. If so, determine the likelihood of the peaceful relocation of the group into Haven's protective walls: un-bloody-likely.

Contact may've been made, but the pathways of communication had been shut tight before they could even get started. Jacob hadn't wanted to discuss anything to do with the null named Annie or her training. And the discussion hadn't even made it as far as relocating her or the dozens of other gifted here in need of training. The cafeteria was practically brimming with power. He could tell because he was getting a bleeding headache trying to keep his shields strong and steady, and even then emotions were slipping in right and left. Unease, distrust, curiosity, anger, and fear—it was all there. The one person who wasn't there was their leader, Jacob. Six minutes ago, and maybe, what, three after Valin's own disappearance, another soldier had shown up, whispered something in the scarred man's ear that had his face turning purple, and sent him bolting out of the room. Bennett just hoped it didn't have anything to do with Valin.

Bloody prat. He was part of the reason this mission was going down the shite-twirler. Valin obviously had other plans than making contact. Or rather, he'd only planned to make contact with one person. The question was why?

Only one way to find out.

Bennett eased up on his shields, trying to pinpoint the exact emotions of the handful of guards who'd been left to monitor him. Most of them, along with their mix of curiosity and annoyance, were actually edging on bored after almost ten minutes of tense inaction. And Aaron, the bloke Jacob had left in charge, was distinctly distracted—had been since Valin left with the mysterious Gabriella, actually. Gabriella the vampire, who, oh, was part-succubus too. WTF?

"Mind if we take a gander? Find my mate?" Bennett asked.

Aaron drew his gaze away from the door, blinking at him. "What?"

"Valin, my mate. I'd like to try and find him if it's not too much trouble." *You know, so I can wring the bastard's neck.* He didn't add that. United we stand, divided we fall, and all that bloody crap.

Aaron hesitated, then meeting the gaze of an African American soldier, he jerked his head toward the door. "Keon, come with us. The rest of you, why don't you go help my brother track down Annie?"

The other soldiers immediately took off, leaving

Bennett reeling at the ease of getting rid of most of his guards. Aaron didn't look old enough to elicit such obedience — early twenties maybe? — nor did he have the same calm confidence his older brother did. So either sharing DNA held a lot of weight here or this Aaron was simply off his stride today.

Probably the whole Gabriella bit. He definitely didn't shine to the fact that she went off with Valin… alone.

At least Bennett knew why Jacob had gone running now. Bennett would pity the null, Annie, but he suspected the hard-ass warrior had a soft spot for family. And if he was any good judge of genetic expression, both Jacob and Aaron here were blood relations to the null. Tall as giants, whiskey-brown eyes, high cheekbones, stubborn jawlines and all.

Aaron turned to Keon. "Shoot him if he so much as twitches wrong."

Keon nodded solemnly, then gestured with his rifle for Bennett to follow Aaron.

"Aren't you buggers so bleeding sweet," Bennett muttered and fell into line. What was it his mate Logan would say about this? Oh, right, what a major FUBAR: fucked up beyond all recognition. Or was that repair? He guessed it didn't matter; it amounted to the same thing. Of course, it couldn't be a total loss. So far they weren't dead.

His hopes of staying that way ended, though, when they rounded the next corner. At the far end of the narrow hall, a naked Valin was facing off with the missing Annie. The look on Valin's face did not bode well; neither did the redhead's cocky pose.

"Get the fuck out of my way," Valin warned.

She smiled, cracking her knuckles. "No."

Bloody fucking hell. That wasn't going to go over well, and sure enough, Valin decided to make her. Valin spun, sweeping out his leg, probably going on the assumption that the bigger they were the harder they fell. Only Annie didn't fall; she jumped into the attack, tackling Valin. She threw a couple punches that Valin blocked. And then they both sprung back to their feet, same sides of the hall, only this time the face-off had been foregone for a good ole downright boxing session.

"Annie!" Aaron charged. Behind Bennett, he sensed Keon tense, his rifle rising to shoulder level.

"Shite." There *were* things worse than a FUBAR. Things like this. Bennett crouched, swiping a leg out and grabbing for the rifle in Keon's hands. Despite Keon's quick initial reaction, the soldier must have been as shocked by what was occurring down the hall as Bennett was, because it was like filching candy from a babe. A split second was all it took for the man to go down, the rifle settling nicely into Bennett's grip as he bolted after Aaron. Multitasking, he ejected the magazine, clearing the slug from the chamber as he ran. When he was close enough he chucked the whole thing and on a push of adrenaline leapt for Aaron's legs. Aaron went sprawling and, jammy bastard that Valin was, didn't shoot the naked Paladin or anyone else on his way to the linoleum.

Probably worried he'd hit Annie.

Scrambling over the pissed Aaron, Bennett stomped the handgun out of the soldier's hand and kicked the Glock away, dashing for the two toddlers playing at war. And that's all it really was—play—because even with the height advantage and the fact that she was actually pretty damn competent, Bennett knew from experience that Valin was a damn sight better. He was pissed. He wanted past. And Annie was stubborn enough not to let him. Thankfully the idiot was at least brilliant enough to know better than to actually harm a lady.

Didn't change the fact that he'd initiated a fight with her.

"Valin, you right piece of shite. Give over, will ya?" Bennett yelled as he forced his way into the barrage of slap downs and blocks. Of course, in doing so he got a nice kick to the outer thigh from the redhead and a fucking fist to the face by Valin, but he figured it was worth it if they all got out of this without any holes.

That stated, the injuries pissed the crap out of him. Bennett smashed a left jab right back at Valin's face. Bugger was too fast and tried to dodge, but Bennett had anticipated and caught him with his right forearm across the throat, driving him into the wall.

"Cor blimey, Valin! What is wrong with you?"

"She got in my way!"

"She's a bloody girl!"

And those were two very pissed-off men who were up and collecting their weapons again. Could this mission get any worse?

Valin's jaw worked, the muscle spasming along it as he drew in deep breaths through his nose.

"Well? What is it, mate? You got a good reason for this? 'Cause if not I might just go help Keon there put his rifle back together."

Valin closed his eyes, rapping his head against the wall behind him. "Fuck." When he opened his eyes again the anger had faded, and for the first time Bennett could sense the pulse of frustration and despair riding his fellow Paladin.

Annie had pulled back in her gift some. Enough for Valin to probably ghost if he wanted. The fact that he didn't said the Paladin might have his head screwed on again.

"What is it?" he asked, easing off a bit. Valin shook his head, removing Bennett's arm with his hand.

"I'm sorry." Valin directed the apology over Bennett's shoulder to Annie. "I didn't hurt you, did I?"

"As if," Annie scoffed, folding her arms across her chest.

Aaron obviously didn't give a shite about whether she was hurt or not. He'd retrieved his gun and had stepped forward, lifting it so it was uncomfortably close to Bennett's face. "Get your fucking hands up, both of you, or I'm going to fucking blow a hole in both your heads."

"Oh, chill, Aaron. He didn't do anything other than stop us. And Valin and I were only sparring. He didn't hurt me, and I learned a lot of cool moves in the process."

"You are fucking warped, you know that?" The comment came from Keon, but when Bennett glanced over at him he saw that the soldier was actually smiling. Annie smiled right back, her wide mouth showing off a spectacular set of pearlies as she performed a little curtsey.

Warped for sure. Though she was also interesting. Bennett could sense nothing from her. No emotions. No nothing. And though that should probably have made him wary, it didn't. It was a bloody relief is what it was. To be able to look at her and not know a damn thing about her or her feelings was a novelty he didn't normally get. He had no idea what she felt or thought of him and all that was going on here. Other than that, she had attitude coming out the arse and a penchant for trouble, it seemed.

Too bad he wasn't going to get the chance to get to know her better. He turned back to Valin. "I think it's about time we took our leave."

Valin shook his head, his bourbon eyes darkening with determination. "I'm staying."

Annie wasn't the only warped mind here. Bennett pierced Valin with a don't-be-a-blimey-idiot look. "Think that's a good idea, mate?" And then when that didn't knock any sense into him he asked, "What do I tell Senior?"

"Tell him I've infiltrated the ranks and will contact him when I'm able," he said sarcastically, but Bennett couldn't help but note that his eyes drifted to a room a short ways down the hall. Aw, crap. A hundred pounds that was Gabriella's room. A thousand on top of it she was the source of both Valin's frustration and his despair.

The troops had sure been falling as of late. Thank the Lord he was made of more indifferent stuff than that. Women were women were women, and as long as he could convince one of them to offer up her soft, sweet body for his pleasure it was all good.

"You're not planning on coming back, are you?" he asked in a low voice, trying to steal some privacy for this rather private conversation.

Valin stared back at him, unblinking.

"Bloody hell, Valin. The kind of mood Senior's in, he'll put a price on your head."

"You looking to collect?"

Bennett recoiled. "God, no. But I don't understand why you're pissing it all away."

"All what? What am I pissing away? You know at Haven I'm nothing more than a second-class Paladin. Only one of lower rank is Roland and you don't see him banging on the doors to get in."

Valin's voice had risen as he spoke. Bennett glanced over his shoulder at the three people doing their best to listen in on the conversation. Other than perhaps Annie—who'd already proven she was a bit touched in the head—there were no welcoming faces there.

"You think it's going to be any different here?" he asked as quietly as he could.

"They'll get used to me." Valin pushed away from Bennett, turning down the hall toward the room he'd glanced at. "Now if you'll excuse me. I'm going to get dressed."

"Goddamn it! Does no one give a shit that I have a fucking gun?" Aaron started after Valin, his steps faltering as he passed Annie. He turned on his heel, walking backward as he pointed at Keon. "Stay with them. And *this* time shoot his ass if he so much as moves."

Keon flashed a brilliant white smile in answer. When Aaron was out of hearing range he turned to Bennett, eyeing him up and down with a pensive twist to his lips.

"You truly going to shoot me?" Bennett asked, a bit pissed at the complete lack of trust. He'd disarmed them, not attacked them, and only then to prevent bloodshed that had the potential to lead to outright war. Valin may've been right that he wasn't high on Senior's favorites list, but Bennett was at least mid-list and they both *were* Paladin…and in Senior's mind these soldiers were not.

Keon lifted and dropped his shoulders, looking a bit chagrined but not really all that pissed. "Might be easier if you hadn't bent the damn cartridge." He held up the magazine cartridge, showing the dented corner at the top. "What are you—fucking Superman?"

Bennett figured the bent corner had nothing to do with him but rather the fact that it was an old gun. It had probably already been bent and just needed a ginger touch to get it to slide home. Kind of hard when your hands were shaking. Despite the bravado he'd shown, Keon was rattled.

"Sorry about that, mate. Didn't mean to bang you up, but I couldn't let you boys shoot my mate full of holes either."

"Yeah, I'da done the same," Keon said, still fiddling with the rifle. Bennett held out his hands. Keon hesitated, but in a moment of stunning trust gave it to him. It took a little bit of coaxing and wiggling, but a few seconds later the rifle was back together and in Keon's hands once more.

"Uh, thanks."

"No problem, mate," he replied, then took up a folded-arm stance against the wall to wait.

Taking a page from Bennett's book, Keon assumed a similar pose kitty-corner across the hall. For show he kept the rifle lifted, but Bennett noted that it wasn't precisely aimed at him either.

Annie, who'd watched the entire exchange, shifted from one foot to the other and then stepped across the hall to take up a bit of wall beside him.

"You know," she said after another blissfully quiet minute, "you really don't act much like the other Paladin."

Bennett turned his head toward her. "And how is that?"

"You're not an ass," she explained.

"And you don't look much like a pain in the arse, but so far, from what I've seen, you are."

"Hmm…" She smiled, her pretty, straight teeth flashing against her rosy lips. "I think I'm going to like you."

He arched his brow. "Because I insulted you?"

"Something like that."

Definitely warped. He shook his head, leaning forward to look down the hall toward the room Valin and Aaron went into. No shots fired yet. That was a good sign.

"So what are you going to do now?" Annie asked, tipping her head forward into his line of sight.

He couldn't help but notice how her tank top dipped invitingly low as she did, revealing just the slightest swell of breast. He swallowed, leaning back against the wall. Valin could damn well take care of himself. Besides, there were much more interesting things for him to pay attention to. Like the woman beside him who was looking at him with—bless the fairer sex—a whole lot of interest in her golden-brown eyes.

"I don't know. Think your bother will go for lessons in exchange for room and board?" he asked with a charming smile. Hell, if he was charming enough, maybe he could get her to convince her brother to give back his knife and phone too. Man, that still buggered him.

Her brow creased, but then lifted. "You mean Jacob?" She laughed, a husky sound that ran down his spine and curled around to his cock. Christ, she had a great laugh.

A bedroom laugh. And those were bang-me legs too. He could just see them wrapped around him as he pile drove her. "Maybe, but probably not."

He shifted, turning so he was facing her as he leaned on his right shoulder. What he really wanted to do was box her in and press his throbbing cock into the soft mound that dipped down into her concave belly, but they did have an audience.

"Don't suppose you'd be willing to put me up." He gave her his megawatt smile, keeping his voice low and seductive.

She gripped her bottom lip with her teeth, running her finger along the collar of her tank top. "Maybe…but I don't think it's a good idea."

"You sure about that?"

She smiled, leaning in closer, but almost immediately drew back again. Out of the corner of his eye Bennett saw why. Keon had shifted, stepping into the middle of the hall, and he looked none too happy.

"Annie, don't you think you should go tell the others that you've been found?"

"Why should I do that?" Annie asked, folding her arms in a make-me gesture.

"Oh, come on, Annie. You know by now what happens when you slip your guards."

Her mouth turned down in a distinct pout. Bennett found himself frowning too. Why did she need guards? Or was this a new development since her break-in to Haven last week? He supposed that made sense. She was the person of interest in the council's mind.

"More like prison guards," she muttered, but then sighed, pushing off the wall. "Well, it was nice meeting you, Bennett. Hope to see you around," she added with a twinkle in her eye.

Despite the fact that Keon still frowned at him, Bennett watched her sashay down the hall. Hard not to, since she did have a fine arse and seemed to be putting just a little bit of extra effort into making sure he watched it as well. The moment she rounded the corner it became impossible to ignore Keon any longer; the soldier's concern was smothering him like a damp blanket.

"What is it, mate?" Bennett shifted, trying to relieve the residual pressure in his pants. "You have to admit she's a looker."

Keon grunted, but nodded in concurrence. "Just don't let Jacob catch you looking at her like that."

"Jacob? Does he not realize that his little sister is a woman?"

"No, I think he gets that Annie's a woman. But I think that makes it worse."

"Why?"

"Because she's not his sister…She's his daughter."

Bennett cursed long and hard, his wanker shriveling long before he was done. "Cor blimey, I'm never getting my knife back, am I?"

—◦◦◦—

What the heck are you doing here, other than freezing your butt off, that is?

"Good question," Gabby muttered to herself as she shifted, trying to ease the tingling feelings in her legs from crouching too long on the roof of the downtown apartment building where she'd made a sport of staring at its overachieving high-rise neighbor across the way.

She wasn't surprised to find that the penthouse windows had already been replaced, and she was sure if she made it inside there would be nothing left of the man she'd spent many an hour watching and wishing she dared get closer to. Her biological father didn't live there anymore. Which was a good thing, all things considered.

Four months ago the Paladin-turned-vampire, Roland, had his top-floor penthouse broken into by the then coven leader—and her own dear stepfather from hell—Christos. And though Christos had since died—yippee ki-yay, mothereffer—there was no way the former Paladin was going to risk his bond mate's life by staying, not after all he'd done to claim her.

You mean all he had to go through to save her after you fucked everything up.

Gabby blew out a deep breath, her chest tightening around the empty ache inside it. Her involvement in Karissa's capture could not be denied, though it certainly hadn't been what Gabby wanted. But what she was and how she'd come to be was exactly the connection Christos and Ganelon had needed to track down Roland and his mate. The fact that Gabby had been further used to lure Karissa out into the open was another thing she would never live down, especially when it had led to the Paladin female's capture and eventual turning.

That betrayal, though done unwillingly, was just another mark against Gabby. It was also the biggest reason why, as much as she might want to, she hadn't tracked her father and Karissa down after they'd moved and done the whole *surprise, surprise—welcome to the family, Karissa; oh, and by the way, I'm your new stepdaughter*. Nope, not a smart idea when she didn't think her daddy had yet to wake up and smell the genetic coding in her genes. Not to mention Gabby's disaster factor. Gabby had figured out long ago that being associated with her was synonymous to inviting trouble. And the last intel Gabby had gotten from her recently deceased vampire spy suggested the new coven leader had no idea where Roland and his mate were. Keeping it that way was the best wedding present she could give them, especially after all the pain she'd given them first, which meant staying far, far away.

Gabby closed her eyes, remembering the intensity of emotions in that mine four months ago. The pure despair that her father had been going through when he'd made the earth-shattering decision to turn Karissa in order to save her life. He hadn't known at the time if what he was doing was right or wrong, but he had known that he loved her so much he would give anything for her. What would it be like to have someone who would move heaven and earth itself for you? The answer to that was something Gabby doubted she'd ever know, especially given the limited amount of time she had left.

Speaking of time, you really need to get off your frozen duff.

With a groan, she stood, shrugging off the memories as she turned and ran for the backside of the building. The edge came up fast, barely time to gain enough speed, but she managed, thrusting off the lip and arm-wheeling it to the next building across the way. She landed with a thump and a grunt, her hands digging down in the filthy coating of smog, dirt, and whatever else sealed the rubber roofing.

Damn, when had she become a complete wuss? There

was a time when she could jump double the distance with no effort.

Standing, she brushed her hands together, ignoring the prickly cry of nerve endings as she headed toward the fire escape at the back of building. Each step brought with it more stinging needles running from her toes up her legs, and her fingers weren't far behind in their Popsicle status.

She scowled, annoyed. It was a cool evening, but still, she should have been better off than this. Yeah, it didn't help that she'd run out of her room without grabbing her hoodie, so the fact she was shaking down to her toes right now was her fault. Though, if she were honest, she could admit that even with a down jacket she probably would still be shaking. And she could put the blame for that, at least, firmly on Valin's shoulders.

Five minutes with the man and here she was, crashing. It was worse than any of the withdrawals she'd experienced after a feeding. Only this time she hadn't even fed, though she almost had. No, she'd almost taken. And not just his blood. He'd offered to let her feed from him, and the desire to do so had been so overpowering, so blatantly arousing, that she could still feel the throbbing pulse not just in her fangs, but in regions of her body that had laid dormant since she'd been turned. Seventy-nine years was a hell of a long dry spell on desire.

As if you could actually go through with it if he took you up on the offer.

Very true. Sex was for power and power alone. She had no desire to give any man, even one like Valin, power over her again. And if he knew that she was the cause of his ultimate pain?

Gabby rubbed her arms, glancing over her shoulder as if expecting to find him standing there, knife in hand. Obviously he didn't suspect how she was connected to the night his wife and child had died or else he would have used that knife on her rather than himself. If she were lucky he'd never find out. Which meant after she'd gotten her meal, if he wasn't gone yet, she'd have to find a way to drive him away too.

"First, dinner," she told herself firmly, putting her foot down on the fire escape. She was going to need all the sustenance she could get if she hoped to set even half the things her screwed-up heritage had caused to rights.

"Still not back yet?" Annie asked from the open doorway.

Valin sighed, heaving himself upright on Gabby's cot. The desire to try and track Gabby down was making him jumpy, so to combat that he'd decided to lie down. Waiting was the best thing he could do right now.

Don't chase a spooked horse. And that's what he'd done, spooked her. Whether it had simply been the offer of his blood or whether it was all the other crap between them that had scared the bejeezus out of her, Valin wasn't sure. Probably both. God knew he understood; he was scared shitless too. Losing Angeline and their unborn child had about killed him; what if he couldn't fix whatever it was that was making Gabby sick? What if she died on him too?

Not going to happen.

"Don't worry. She'll come back. She always does," Annie said, coming completely into the room.

"Yeah? When?"

Annie shrugged. "When she's ready."

"Fucking spectacular."

Annie smiled and moved over to the desk, hiking her butt onto it. And yeah, way to make him feel even shorter. Whoever had named her Annie must not have been thinking very far into the future. Tall genes did not grow on trees, unless it was the family sort. Surely her parents could have guessed that she might eventually hit cloud levels and given her a name that didn't bring to mind scrappy little orphans in red dresses.

"So, how did you and Gabby first meet?" she asked.

Valin narrowed his eyes. He'd gotten the impression from their little encounter outside Haven last week that Annie already knew about him. He'd made the assumption—okay, he'd hoped—that was because of Gabby; it seemed he may have been wrong. "Gabby didn't tell you?"

She rolled her eyes. "Gabby isn't too big on the sharing thing. What she does excel at is stomping around and putting her nose in other people's business."

"And you're her best pupil."

"I strive for A's across the board."

Valin decided to not say what was on his mind. Besides, he wasn't exactly expunged of guilt on either subject himself, though he liked to think he pulled off the stomping bit with more style and grace.

Yeah, sure you do, Valin. Except maybe when you're tackling women in hallways.

"So…" Annie drew the word out, tapping the metal desk with her short-trimmed nails. "Wanna tell me why Gabby was running from you?"

Not really, no. But then again, Annie did seem to have

a real familiarity with Gabby. She certainly seemed comfortable in Gabby's room and to be able to imitate the same cocked-hip attitude stance so well, she must spend a fair amount of time around her too. Even if she didn't have any real answers, maybe the girl at least had a theory as to what the heck had happened to Gabby.

"How long have you known Gabby?"

"A little over two months." Annie shrugged. "But she's only been staying here the last few weeks or so."

"Why?"

"I don't know. I think she just loves torturing us."

"Torturing you?"

"Yeah, she helps my dad out with the training. She has a real love of the whip." She snapped her hand out and back in front of her. "Whipcha!"

"So she's been spending more time here in order to train you guys."

"We were a pretty sorry lot. At least when it came to properly utilizing our other sides." She quoted the air with the word "other." "And we've had a lot more recruits since she showed up."

"Recruits she helped find?"

Annie nodded.

Valin frowned. Everything Annie was saying sounded exactly like what he'd expect from the Gabby he'd met in the mines. Yeah, the vamp played hard and tough, but she'd given away that day just how much she cared about others when she'd attempted to sacrifice her own life for Roland's and Karissa's. What it didn't explain was that dark taint on her.

Annie rapped the desk with her fist, drawing Valin's

gaze back to her. "Okay, pretty boy. I've spilled. Your turn now."

Valin narrowed his eyes. "You called Logan that too. Back at Haven."

Annie frowned, but then a look of enlightenment crossed her face. "Oh, you mean Gabby's Paladin friend."

"Yeah…The Paladin friend you had a message for." A message that had come too late. Poor bastard. The unfairness of the whole thing was something right out of a damn soap, only worse. Because not only had Logan found his bond mate, who was human, but she'd died way too fucking young.

Not the only one. And not the only poor bastard left behind, either.

Annie made a sound like she had something stuck in her throat, her cheeks flushing as she pointedly looked away from Valin, her gaze catching on anything and everything that could be considered halfway interesting, which wasn't much. He didn't think it was his morose thoughts that had made her uneasy, though.

"Gabby didn't actually send you, did she?"

She gave a little lift and drop of her shoulders. "I overheard her talking to my dad."

"Your dad?"

"Jacob."

Valin fought to school his face. Jacob did look older, but not old enough to be her dad. Either he was really young when he'd knocked Annie's mother up, or he'd inherited some of the Paladin longevity genes.

"Okay, so did Gabby call him pretty boy to your dad or something?"

"No. I called him that. You have to admit he is damn

fine to look at." She dragged her gaze over him. "I'm thinking most of you Paladin are."

Valin shook his head. "Fucking twins."

"What?"

"You and Gabby. You've emulated her so well that you're like her damn twin."

Annie's mouth thinned, her body going completely still. Nope, despite the fact that she obviously looked up to Gabby's badass attitude, she didn't appreciate being called a copycat. Which had been Valin's hope. Stirring up the pot almost always yielded interesting things in its depths.

Valin folded his arms across his chest to wait. Annie hopped off the desk, letting her agitation out by moseying around the room, touching Gabby's things as she did. It took all Valin's self-control not to leap up and slap her hands away when she started playing with Gabby's weapons. They were Gabby's weapons, not hers. And a weapon was everything to a warrior. Valin would know, since he so often had to do without his when he took to the shade.

"I'm not like Gabby. Despite the fact that you're being an asshole, I'm not running, now am I?"

"Well why don't I just award you some bonus points, since Gabby's not here to do it?" He cocked an eyebrow. "Or should I deduct them?"

"Well, if we're deducting points I have to give you a big fat fail for not answering the question."

"Oh, which one is that?"

"What did you do to drive her off?"

He ground his molars, his jaw aching he clenched it so hard. The accusation, that *he'd* driven her off, didn't sit well, even if it was true in its own way. "I offered her my vein."

"Get the fuck out."

Valin snapped his head around, but she wasn't actually trying to kick him out; her mouth was hanging open with incredulity. She managed to recover, shaking her head as she pulled her mouth back together. "Oh, wow. That would do it too."

"I take it I'm not the first one to offer." And why did that piss him off even more?

She shook her head. "Uncle Aaron offered just the other night. Put her in a real weird mood."

Aaron. Valin took a deep breath. Of course it had to be him. Valin had really been hoping that he wouldn't have to kill the fucker, but this cinched it—Trigger Happy was dead.

Later. Right now he had to concentrate on the more important thing: Gabby's health. "So I'm also not the only one that sees she can't be feeding enough."

Annie pursed her lips, looking uncertain. "I don't know. I thought that too, and I do think it contributes— that and the inconsistency of her feedings—but that theory isn't settling."

"Why not?"

"Because sometimes after she feeds she seems worse."

"Worse?"

"Yeah, I mean she has more energy, sure, but it's not a good kind. And then when it fades?" She shrugged. "Well, she looks worse than before. Like housing all that yucky energy is draining the life right out of her."

"Fuck." He shook his head as the enormity of the problem hit him. It wasn't a onetime incident that had put the stain on Gabby; it was an ongoing thing. Whatever or however Gabby was feeding, if this accelerated aging was the result, then she was destroying herself when she did. "Fuck me."

"You know what's wrong?"

"Not exactly," he pushed up off the cot, checking to make sure his knife was strapped on tight, "but in the end it doesn't really matter, does it?"

"Doesn't matter? Why not?"

"Because I'm going to put a stop to it."

"How?" Annie asked, following him to the door.

"Easy." He stopped, knuckles white as he gripped the doorknob. "Tonight she'll be feeding from me."

Chapter 5

BENNETT SAGGED DOWN AGAINST THE TREE, THANKFUL for the strong hardwood and its supportive capabilities. He'd only had a couple of shielding sessions with Karissa, and reaching out across such a great distance to find her and link up had not been easy.

Would have been easier with his fucking phone, but though he'd been allowed to stay in the base, his phone and knife were locked up tight somewhere. He was sure it was Jacob's idea of an insurance policy. The man wasn't stupid, and there were enough gifteds with the sensitive aspects here to know the knife they'd taken off him had power. Bennett wondered if they knew it wasn't the average everyday magical kind but rather power bestowed on the weapon by the Almighty One Himself. More so, he wondered if any of them could actually draw the power from the heavenly blade without getting hurt. That right there might convince the council these soldiers weren't as inferior as Senior Calhoun seemed to think.

The council's stance on these part-breeds frustrated Bennett. He had too much of his own diluted blood to consider these soldiers anything less than lost cousins, and as such had taken the assignment as much to prove Senior wrong as anything else. He bloody hell wasn't a kidnapper, that was for sure, so if Senior Calhoun thought Bennett would actually take the pointed suggestion to obtain the null and bring her home by any means necessary, the elder was as warped as the rest of them were.

Speaking of warped minds…Bennett lifted his head, squinting against the dappled sun pouring through the maple tree to focus on a stretch of grass in the center of Fort Greene Park. And sure enough, he'd been right earlier when he'd about dropped the link in shock. That was Annie soaking up the warming rays of the fall sun as she sat in the clearing, sipping something out of a straw cup as she dug her bare feet into the blades of grass. The question was where were her guards? In the thirty-six hours or so since he and Valin had forced themselves into the status of unwanted guests, Bennett had noted that she was rarely alone—at least when he or Valin were around.

Think maybe there might be a reason for that, like, oh, maybe her father doesn't trust you?

Well, he supposed there were a couple ways to earn the man's trust, and bringing his daughter home seemed like a good start.

Pushing back his exhaustion, he straightened and made his way across the park to her. She didn't notice he slipped up behind her until his shadow fell upon her, cutting off her sun rays, making her shoulders tense.

"Does your da' know you're out here?" he asked and watched those shoulders relax again.

She tipped her head back and wrinkled her nose as she shaded her face to look up at him. "Hopefully not. But he probably knows by now that I'm gone."

Which meant she *was* alone. Crap. "Why are you out here?"

"Why are you?" she asked, stuffing her feet into a pair of Converse. She stood, gesturing for him to walk with her down the path that led toward the north end of the park. "I find it hard to believe Dad would have sent *you* outside the base to look for me."

He shrugged, falling into step beside her. "I had some things to take care of."

"Things..." She pursed her lips, eyes narrowed. "Things like contacting your buddies back at Haven and telling them where we are?"

The only thing about the question that surprised him was that he hadn't heard it from any of them before. But no grilling had occurred yet, leaving Bennett to assume that Valin had somehow either managed to pull some charm out of his arse or Jacob had been even more desperate to cut a deal than Bennett had figured. And if that were the case, Bennett just hoped it was a deal that he, and the other Paladin, could live with.

He sighed. There was really no reason not to tell Annie what he was doing out here. And the first step on the road to trust was truth, and the truth was he wanted to find some way to make this a win-win for everyone. Whether the council saw it or not, he knew deep in his gut that he and his brethren needed these distant cousins of theirs on their side in this war. Just as he knew the way to winning them over wasn't by forcing their hand, but by showing them they could bend, even go so far as to give if the need arose.

"No. Like contacting Karissa and telling her."

Annie gave him a hard stare.

"We've been gone longer than normal without checking in. I thought it prudent to avoid any sort of search parties. Karissa has no allegiance to the council. She will pass the message to Haven that we're safe, but she won't tell them where we are."

He waited for that to sink in, figuring she was smart enough to read between the lines and realize he was playing in shades of gray for them now. "I'm not going to give up your safe house. If your father determines he's willing to open the lines of communication, then I hope he'll consider me a mediator. Meanwhile, I am satisfied being given the opportunity to live amongst you."

"Hmmm…" She tapped her cup. The sides were dewed from the exceptionally warm fall day. A perfect day, really. He almost hated having to begrudge her being out in it, but on this point he, the council, and her father all agreed: Annie's safety came first.

"So why are you out here?"

She raised the cup. "I wanted a slushee."

"And that's a good enough excuse to worry your father?" Not to mention putting herself, and thus everyone else, in danger.

"I know, I know. I'm just so sick of being a prisoner. I know I'm being selfish, but occasionally I just have to get out of there. Otherwise I think I'm going to just start screaming."

"I understand." He did. With his gift there were more occasions than not that he wished he could just take off and drive, not stopping until he was completely alone. He didn't, though. Not when so many others counted on him. So he got his outlet in other ways: fast cars, fine clothes…women. Still, if catching some rays were so important to Annie, he didn't get why she risked her safety for it. "But why don't you bring someone with you? Doesn't your dad give you guards?"

"You think even with a dozen guards my dad would let me out? Especially now, after you guys burst his little safety bubble the other day?" She shook her head. "I'm lucky he hasn't locked me in my room and posted full-time guards."

That was a point. And because it was a good one—not to mention a likely possibility once he brought her back—Bennett decided not to rush her and slowed his pace slightly. She didn't comment, but threw him a smile in thanks, tipping her head back to catch some more of those rays. The sun caught in her short tussle of hair, teasing the color from pure red to blond, chestnut, and copper. It made him itch to touch it. Touch her. Sink into her mind and steal just a little bit of the pleasure she seemed to be indulging in. What would it be like to be able to wall off your worries, if only for a moment, and simply enjoy?

But he couldn't, now could he? She was a null, which meant that the moment he touched her, his gift would go dormant. And because of that fact, the urge to reach out and touch her became almost unbearable. Contact always increased his gift. When he touched people he tended to take on their emotions. It's one of the reasons why he both craved and hated sexual encounters. The high he got off a woman's desire was fucking amazing, but it also made him feel sleazy. More often than not when he left their realm of influence, he realized that there had been no actual attraction on his part and he had simply been feeding off theirs. Yet he was definitely attracted to Annie. If he reached for her now, would he experience the same sexual zing as he did with other women? And if he did, would it be better or worse because it was his and his alone?

But is it your own? Isn't it possible that she's turned her gift off and you are feeling her attraction?

He tried to reach out but felt nothing. In fact, he was either more exhausted than he'd thought, or she was running hot. He couldn't sense anyone anywhere. And wow, wasn't that amazing. "I thought you were on orders not to use your gift, especially outside the base."

"Ugh, sorry. It's because you're so close. I'm not trying to pull, but it's hard to be a perfect island."

He nodded, knowing he should be concerned about his lack of the extra sensory input, but it didn't seem to dampen his innate satisfaction that his attraction was all his own. He glanced over at her, the insane thought to touch her rising back to the forefront. How many other opportunities would he have? The moment they walked back into the base there would be guards and the overprotective shadow of her father.

They came to a fork in the footpath. Without even making the conscious decision he reached out and cupped her elbow, pulling her slightly toward him as he directed her onto the right fork. And damn if that wasn't a zing. A pretty huge zing that ran straight up his arm, bounced up to his brain, then headed south fast to Mr. John Thomas.

She sucked in a breath, her gaze flying to his face. He immediately let go, making an excuse of scanning the area so he wouldn't have to answer the question in her eyes.

That had been stupid. Right fucking stupid. Like eating just one sweet…you always wanted more. And though Annie certainly was of age, she was bloody young.

While he was berating himself, his gaze caught that of a man who'd stopped on the footpath a dozen or so yards in front of them. As tall as Bennett, but bigger, more like his brother Alexander's type of muscle mass. He had dark hair, dark olive skin, and the type of face that women would probably drool over. He was also staring at them like they were Hollywood celebrities or some such nonsense.

Bennett leaned closer to Annie so that his voice wouldn't carry further than her ears; trying to keep their pace steady, they approached the man while also using his body to edge her off the footpath. Annie looked over at him, a question in her eyes.

"Know him?"

Annie followed his gaze, then chuckled.

"Well?"

She leaned in toward him, lacing her arm through his—damn bloody distracting—and put her head together with his. "I think maybe I should be asking you that. He's checking you out, not me."

"Huh," Bennett grunted, noting that Annie was right. The man was definitely focused on him now and he supposed Annie's assumption that he was gay and "checking him out" might explain it. But the unease running up his spine wouldn't pass. "Seems awfully interested considering we're walking through the park together," he said when they were fully by him.

"Maybe he swings both ways." Annie shrugged and lifted her slushee, sucking hard on the straw so her cheeks dipped in. And wouldn't you know, Mr. Thomas responded to that too.

Focus on the job, mate. Like figuring out what that man is about and getting Annie home safe.

By the time he'd reprimanded his dick and looked over his shoulder, the man had moved on, taking a short-cut across the grass toward a cluster of trees. Bennett frowned, torn between the urge to race Annie out of there or get far enough away from her to make sure there was nothing beyond just a bit of strangeness to the guy.

"What's wrong?"

"It occurs to me that for all I know he could be a demon or a merker. In fact, for all I know we're surrounded by them right now."

She shook her head. "We got close enough to him that if he were a demon, any glamour would have fallen." She nibbled her lip, her brow furrowing. "What *is* a merker, anyway?"

Bennett sucked in a breath. Cor blimey, these people knew nothing, did they? What had Valin's little vampire been teaching them anyway?

"Uh-oh, I said something really naïve, didn't I?"

"You have no idea."

She glanced over her shoulder, her eyes narrowed as she tracked the progress of the man walking in the other direction. After a moment she sighed.

"Well then, there's no hope for it." She chucked her drink in the nearest garbage can and tugged on his arm, directing him off the path and cutting toward the western side of the park.

"Where are we going? I thought we were heading back."

She nodded. "We are, but first we have to cover our

asses by making a few stops on the subway." She leaned in, her breath fanning across his ear. "You know, just in case hottie over there is a demon in disguise."

"Hey, watch it!"

Christos growled, flashing enough fang to send the rude human who'd had the gall to not move out of his way scurrying back from the edge of the subway platform. Not that the human's hasty retreat mattered now, for the train carrying Christos's object of interest was already pulling away. He narrowed his gaze, air sucking through his teeth as he watched the young, redheaded woman lean in closer to her companion as their car slid out of sight into the tunnel.

What would a Paladin be doing this far from their normal stomping grounds, unless…the woman. A gifted human. Though perhaps the more accurate terminology would be a gift thief. Christos had almost missed the fact that she was a null when he'd first looked up from his brooding mosey through the park and seen her. That hair…cut short, but the color? A deep red that practically glowed. For a moment his heart had skipped, until the woman's height registered. Walking shoulder to shoulder with her companion, she was way too tall to be Gabriella.

Christos's disappointment at having his reunion with his vampire-child postponed was quickly tempered when his gaze had moved on to her companion. He'd been stunned into inaction, his fangs throbbing with the memory of another Paladin with the same strong jawline who'd stubbornly refused to give up the hiding location of his wife and son, even though he must have known it was only a matter of time before Christos's vampires tore the house apart to find them—time that was quickly slipping from the Paladin as Christos bled his life force away. Maybe that stubbornness had been worth something, as his coven had never found the son, though at least the mostly human woman had been a tasty dessert.

Christos had half a mind to grab the next train and try to track the Paladin and the woman to their destination. Finish the job he'd started with the Paladin's parents, then take the null and see if she couldn't be of some use. It would have to wait though. He'd gotten the impression from the way they'd quickly altered their course back in the park that this subway station had not been their original destination, making him think the null's home must be closer to his present location than anywhere the rattling box of metal might take them. Besides, now that he knew she was out there, all he had to do was keep a mental eye out for the lack of an energy signal and he could find her again. If he was doubly lucky the Paladin would still be with her when he did.

With a smile on his face, Christos turned and stepped onto the escalator that brought him back to street level. To the blaring orchestra of car horns and screeching brakes, he spilled out onto the sidewalk and into the midst of anonymous humanity and car-corroded air. Ah, to breathe again. To feel the morning sun radiating down upon his face. It was the former he'd missed the most while his soul had been trapped in the burning fires of hell, possibly because it was freshest in his memories. But the latter…that was going to be what took him from the demigod status of his past life to godlike. He was reborn. And this new body held all of the perks and none of the hindrances of the last. The skill and speed of the vampire, the seductive powers of his mother, Lilith, and this time, no tells to give either away. He could go out in the sun, and because over half the souls Lucifer had used to resurrect his own were merker, he'd inherited their constitution too.

He couldn't wait to meet Roland again. Let him try and kill him now. But first? It was time to rattle the status quo and oust the imposter who'd been sitting in *his* seat at his father's right side. And after that? Well, he had a mind to see to his disobedient daughter before teaching any more impertinent Paladin their place. Family *was* the most important thing, after all, and like his mother before him, he wasn't above lying, stealing, cheating, or killing to ensure his family's deference to his will.

With a smile on his face and a spring in his step, he stepped out to the curb, whistling for the next available taxi.

Chapter 6

"Damn it, Valin. Do you have to follow me everywhere?" Gabby snapped, not caring that her voice was loud enough to turn heads. On top of everything else this morning, dealing with Valin was not what she wanted to do. But he'd been there hovering in the hall outside Jacob's offices the moment she stepped out of the impromptu meeting. Which, to be truthful, was the source of her real frustration: Jacob was on the warpath. Annie was missing—again—and since Gabby seemed to have a knack for spotting the vacuum bubble of non-magic that always surrounded her, Gabby was going to have to find her, despite the fact that it was barely past ten a.m.

Why couldn't Annie at least wait until after noon to slip her collar?

Valin smiled, not exactly friendly, more of a bite-me kind of smile, and said, "Get used to it, cookie. Consider me your shadow."

Gabby growled, pushing past him and marching toward the front doors. She was not at all surprised when he fell into step less than a length behind her. His metaphor was apt. He *was* like her fucking shadow. She couldn't turn around without him being there. Oh, he'd been smart enough to get his own room—one door down from hers in a barely big-enough janitor's closet…that he left the door open to…and slept with his head in the opening so he'd immediately sense any movement in the hall—but he was making a pure nuisance of himself the rest of the time. He was worse than Aaron. Not only did Valin show up anywhere and everywhere she was or planned to be—including her damn dreams—but he wouldn't let things rest, either. Aaron at least had brains enough to not ask her more questions after being given a blatant shutdown. But Valin's current favorite topic of discussion was her feeding habits, which *so* wasn't happening.

Gabby had managed to feed the other night before Valin found her, but the moment they'd run into each other he'd been all over her the whole way back to base. Demanding to know why she'd run, whether she'd fed, *who* she'd fed from, etc., etc., etc…He'd sounded like a damn jealous boyfriend. So she'd blatantly ignored him, slamming the door to her room in his face when he looked like he might follow her in. She'd thought for sure he'd either jimmy the lock or just plain ghost in, but he hadn't.

And she hadn't been at all disappointed over that fact. Nope, not at all.

"So, do you have any idea where Annie might have gone?" Valin asked, proving he'd been eavesdropping too. Why was she not surprised?

Gabby ignored him and pushed out the front doors, the sun greeting them with her warm rays. Gabby couldn't stop herself from taking a huge breath. Until four months ago, she'd forgotten how much the sun could warm the air, even on these shortening fall days.

"You think she'd come out here?"

"Probably out for coffee," she said and started down the steps, leaving a surprised Valin at the top.

"For coffee." Valin double-timed it to catch up with her. "Are you kidding me?"

"That or a slushee or a milkshake or some chai tea." She sighed. "As long as she gets her fix of oxygen, she doesn't much care what the beverage is."

"It's a wonder her dad doesn't cuff her down in the boiler room." He frowned. "Is there a boiler in the school's basement?"

Gabby shrugged. Didn't know or care. Nope, the only thing she cared about was the familiar redhead strolling down the street arm in arm with...damn, was that Bennett?

"Looks like your mate *found* her." She quoted the air with her fingers. It hadn't escaped Gabby's notice that Annie had been spending a lot of time loitering in whatever area of the base that the blond warrior happened to be in—using the excuse of studying his shields, of course. Not that the Paladin could teach Annie anything beyond what Gabby could—which was close to nothing unless Annie could learn to completely check her gift—but hey, the Paladin, with his golden good looks, was probably more enticing than Gabby's own grumbly nature. The problem was Gabby didn't think Annie's interest had escaped Jacob's notice either. The Paladin might not know it, but he was holding a grenade in his hand, without the pin. One wrong move and the thing would blow up in his face.

Valin glanced over at her, brow raised. "Bennett wouldn't have helped Annie escape if that's what you're implying."

"Maybe," she conceded. "But they seem pretty chummy, don't they?"

"And you care that they're getting along because?"

Gabby gestured sharply at the cozy scene. "Because Jacob's going to be pissed if he sees them like that, that's why."

"Ah…yes…because daughters, even grown ones, should never have any interest in a man. Especially one as ugly as that British bloke."

Gabby blew out a breath that bellied her exasperation. "That's not what I meant. And Jacob wouldn't have anything against him being British."

"Just a Paladin?"

Gabby didn't answer. Not because she wanted to spare Valin's—or Bennett's—feelings, but because the truth was she didn't know. She had to admit the impression she got from the gifteds at the base was that the Paladin had turned their back on them long ago, and thus they had no intention of going out of their way to make friends. But did they actually harbor resentment toward them? Gabby wasn't sure.

Feeling moody, she stomped the rest of the way down the stairs, and then, with her arms folded across her breasts, carefully scanned the street while she waited for Jacob's lost lamb to be shepherded home by Bennett. And that was what he was doing. Despite the fact that their arms were linked, there was a set scowl on his face that was punctuated with more than one worried glance over his shoulder. Valin noticed too that the knife, which Valin wore wherever the heck he went now, was loosened in its sheath, his knuckles tightening around the jewel-encrusted hilt.

Fucking Paladin blade. The thing was an early grave maker. "You better be careful if you have to draw that thing around me."

He looked over at her. "I told you that you never had to worry about this blade being used to harm you."

"Accidents happen."

His mouth pulled up in a smug, lopsided smile. "Not unless I want them to, cookie."

"Stop calling me that."

And the other side of his mouth followed, forming a full-fledged grin that made her blood heat in her veins.

Damn the man. How did he get to her so easily?

"Were you followed?" Valin asked when Bennett and Annie got close enough, beating her to it.

"Don't think so. Though it's hard to tell around her." Bennett jerked his head toward Annie.

"Hey!" Annie yanked her arm from his, her lips pulling into an offended pout before turning to Gabby. "If we were, we lost them. We played the subway game for a good half hour."

"You better hope you did." Gabby jerked her head toward the stairs. "Inside. Now. Before your father comes roaring out here."

There was some mild grumbling, but Annie fell into step beside Gabby and the men behind them as they climbed. With each step, Gabby felt her frustration boil closer to the top. Annie pouted as if her foolishness wasn't the cause of this, Valin was watching her ass (she could feel his damn eyes skimming over her curves), and on top of all that she was tired again. Which meant, damn it, she was going to have to slip out from under his watch to feed again.

"Damn it, Annie. Do you have to pull this crap when I'm around?" Gabby snapped and then immediately felt guilty for taking out her frustrations on her. Not that

Gabby should. It was Annie's fault she was up this early. Her fault too that Valin was here, since it was Annie and her cohorts who'd drawn the Paladins' attention.

"You make it sound like it's a personal affront to you," Annie grumbled.

"Maybe not, but when you do it when I'm around, I have to deal with your father." Gabby glanced up the stairs. "And, crap, there he is."

Jacob was indeed pissed. And the moment Annie got within reach he took her by her elbow and walked her briskly down toward his office. It was a testament to how smart Annie actually was that she didn't give her dad any of the lip she normally gave Gabby. Still, Gabby just *knew* she was going to hear about this later.

Jacob was desperate to keep his daughter safe, and when the options he presented to Gabby had come down to either eliminating the two Paladin or keeping them close until their trustworthiness could be determined, Gabby had urged the latter. She might have wanted Valin gone, but that didn't mean she wanted him dead. Unless it was by her hand, that is, and right now she was severely tempted.

It was on her word that Valin and Bennett had been allowed the freedom Jacob had granted them. Jacob knew she had past dealings with some of the Paladin and had trusted her assessment that Bennett was too honorable to break a vow and Valin (whom she wouldn't put it past to break a vow) was simply too willing to thumb his nose at authority and wouldn't give them up to the wrath of the stuffy old council. How stupid had she been? There were only two reasons for Bennett to be outside at the same time Annie was, and despite what she might have implied to Valin, she knew it hadn't been as an accomplice.

"And you!" She rounded on the frowning Bennett, who stared down the hall after Jacob and Annie.

Bennett blinked, turning back to her. "Me what?"

"Who were you chatting with out there?"

"Chatting with?"

Gabby couldn't tell if he was being deliberately obtuse or not. "I could sense you reaching out across the miles. But once you tapped in I couldn't make out much of anything."

Valin stepped closer, his gaze narrowed on her. "You're able to pick up shielded projected thoughts, by people who aren't even near you, and through the base's shields?"

"Shields I made," she reminded him, then sighed when both men continued to stare at her. "Yes, okay?"

The men exchanged looks, which had her squirming. And how the heck had the tables been turned on her?

"What?" she snapped.

"Nothing, cookie. Just impressive for a merker."

Her jaw dropped open, her breath momentarily hung up in her lungs. "Merker?" she finally managed to gasp out. "You think I'm a damn merker?"

She could feel her face heating. Her entire bloodstream was heating. How could Valin believe that? And if he really did believe her to be Ganelon's child, then why the hell didn't he use his damn knife on her?

"Or…uh…maybe just part merker." He at least had the decency to look a little bit remorseful for saying it, but he still said it, damn him.

She glared at him, hard, and wondered why he didn't

fall down and bleed out on the pavement. Probably his superhuman Paladin genes made him resistant to the daggers she was sending him out of her eyes. He did get all defensive though.

"Roland said once that your mother was pure succubus and, well, your daddy couldn't have been human if you can do what you say you can do."

"If I say I can?" And now he thought she was a liar too? And, okay, she could maybe see why he might have come up with the conclusion he had. Succubus were nothing if not liars, using their seductive powers to imprint ideas in the heads of naïve fools across the globe. But they couldn't actually project or receive exact thoughts. Still, it pissed her off that his only conclusions were either the grand title of Liar or having Ganelon's blood in her veins. Not that her mommy's demon blood didn't make her heritage pretty questionable, but somehow being the daughter of a succubus seemed a lot better when she knew her real daddy had been a Paladin. Ergo she had no relation to Lucifer's right-hand bastard, the betrayer Ganelon.

"There are a lot of other possibilities besides human," she told him in a dangerously quiet voice. "But whatever, you're going to think what you want."

Valin started to open his mouth to speak, but she turned her back on him—she'd deal with him and his holier-than-thou thoughts later—and directed her gaze at Bennett. "Now that your matey here has gotten me even more pissed off, maybe you want to make nice and tell me who you were chatting with."

"I told Annie, but if it eases your mind, I'll tell you also."

"Thank you," she ground from between her clenched teeth. Righteous bastards. Both of them. She'd let Jacob deal with Bennett after she determined the extent of his indiscretion, but Valin? Well, she hoped he had his will in order.

"We've been gone long enough I thought it best to check in with the council, else they might start wondering and searching."

"You thought it best," she sputtered. "Even though both Logan and his daddy could doubtlessly tell exactly where you were contacting them from?"

"I didn't contact either Calhoun."

"No?"

"I contacted Karissa."

She worked her jaw, not sure if that still pissed her off or not. Yes, Karissa might be able to figure out where Bennett had been—the woman's shields had certainly gotten better if Gabby hadn't been able to sense it was she whom Bennett had been speaking with—but Karissa was much less apt to pass that information along to her estranged father. She might tell her brother though, and she said as much to Bennett. "You don't think she'll tell Logan where you guys are? No offense to pretty boy, but I don't think he'd stand up long against his father if Senior really wanted the information."

Both men shuffled uncomfortably, exchanging looks.

"What?"

"Gabby…" Valin reached out, taking her hand in a gesture that was not so alarming for the contact, but the fact that he felt the need to do so.

"What?" She stomped her foot.

Another set of exchanged glances, and then Valin

cleared his throat. "Logan isn't, uh, in any sort of state to be speaking with Karissa right now. Or his father."

"Why the hell not? Is he hurt?"

"Not exactly, well, sorta."

"Not exactly, well sorta?" she repeated. Damn, her chest was feeling tight; didn't stop her from raising her voice though. "What the hell does that mean?"

"His mate died last week."

"Last week," she repeated him again, as if she were having trouble with the words penetrating her obtuse skull.

"Ten days ago to be exact."

Gabby's blood went cold. Ten days. That would be right after Annie and the boys had broken into Haven. Gabby had been pissed over the girl going behind everyone's back to deliver her message, but secretly she was also glad. Logan had always been nice to her. He'd also been the only one to stand beside her father when he'd been expelled from the Paladin order. Logan didn't deserve to be punished with the loss of his mate. Yeah, life in general sucked. Nothing was fair, but this? Logan had been nothing but faithful in his belief in the Paladin mission of eradicating evil, further proving his honor by his loyalty to his friends.

And look where it got him.

Gabby shook her head, swallowing back the lump in her throat. Better to take what you want. Even if, for her, all she wanted was revenge. For her. For her daddy. For all the stupid naïve humans affected by this war. And now for Logan too.

"Excuse me," she said, easing her hand from Valin's grip. "I need to be alone." And for once, Valin didn't follow her, though damn it, wouldn't you know that this one time she wished he would.

—*∿∿*—

The doors banged open. Ganelon looked up from his perch on the chaise lounge chair at the back of the covens' entry hall in time to see Christos stride in, his pretty new face a thundercloud as he shouted orders left and right.

"I want a meeting in the dining hall now! And I want that worthless excuse for my second laid out on the table before me. And why is it so fucking cold in here? You couldn't light a goddamn fire?"

His orders weren't met with the immediate obedience he probably expected, but rather a collective response of hisses and curses as the daylight speared into the dark, and yes, rather chilly interior. A few moments of chaos ensued as any vampire in the area scrambled to get out of range of the deadly rays. Ganelon sat unmoving, admittedly thankful for the warmth of the sun—even if it did make him have something in common with the idiot fuming his way across the grand entry hall.

"Stupid weaklings." Christos shook his head as he stomped his way across the black marble tiles. It wasn't until he had practically passed by that he caught sight of Ganelon and drew up short. "What the fuck? Who let him in?"

When no one answered—probably because no one was there to answer—Christos planted his hands on his hips and glared down at Ganelon. "Well?"

"Tired of being back in charge already?" Ganelon

asked Christos, nodding pointedly at the doors that he'd left open during his rampage.

Christos grunted. A moment later a human lamb rushed in and slammed the door closed, cutting off Ganelon's sun. Too bad.

"What are you doing here?" Christos directed the question at Ganelon this time.

Ganelon inspected his nails in the flickering gaslight, digging out some dried blood from his recent... persuasion...session. Christos huffed and Ganelon had to suppress a grin, secretly enjoying the waves of irritation coming off the vampire king. He drew the pause out as long as he deemed necessary to reestablish his superiority, but not so long that he'd drastically increase the amount of time he'd have to suffer being here. Though frankly, anything over nothing was too long.

Ganelon ground his teeth, chafing at the orders that had made his presence here necessary. How was it that Lucifer actually believed this idiot would be instrumental in bringing about the Paladins' demise? Christos was not suited for the subtleness the task required. Besides, a one-line prophecy made years ago about some child conceived of light and born in darkness being the key to breaching the worlds did not necessarily mean the destruction of His warriors, Lucifer's sworn enemies.

"The liege lord sent me," Ganelon said, flicking the loosened blood from his nails onto the floor. "He wanted me to make sure you didn't need anything."

Christos scowled, not appreciating Lucifer's lack of confidence. At that moment, the lamb who'd closed the door made to scurry by them but stopped short when

Christos turned his gaze on it, making it shiver in its shredded clothes. "Wine for me and my brother. You may tell Stephan that he's been granted a reprieve."

The lamb nodded and bolted by. Doubtlessly glad the request was wine and not blood.

"Trouble on the home front?" Ganelon asked.

"My second is an incompetent fool. One task he set out to accomplish in the last four months while I've been gone and even that he screws up! How could he have not known about the girl?" He frowned, the skin around his eyes and nose pinching in anger. "At least he better not know about the girl."

"Must be some girl. Where did you see her?" Ganelon asked, taking the glass of wine that the lamb had returned with. As soon as he'd clasped the cup, the lamb went rushing out again.

Christos sneered at the creature's fleeing back and then grunted, flopping down in a wing chair that flanked the chaise and propping his feet up on the end table. "In Brooklyn. By that Martyr's Ship Monument or something," he added, waving his hand.

Ganelon blinked. "You were in a park? In Brooklyn?"

"I've been visiting the other covens in the surrounding areas. Putting to rest the rumors of my...demise."

"But the park?"

"Antoine has a flair for the gothic. He found it amusing to convert a few key humans in order to build a hidden set of chambers while the crypts beneath the monument were being constructed."

"How cliché."

"Isn't it?" Christos shook his head, then sighed pensively. "She was walking with a fucking Paladin."

"A Paladin?" Ganelon prompted, realizing they were back on the topic of the girl.

"At least I'm pretty sure he was. He was older, but he looked an awful lot like the adolescent brat that escaped the Oxford cleansing."

Ganelon nodded, well aware of the incident Christos spoke of. It was one of those events that Lucifer had raved on and on about. How Christos, Lilith's son, had captured, tortured, and killed a half-dozen full-blooded Paladin and their part-blooded children. After Lilith's death, Christos had taken on her position as the vampire leader. He'd left a few of his mother's best men with a handful of vampires to hold Europe and Asia, but he'd taken the bulk of his coven here to America. That had been back in the 1800s, so the adolescent Paladin would be full grown by now. Still, Ganelon thought Christos should be able to tell for sure if it was the same man, unless, of course, Lucifer had been wrong in his belief that he'd managed to infuse Christos's new body with some of the sacrificed souls' gifts and talents.

"You could not tell for sure?" he asked, calmly sipping the wine. It would be poisoned, of course—Christos was ever the opportunist. But it didn't matter. First, his lovely genetics made him resistant to things that would kill a normal man, and second, he'd made a point of increasing his resistance further by building an immunity to such things.

He shook his head, a growl rumbling in his chest. "The damn girl. She must have been a null. I could sense nothing from her!" He pounded the table. "I couldn't even sense that half-wit Paladin and I was practically on top of them both before I noticed them."

Ganelon tapped the table, his heart racing in concert as he thought about the possibilities…assuming Christos was actually correct, which was a big assumption, given the vampire's track record. "Being able to nullify the magic in one's surroundings is a pretty powerful gift. Something more than I thought a mixed-blood human could achieve."

Christos shook his head. "If there is one thing my second did right in my absence it was hunting down the part-breeds. There is a whole crowd of them with some pretty impressive gifts. He suspects they've even started their own recruitment methods and are creating a little army of gifted soldiers."

"And you think you saw one of them today with a Paladin."

"I know I saw one. You don't create that sort of energy vacuum around yourself without being a null."

Ganelon rubbed his chin. "So it's possible they've joined with the Paladin, then. If this…man…is who you think he is."

"I would bet my second's head on it."

"But not your own?"

Christos shrugged, a sly smile twisting his lips. "I'm a big believer in delegation."

"Hmmm." Ganelon used to think that way too. He was learning lately that allowing minions to do the important work wasn't always a good idea. At least not without a heavy hand leading them. He was still pissed over the failure in his last endeavor. He hadn't gotten the key that would allow him to infiltrate Haven. What's more, Logan was being stubbornly stoic in his grief and that stubbornness seemed to be his anchor for his sanity.

Calhoun Junior hadn't fallen yet. Ganelon was really kind of pissed at that. He'd expected the Paladin to go on a rampage within hours, if not days, of his mate's demise. But it had been almost ten now and all the big bastard was doing was sulking.

Should have killed him. That would have been the best way to stick it to the Calhouns.

Luckily he had someone to take his frustrations out on. His wayward son Damon was proving to be a willful bastard and Ganelon was enjoying reminding him of what proper deference meant. When Ganelon finished with him he figured his son would either have regained his place as dutiful minion or not. And if not? Well, the liege lord always had souls that he was hoping to resurrect.

"They headed for the subway, but I got the impression that was a change in plans. It's likely that their base is there near that park," Christos said, though he appeared to be mulling things over rather than speaking to Ganelon. Still, Ganelon didn't want to appear unhelpful, not when Christos would probably go and whine to Lucifer about his lack of assistance.

"Do you need my services to help you locate it?"

Christos curled back his lip, flashing fang. "I am perfectly capable of handling a bunch of wannabes."

"All right then. You know how to reach me if you change your mind." Ganelon stood, smiling as he offered his hand to Christos. Christos glanced down at it in disgust but ended up taking it. "Take care, brother. May your hunting meet with great success."

"No worries…brother." Christos's pupils flashed fire as he met Ganelon's gaze. "I'm quite sure it will."

Ganelon nodded, taking his hand back and rubbing it on his pants before he made his way out of the room. A lamb rushed ahead of him to open the great wooden doors, just enough for him to slip through. The warm sun greeted him with enthusiasm, and damn if it didn't feel brighter today than normal.

Turned out his visit with Christos had been the pick-me-up he needed. He would, of course, send his own scouts in, but in the end he'd let Christos call the shots on this. It wasn't like Lucifer could find fault with what Ganelon was doing either. The liege lord had made it perfectly clear to Ganelon that he was to treat Christos as an equal, and so Ganelon had. He'd reached out and welcomed his brother back, even offered his aid, and Christos had refused, which suited Ganelon just fine. Let Christos soil his own bed with another screwup. It was just the sort of thing Ganelon needed to shore up the foundations of his status with the liege lord. And then, after, he'd be there to collect the bounty. Oh, yes, that null was going to be very useful indeed.

Chapter 7

SHOULD HAVE FOLLOWED HER. THE ASSUMPTION THAT Gabby wouldn't try to slip out until the sun went down had been a stupid one on his part. When she'd headed back into the base after claiming she wanted to be alone, Valin had thought to allow her a moment and take care of some other business while she was safe—and most likely sleeping—in her room. That's what vampires did, after all: sleep during the day. But Gabby wasn't beholden to such necessities anymore. And though she'd spent most of yesterday doing just that, he shouldn't have assumed she'd do so again.

With his options dwindled to trying to hunt her down again or trusting that she'd return, he'd decided to show some faith and spent the day making plans. Plans that started with buttering up the other recruits in the base and making nice with some of the more established soldiers in hopes of learning what sort of strategy might get him in Jacob's good graces. Not that he really gave a crap what the tight-ass thought of him, but he figured he should make the effort. Gabby might not want his blood—or anything else to do with him, for that matter—but if he were to become a standard fixture in her life she might just start to relax around him, at least long enough for him to infiltrate her defenses.

And that was working out so well too. Hard to become a standard fixture when she wasn't there.

Valin took a deep breath, concentrating on stretching his awareness on another sweep of the area around them. Nothing. Not a hint of an evil presence in a ten-block area. Which meant there wasn't a hint of Gabby either. Not that he'd expected her to be nearby, but when the day had worn down and he'd agreed to Jacob's suggestion of a little patrol to get a feel of his and Bennett's skills, Valin supposed he'd been harboring some sort of hope he might find her.

He frowned, thinking of the dark stain on Gabby's soul and his little foot-in-mouth routine that morning. He'd called her a merker. And though he hadn't really put much thought behind her heritage, he realized that he had, in fact, assumed she was at least partially one. From the little he'd gathered from Roland and Logan, Gabby's mother had been a highly ambitious sort when it came to rising up the ranks of Lucifer's army. Valin had just assumed that someone who was willing to trade her daughter's life to gain the good graces of the vampire's leader would have been more than happy to spread her legs for one of the more powerful merkers out there, if not Ganelon himself. But thinking of his current batting average, Valin now realized that might have been yet another bad assumption.

He hadn't met a merker yet that didn't have a stain of evil. And before Gabby had pulled her disappearing act in that mine, her soul had been about as pure as new-fallen snow. Okay, maybe not quite—there had been some real roughness about the edges—but where it counted there had not been anything intrinsically evil to it. Was his guess on her heritage really that off? Valin wouldn't care either way. The only thing that he actually cared about was how that stain had gotten there—and how to get rid of it.

Merker blood or not, she certainly wasn't tapping into her succubus heritage. Granted, he hadn't gotten that much time to observe her, but it was enough to see she made a point to suppress her natural seductive powers. Not that it seemed to put a dent in Aaron's little puppy dog interest. He was still trying to worm his way into her presence at every opportunity, and the drop-dead glances he reserved for Valin were becoming hard for even Valin—who didn't give a shit—to ignore. Only reason Valin hadn't bloodied him up yet was that Gabby hadn't reacted at all to his less-than-stellar advances. He better fucking watch it, though.

He glanced over his shoulder to where Aaron was bringing up the rear with Bennett...and received a dagger-eyed glare for his trouble.

Beside him Jacob cleared his throat. "Remind me in the future not to place you two on any patrol shifts together."

Valin raised his brow. "Does this mean we pass?" He figured the only reason Jacob had let them come out tonight was not so much to "get a feel" for their skill level but because the man wanted to test them and see where their loyalties lie.

"Not yet, but so far so good. And if you and Aaron both make it back without bloodied noses—or worse—I think we can consider this a success."

"Wonderful," Valin drawled and received an inquisitive look from Jacob. "Good to know you trust me."

Jacob chuckled. "Hell no, I don't trust you. But I do trust in your nature."

"And what is my nature?"

"To protect your mate. Which is why I'm going to reiterate to my brother that he needs to back the hell off you and Gabriella."

Valin felt like the air had been sucked out from around him. For a moment all he could do was blink at Jacob—as if clearing his eyes would reveal a two-headed demon rather than the soldier that walked beside him.

Jacob cocked his brow. "The hovering around her all the time, the I'll-kill-you glare you give any man that comes near…that crazed look in your eyes whenever you don't know where she is? You're not going to tell me I'm wrong, are you?"

Valin blew out a breath and nodded. "You're not wrong."

"Then why are you so surprised? You don't think I would try and spare my brother the heartache if I can?"

"No, I'm just surprised you know about the mate bond." The mate bond was a once in a lifetime kind of thing for a Paladin. Beyond silly notions of true love, kindred spirits, or even a human's idea of soul mates, it was a bond between two souls that was designed by the Big Guy Himself. The original angelic volunteers who'd come to earth to pick up weapons against the fallen Lucifer's evil hordes had thought it their reward for the sacrifice they'd had to make to take up those arms— the peace and completeness a Paladin received from the mate bond being the balm for a soul that had been rendered incomplete at the removal of its wings. But as more time passed and less mate bonds were forged, the golden glow of that idea faded as newer generations of warriors were forced to search out compatibility pairings in order to ensure the continuity of their order. In fact, most of the Paladin alive today had never found their mates. And when they did? Well, look at what happened to Logan.

Jacob heaved a large sigh, shifting the belt of ammo strapped over his shoulder under his trench coat. Valin wondered briefly if the man wore the coat in the hot summer months too, and if not, how he hid the virtual warehouse of weapons he toted around from the general public.

"My parents were mated," Jacob said, causing Valin to do the blinky-blinky headlight thing again. "Oh, they didn't call it a bond, just soul mates. My father told me it was far more than simple love. I always thought it was kinda kooky until Mother died. He died a week later. Stupid thing, really; picked a fight with one of those half-demon creatures. I think he knew he wasn't going to come out of it alive and I think he was glad for it."

Valin nodded, swallowing the jagged shard of lead that seemed to have magically appeared in his throat. "It's common, actually. The loss of a bond mate has been known to drive the remaining mate to insanity. Especially if they feel like the other's death could have been prevented."

"Prevented by them, you mean."

Valin nodded again, not even able to respond this time. If he hadn't been off skipping around the shade that night…if he had kept a tether open rather than clamping tight on his shields…

Jacob frowned, studying him. "Is there only ever one soul mate, or can a Paladin move on?"

Valin took a deep breath, pushing away the what-ifs. Even if Angeline had been able to reach him in her need, it was unlikely he would have gotten there in time. "A Paladin can live if his will is strong enough, but not move on," he answered, surprised at how calm and even his voice came out. Though it must have been too even, too measured, because Jacob was staring at him knowingly.

He gave a barely perceptible shake of his head. *Don't ask. Don't make me relive that.*

Jacob frowned, coming to a complete stop under a flickering lamppost. "You've lost someone."

Not a question, but a statement, and one that had the other man obviously struggling to fit in with the little he thought he knew of mate bonds and what Valin had just supposedly confirmed about his feelings for Gabriella.

Valin turned to look at him, well aware of the fact that Bennett and Aaron had drawn close enough to hear. Didn't matter. Bennett already knew and Aaron, well, right now he didn't give much of a fuck about that prick.

"I lost my pair bond. She was my best friend and we were compatible enough to be given His blessing and form a pairing." He swallowed, looking forward. "However, I was not blessed enough to share her life for more than a few years." And never Peanut's. He'd never get to hold his unborn child.

"Valin?"

He sensed more than saw Bennett come up beside him, his hand hovering awkwardly above his shoulder. Valin shook his head, stepping away from the Paladin's offer of support. It was too fucking close to comfort and might very well break the dam on the grief that he'd shored up so very long ago.

"I thought we were on patrol," he snapped as he spun around and stalked toward the next intersection, the other three falling in line. Their silence was so thick that the flapping wings of a pigeon taking off from the roof of the boarded-up building beside them had him practically jumping out of his skin.

Stupid. How long had he stood there pouring out his heart and opening old wounds? More important, why had he let Jacob peel back those scabs? He rolled his shoulders, closing his eyes briefly as he sent out his consciousness for another sweep. What trickled across his senses had his muscles tensing into hard knots. "Oh, shit."

"What?" Jacob asked, his hand shifting into the folds of his trench coat.

No need to answer when two merkers rounded the corner less than ten feet ahead of them. Unfortunately they weren't the only ones who'd just pinged on his radar.

<<*Bennett! The roof!*>> he yelled, hoping the projective blast would distract the merker enough to make him hesitate. But it was too late. That was a pyrotechnic merker back there, and this time hell had come from above.

Gabby fought for breath, her knees buckling as she reached out for something to catch herself on. Nothing was there. She stumbled to the sidewalk as the blast of Valin's projection wrenched through her mind, tearing at both her shields and her grasp on consciousness. For five long seconds she battled the pounding wave of fear and alarm that rolled in like a tsunami after the initial stab of contact, concentrating instead on the gritty feel of the cement beneath her fingertips. Couldn't think. Couldn't breathe!

Finally she was able to gasp in air. For once, the sweet ache of gas fumes and rotting trash filling her lungs was a welcome sensation, as was the fact that she was alone in her mind once more to enjoy the return to her own reality and the comforting blanket of her shields snapping back in place. That is, it was reassuring until she realized that she had no fucking idea what had happened.

Holy crap, Valin packed a powerful punch. How had he breached her shields like that? Why had she caught the thought that had obviously been meant for someone else? And how the heck had he managed to project what he was feeling along with the thought?

Gabby wasn't an empathic. Nor was Valin. And projective thought did not convey that level of emotions. Not that she cared about the how right now; what was important was the thought and emotions themselves. Alarm. Fear. For who? Bennett? Or was that fear possibly for himself?

She sucked in a breath, the cool air chilling the sweat that had beaded out on her exposed skin. Whoever the fear had been for, someone was in danger. Given the power behind the projection, they couldn't be that far away, which meant she was most likely the closest one to providing aid.

Flat-out ignoring the street bum staring at her from his hidey hole in an alcove across the way, she pushed herself up and broke into a run. The residual throbbing in her head made the pounding pace difficult, but with each stride she found an inner strength that pushed her forward faster.

Not far. Can't be far. Two, maybe three, streets over?

A scream cut through the air, her gut tightening and twisting at the grating scrape of pure agony. Definitely not far, but more north than east. Ducking between two badly parked hunks of junk, she cut across the street, aiming for the narrow delivery entrance across the way. She knew from patrolling these streets for the last few months that it backed up against the brick wall of the building behind it, but the building itself was only a few stories high, had lots of hand and foot-holds in it, and conveniently sat across from an even shorter building.

Without thought to who else besides the bum might be around, she gathered her muscles and leapt for the narrow ledge framing a second-story window. It took her longer than she wanted to scale the building, but the wasted time was easily made up when she sprinted across the rubber roofline, grasped onto the brick lip on the far side, and pushed off, drawing on her supernatural strength and the willpower of desperation.

The street flashed beneath her—a streetlamp, a couple scurrying pedestrians in dark hoodies furtively heading in opposite directions, an idling car with its lights off down at the corner—and then she was land-ing, the impact forcing her down onto all fours as she fought to keep moving forward. This roof wasn't as well cared for, the cracked rubber pitted and covered with a skin-abrading combo of tar and fine asphalt. Ignoring the sting, she went into a tuck, rolling up into a crouch, then spun around a rotating vent that popped up in her way, only to come up against the short lip of the backside of the building. Unfortunately, this is where her shortcut ended. Grasping onto the edge, she vaulted over, dropping down onto the sidewalk below with a teeth-rattling jar.

"Gabriella!"

She jerked her head around, spinning on the balls of her feet toward the sound of Jacob's voice. A hundred yards distant came Jacob and Bennett, their pace frantic but stunted as they half-dragged, half-carried Aaron between them. Aaron gritted his teeth, but he couldn't hold back the grunts and moans of agony as the two men dragged him along.

Gabby sucked in a breath, her gaze dragging over his wounds. His favored gray T-shirt and cargo pants had been singed until they looked like the equivalent of charred Swiss cheese, each gaping hole exposing glistening red flesh. The burns ran up the side of his thigh, stretching across his torso and the entire right side of his face. He looked like something out of a Batman comic—or a war zone.

"Aaron..." She shook her head, choking back the keen of misery that rose. Just as sharply fury followed. No one harmed what was hers. Yeah, she might have wanted to rough up the idiot more times than she could count, but that was her right as his friend and mentor.

"Who did this?" she demanded, rushing over to them.

"Bloody pyros..." Bennett shook his head as he made to shrug out from under Aaron's armpit. "Here, help get him home. I need to go back."

Her gut clenched. Bennett wasn't like her. He was more of a practical sort and didn't appear to buy into petty things like revenge. So the only reason she could think of for him to be going back was..."Valin?"

He nodded. "He stayed behind to protect our retreat."

Against a pyrotechnic merker, and Lucifer knew what else. "Oh god, no…"

Ignorant of Bennett's swearing, she bolted down the street.

Chapter 8

VALIN DODGED ANOTHER FIREBALL, FEELING THE CURL of the hair on the back of his calf as he dove behind a jacked-up van missing all four tires. Protected from sight, he immediately shifted into a formless shadow and, taking advantage of a gust of wind and the scattering of leaves it kicked up, made his retreat to a nearby Dumpster. The van, already coated with graffiti, inherited another coat of dark char as the pyrotechnic merker worked to ensure that Valin wouldn't be coming out of there alive again. Amazingly enough, the van didn't blow, showing that tires weren't the only thing to be lifted by the locals, but gasoline too.

"Sorry, buddy, no boom-boom today," Valin muttered from a safe distance of a couple dozen yards away and settled down to wait.

Damn, that had been close, though not as close as the previous round they'd played. If he wasn't careful he wasn't going to make it out of here at all. Not that getting out of here was his goal at the moment, but ultimately it would be nice.

He flexed his elbow, wincing at the pull of pain that came from stretching the burnt skin and muscle. Damn if it might actually scar. Though he should be thankful it wasn't his face. Poor fucking kid. As much as Valin didn't like puppy dog's attitude, he didn't harbor Aaron any real harm. But because Valin had screwed up and lost his focus, the kid was going to go through life with a messed-up face…assuming he lived that long.

He'll live, but only if you keep these fuckers off their asses. Speaking of which, where were they? He and the pyro had been playing cat and mouse for the last five minutes, which given the extent of Aaron's injuries was probably another five short of long enough for Bennett and Jacob to drag the invalid far enough away that these merkers wouldn't give chase.

Valin's stalling techniques had consisted of the classic strategy of pissing them off (slitting two of their throats in quick succession would do that). He'd stuck around long enough to finish the job on one with a good carving session with his pretty knife to both head and heart, but had to skip off into the shade before finishing off the merker's temporarily immobilized buddy for fear of getting fried. After that the game had really started. With one down, one recovering, and the last out for blood—his, to be precise—Valin had made a game of wagging his naked jangles in the universal taunt of the ages…then hiding and ghosting in time to avoid becoming a crispy critter. At least mostly un-crispy. More like the original recipe perhaps. But levels of doneness aside, this time his pyromaniac buddy didn't appear to be seeking, which was simply not acceptable.

If he thought he could ghost in close enough to sneak up behind the bastard and take him out, this would all be much easier. Unfortunately his options were vastly limited, given that he'd had to ditch his knife the moment he'd first shifted into the shade.

A longing glance at the inert knife on the sidewalk halfway down the street showed the other merker staggering to his knees, one hand clamped tight to his throat, the other pressed hard against the nearby lamp-post. Aaaannnnnd so much for almost-even odds. If the merker was up, it wouldn't be more than a minute or so before he was running too. Too bad it wouldn't be away.

Taking a deep breath, Valin took stock of his options, which yielded about the same amount of return as his recent investment in the stock market—far less than stellar. If he thought he could ghost over there, grab his knife, and do a little slice and dice before the pyro could join the round, he'd go for the kill. But he didn't trust the pyro's scruples enough to not indulge in a little friendly fire if it meant taking out his intended target, which, um, yeah, would be Valin.

He had just about come to the conclusion that making like Speedy Gonzales and vamoosing in hopes they'd follow was his only option, when a guttural cry erupted from the cross street. Who the hell?

Risking exposure, he ducked his head back out, then sucked in a breath. That was Gabby, knife drawn, and running all out at the pyro.

Fuck. No…

"Gabby!" He leapt up from his hiding spot, then cursed and ducked as his own knife sailed toward his head.

That was just so wrong: a merker using a Paladin blade against him. He hoped the cost had been a nice burn on the fucker's hand at least.

Valin was torn between ghosting to where the pyro was patiently waiting for Gabby to get close enough and grabbing for his knife, but his decision was made when the second merker simply disappeared, only to immediately reappear directly in front of him.

Fuckingcraptastic. A teleporter? Boy, was Senior going to be pissed to find out Karissa wasn't the only one with those skills.

Knowing the merker would simply be on top of him again the moment he reformed from the shade, Valin dove for his knife, simultaneously tossing out a warning to Gabby. <<*Get back! He's a pyrotechnic!*>>

He hoped to hell she heard, prayed even harder that she'd actually fucking listen to him and get the hell out of here, but he didn't have the time to make sure as his hand had barely closed around the blade when the second merker was on top of him, its iron-heavy fists pummeling into him like goddamn battering rams.

He rolled away, ignoring a sharp crack from his lowest rib as one of the blows grazed his side just right, and scrambled to his feet, quickly putting some distance between them. He'd barely had time to settle his grip on his blade when the merker flashed in directly in front of him. Luckily Valin had anticipated that and got in a good stab to the merker's midsection. The merker roared, immediately flashing. Only the stupid fuck forgot that anything touching him went with him, which meant both Valin's knife and Valin went with Star Trek boy too. A split second and a disorienting fifty feet later, Valin and the merker staggered away from each other, each clutching at their most recent wounds.

"Wanna try that again?" Valin asked, stalling as much for a chance to clear his head as anything else.

"Want to die so soon?" The merker sneered back, then, rude bastard that he was, charged before Valin could retort with his own quippy comeback.

Probably not a bad thing; would have been pretty lame anyway.

Valin crouched, readying for the impact, only at the last second the merker flashed out. Instinct had Valin spinning, his blade rising in a defensive arc. Good thing too, as the merker reappeared a couple feet in the air behind and above him. Because of his quick thinking, gravity turned into his friend and the merker received another hole in his body, this one a deep gash across his thigh as Valin continued to spin out from under him.

With the merker howling obscenities, Valin risked a glance toward Gabby, then wished he hadn't as his heart came to an abrupt halt in his chest. As he watched, she leapt onto a car, pushed off, her body twisting, feet flying out like a fucking ballerina as she whizzed over the pyro's head, the arc of flame chasing her through the air. One of those feet connected, the audible crack of bones fragmenting a welcome sound in the pandemonium of the dual fight. Sensing the second merker bearing down on him, Valin rolled out from under another attack. Valin barely caught the movement of the pyro slumping out of the corner of his eye.

Still, he needed to end this.

On a gamble, Valin heaved his knife into the air, the sharp blade all but disappearing from sight as it sailed up, up, up into the darkness. It was hard to miss the merker's what-the-fuck expression. For a split second pure shock rooted his feet to the spot as it tried to decipher why Valin would toss away his only weapon.

"So I can kill you, fuckwad," Valin muttered. He knew he had to time this right. The knife reached the pinnacle of its arc a good dozen stories up and began to fall. He waited. The one thing that could screw up this plan would be if the merker looked back his way, but the stupid shit never took his eyes off the knife to see Valin shift. If Valin had enough substance to shake his head, he would have as he watched the switch from confusion to determination cross the merker's face as he prepared to teleport. Valin thrust his essence across the expanse toward the knife. The next part was tricky and he had to concentrate hard to twist just enough of his ghostly substance back into semi-solid mass. The knife settled into the shadowy form of his outstretched hand.

Pulling deep from his own energy stores, he kept the blade aloft, thrusting the knife forward before releasing the agonizing hold he had on the rest of his substance that wanted to follow his hand's example and reform. It all took but a split second. Just long enough to drain the hell out of him, but long enough for the ultimate pay-off. The merker popped back in. But because Valin had shoved the knife's trajectory that foot and a half forward before fully reforming, the merker's hand didn't grasp onto the knife, but rather Valin's arm—which, what do you know, happened to be attached to the blade now lodged deep in the merker's chest.

"Sayonara, A-hole." Valin smiled, calling forth the light that had been infused within the heavenly forged blade. Like lightning, it shot down the sharp-edged metal into flesh. The merker roared, his iron hands clamping down around Valin's forearms. Within its chest the blade continued to burn away at the merker's blackened heart. Unfortunately, like all things wonderful in Valin's life, this moment of joyous fuck-you was rudely interrupted too—by the hard-ass smack of reality called gravity.

Oh yeah, hitting the ground from that far up was a bitch. He tried to take away some of the shock by absorbing the impact by bending his knees, but that didn't stop the blast of you-stupid-fuck agony from shooting up his legs and driving a railroad spike of crap-that-hurts through his back and into the base of his brain. The only good news was it seemed to have a similar effect on his half-incapacitated buddy. The merker crumbled, his grip falling from Valin's arms and his body slipping from the blade as he fell ass backwards, his skull cracking most satisfyingly as it struck the asphalt. And yeah, minus the fact that his entire body was still cursing him out, things didn't get much better than this.

Valin smiled, straddling the merker, who was sprawled like an offering before him. Lots of practice made short work of the next step, and seconds later the merker's smoking skull lay detached from its body, the creature's soul obliterated with His light.

Damn, that had taken way too long.

Heart thudding, Valin spun, his gaze immediately searching out the dark shadows where the pyro had fallen. It was still there, only shit, so was Gabby, her slim body sprawled over the crumpled form of the unconscious merker.

"Gabby!" he choked out. Had she been hit by that last blast of fire? Images of her charred body flashed through his brain, pumping adrenaline through his system so that all pain and exhaustion were forgotten. The jolt allowed him to sprint across the expanse as fast, if not faster, than he could have in ghost form.

Scared to death of what he might find, he grabbed onto her shoulders and pulled, only to meet resistance.

"Gabby?" He tugged again, then recoiled as she snapped her head around and hissed at him. Wild eyes, blood-drenched fangs. Holy fucking hell, was she feeding from that thing? His question was immediately answered as she turned back to her meal, fangs flashing as she lunged at the merker's already gaping throat and sank in. The shock had him standing there like a dumb-ass, not moving, hardly breathing, just watching. He wasn't even aware of time passing until the world started to spin and he had to consciously draw in a long pull of air.

Way to go. Why don't I just pass out while she's vulnerable to any backup that happens to be on the way?

His oxygen-sucking routine must have startled Gabby because she leapt off the merker and staggered a few yards away.

Still feeling like the world was off-kilter, Valin stepped forward with his knife. Only, crap, the merker looked damn dead already. He squatted down, fingers fumbling at the merker's torn throat as he searched for a pulse. Not finding any, he reached out with his senses, but all he could feel from the merker was a fading stain of evil, not the pulsing taint of dark energy he'd expect from a live creature.

"What the fuck?" He stared at the blank eyes of the merker, his grip tight on the hilt of his knife. Any second now the creature was going to blink and pull one of its walking dead reanimation routines. Only it wasn't; it just laid there in a pool of its own blood, its dead eyes staring at nothing.

Holy crap. She'd killed a fucking merker! Drained it of not only its blood but its life energy.

There was a scrape from behind him, like boots scuffing on pavement. He spun on his heels, half-expecting to see one of those backup merkers he'd feared coming up behind them, but met, instead, with the vision of Gabby's backside as she half-ran, half-staggered down the street. Like she was, holy fucking hell, running away from him again.

He didn't even think. Dissolving into the shade, his knife clattered back to the ground as he sent the particles of shadow that held his essence after her. He reformed behind her, his frustration and anger propelling him forward so that his grab for her shoulder turned more into a tackle. She hissed, a sharp elbow digging deep into his already screaming rib cage as he tried to twist midair so as to take the brunt of the fall. Bad idea. The combo of her hit and the sharp smack of the hard pavement sent the air right out of him and his grip slipped. She rolled off him, her boots smacking pavement by his head as she bolted once more.

Goddamnit!

Valin rolled over, sucking air as he watched her crouch, all that compact strength pulling in as she sighted and locked on to her intended escape route: a narrow three-story brick building pinned between two taller cement monsters. Having seen Roland in action, he wasn't surprised she'd look to the rooftops to elude him, though he was a bit insulted that she thought it might work.

With a sigh, he took to the shade once more. His little minx was going to have to learn sometime that he wasn't going to let her run from him and now seemed like a damn fine time.

Thankfully Valin's second tackle went much better. Probably because she'd paused to catch her breath on the second rooftop she'd clambered up on. He'd barely reformed before he snatched her right wrist, twisting her around.

Her lips peeled back, exposing elongated fangs. Not at all intimidated, he grabbed her other wrist. Both hands in his firm grip, he spun and smashed her back into the roof's access door.

"What the hell is wrong with you?" she snapped, using every muscle in her tiny, pint-sized vampire body to try and dislodge him.

"Me? Where the fuck did you think you're going?"

"Oh, I don't know…wherever the hell I want?" She jerked her arms against his grip, then when that didn't work, used the metal door to try and lever her body into an arch. It took all his strength to keep her pinned, and all his willpower to not rub himself against the amazing set of curves that she was wiggling so deliciously against his naked self. Finally, with a muffled growl of frustration, she collapsed back against the door.

He was still trying to convince his little brain that this was not the time or place when it finally clicked in his head that she was shaking, badly. Concern that maybe she'd taken some injury during the fight that he hadn't seen had him loosening his grip. "Are you all right?"

"I'm fine," she hissed, her eyes flashing daggers that would have cut him open if possible. That look and his muscles that still ached from the effort it had taken to catch her should have been sufficient reassurance, but he still didn't like the trembling that shook through her thin frame, rattling everything from her teeth to the bones in her toothpick ankles.

How the heck could she be feeding like that and still be so damn skinny? Unless it was because it was merker blood. Maybe her body couldn't process it properly. Maybe...

He sucked in a breath as a horrible piece of the puzzle clicked into place. "Crap, Gabby, is this what's making you sick?"

"What's making me sick?"

"That." He jerked his head back in the direction of the fallen merker. "Are they what you've been feeding off of?"

She raised her brow and blew at a stray lock of hair that had fallen into her face as if wrapping up a *duh* and a *what do you care* all into one.

"Scratch that, of course they are. Do you always have this sort of reaction to them?"

"I don't know what you're talking about."

"Come on, Gabby. The shaking? The sweating?" *The oily slickness of evil coating your skin.* He didn't say the last part out loud. Still she sucked in a breath, clamping her pretty white fangs down on her lower lip as she averted her gaze. "Aw, fuck. It is, isn't it? You've been feeding off those things and it's making you sick." He shook his head. "You must realize the harm you're doing to yourself. Why, Gabby? Why are you doing it?"

"Maybe because I like it," she said, her voice lowered in a sibilant whisper. "Maybe because I need it."

"Need?" That she needed blood was a given, but to wreak such devastation upon herself?

"Oh yes, I need." Her gaze moved past him, her eyes sparking crimson as they looked back toward where the merker had fallen. "Before I die I'm going to see as many of those fuckers dead as I can."

Chapter 9

GABBY COULD TELL SHE'D SAID SOMETHING WRONG. Not that there could be much more wrong with this moment, and being pinned up against the flaking metal door was the least of it. She never let anyone see her feed, and this was why.

Humiliation burned along with the blazing bonfire of self-disgust. She didn't feed in front of anyone because she didn't want them to witness the sick pleasure she got from her bloodlust. Didn't want them to know how much she craved the dark energy that filled her after exacting just a bit more of her revenge upon Ganelon and his deceased maker.

Only with Valin it seemed infinitely worse. The dark anger in his gaze made her want to shrivel into a puddle of shame at his feet…or kick him in the nuts so as to see something else there.

She jutted her chin up instead. "What? You have a problem with that?"

His jaw clenched, obliterating the devil-may-care magnificence of his face into something far darker and strangely erotic.

That's the succubus in you talking, Gabby.

"You're not going to fucking die," he growled and then crushed his mouth to hers. Shock had her not reacting; otherwise she would have taken that kick to the boys. At a minimum twist her head away before she could compare the hard press of his lips from her recent imaginings to the reality of the man consuming her now. But she didn't, and he did, and it didn't take her a split second to realize how very wrong those fleetingly brief and definitely unwanted thoughts had been. His kiss wasn't hard and punishing but rather an invitation. Or more aptly, a challenge to explore the deliciousness of his mouth with her own.

Gabby had never been one to back away from a challenge. Challenges had to be met head-on—or at least circumvented through sly planning and sheer will. This didn't call for such finesse, so she threw herself into the kiss, battling his tongue for possession of their shared taste. He growled, the sound rumbling deep in his chest and vibrating against the softness of her breasts as he pressed himself tight against her.

Her heart thumped—hard—against her ribs. She tried to convince herself it was fear that made the organ seize up, fear of being trapped, fear of not being totally in control, but she knew it was a lie. This kiss was not about winning some sort of damn power struggle but about fulfilling a need. She needed him. Needed his mouth on her. Needed to taste the dark bitter chocolate of his tongue. Needed the warmth of his body pressed tight to hers. She'd been so cold for so long.

As if to punish her for even thinking as much, she felt him start to pull away. A sound strangely like a whimper rose from her throat as her body treacherously followed.

"Hold on, cookie. Just let me…" His hands lifted from her wrists. Still fearing he meant to end the delicious torture of her senses, she immediately wrapped her arms around his neck, lacing her fingers into the silken luxury of his thick hair. Only he wasn't leaving because almost immediately the warmth was back in the tight fit of his body against hers, and the blazing heat of those skillful hands working their way under her shirt.

Gabby sucked in a breath, then let it out as his talented fingers skirted a path of warmth up the curve of her rib cage. She hardly noticed the chilling tease of the breeze as he rucked up her tank top, exposing her torso to the night. She only knew that if he would just keep on touching her, keep on tasting her, that she might possibly find the heat she'd been missing in all those power games she'd been forced to play.

You really think this is anything more? You think it can be?

She bit her lip, searching out his face for signs of duplicity and manipulation, but found nothing but heat in his gaze as he took in the view he'd uncovered. What was it with men and boobs?

"God, Gabby..." He pulled at her bra, popping her breast above the constricting fabric. Strangely, looking at her like that was admittedly hot, not vulgar.

"I have to taste you. I have to know," he said, the words rumbling thickly in the back of his throat. And okay, yeah, that warm, slick heat pooling between her legs in response was a double-hell-yes-that's-hot from her body.

She was practically panting, but before she could clear her fogged brain enough to convince herself how embarrassing that was, his hand latched onto her ass, hoisting her up against the door. A moment later the delicious ridge of his erection pressed against her pelvis as he lowered his mouth to the straining tip of her nipple.

Pinned between the door and his hard body, she arched toward him, biting back a scream as he drew her areola deep into the heat of his mouth. Pleasure rippled from deep within her core, another rush of slick heat coating her most intimate of places and making her burn for the press of his erection against her. But the angle wasn't quite enough. She needed to tip her hips just a little more, only she was pinned so tight she couldn't move.

"Ugh, Valin, I need..." She squirmed.

He chuckled, then obviously reading her mind, he shifted again, this time clutching the cheeks of her ass in both hands to hike her up further. She wiggled, parting her legs and wrapping them around his waist, and holy-fucking-crap that felt so good. He was so hard and thick and if she could somehow just genie-wish away her clothing this might actually be enough.

"Fuck, you're sexy," he growled, then went back to torturing her with his mouth on her breast. She arched against the heat of his tongue and was immediately rewarded by a groan as he rubbed himself erotically against her. A tremor racked through her body, starting at every point of contact between them and flaring out in a wave of heat until even her toes were tingling with a promised sort of release beyond anything she'd experienced. Sure, she'd brought herself to orgasm before, had forced herself to learn her body so that she might use it as a weapon when needed, but never had the ripples of pleasure left her panting for breath before. His talented hands, his devilish mouth, his rigid length rubbing against her center—she needed more. More of this, more of him. She needed to taste him, needed to...

She dropped her gaze to the top of his head and became mesmerized by the glint of the city night lights off of the thick dark strands. He'd trimmed it since the cave four months ago, a half-ass job wrought with uneven fringes that somehow pulled together into some of the most enticing waves around the back of his neck and ears.

"Damn, Gabby, you taste so good," he murmured against her breasts, pulling back until her nipple popped out, the coolness of air evaporating the hot moisture left by his tongue. Before she could protest, he switched targets, his head lowering to the other breast, his tongue laving her nipple so that she gasped and clung on tighter.

Oh, yes. She liked being tasted. She wanted to taste him too, if only demanding the freeing of his mouth wouldn't mean ending the luscious sensations to those other parts of her.

He'd tipped his head when he'd altered his attentions to her other breast, exposing the strong curve of where his neck met his shoulders. His skin glistened with the thinnest coating of sweat and made her wonder what he would taste like. Salty? Musky?

Delicious.

She licked her lips, saliva pooling on the back of her tongue. Before she realized what she was doing, she lowered her head, breathing in deeply. Intoxicated on the scent, she dipped her tongue out, gliding over the hard muscles and corded tendons, and eliciting a moan at the salty tang that danced across her taste buds. Not enough. She trailed a path up his neck, briefly nibbling his earlobe before deciding she liked the heady flavor of the pulse at the crux of his jaw and throat better.

Warm blood, sweet salty heaven. Her mind conjured an image of what it would be like to graze her fangs over the smooth skin, the blood welling, then the strike. She licked her lips, dipped her tongue out once more, shuddering at the throb of his pulse skittering against the moist tip of her tongue.

He stilled, but then tipped his head further to the side, granting her better access to the accelerating throb of blood in his vein. She didn't think, instinct overtaking her as she opened her mouth wide and pressed down. Her sharp fangs broke through the surface of his skin, the warm blood welling against her lips. For one blissful moment she gave into the pleasure of it, her entire body shuddering at the thick sweetness of his life-giving fluid coating her tongue, but then awareness of what she was doing sunk in and she jerked back in horror.

"It's okay, Gabby." His hand sank into the hair at the back of her head, as if trying to draw her back to his neck. "Don't fight it. Let me sustain you."

Sustain her? She could kill him. Even now, with the horrid realization of how close she'd come to giving in and losing herself to the bloodlust, her body shook with the need to agree to his encouragement, sink her fangs back in, and drink her fill. She couldn't do it. Couldn't give in. Knew that the moment she did there would be no turning back. Knew that the heady blood-lust wouldn't ease but become worse and worse until that was all there was.

Her legs dropped down from around his waist, the hands that had been linked in his hair lowering to push against his chest. He growled, grabbing her face in both his hands, forcing her gaze to his own.

"Gabby...don't. Don't pull away from me."

She shook her head, her eyes stinging from the effort it took to keep them dry. She had to push him away. He was a temptation she couldn't have around. Not without risking both their lives. "Why are you doing this? Why would you want to help a monster like me?"

He shook his head. "No, Gabby. You're no monster. Christos was a monster. Ganelon's a monster. But you're not."

"But you think I have Ganelon's blood in me."

His anger slapped against her, riding the link created by the trickle of blood that still ran down the back of her throat. "Don't do that."

"Do what?"

"Don't pull away from me." He yanked her close, his breath fanning over her ear as he ground his erection against the hollow curve of her belly. "No more running, Gabby. No more denying. There's too much between us for you to be pulling that sort of bullshit anymore."

A chill settled into her bones, erasing the warmth that had filled her with his touch. Too much between them. Too much lust? On that she could agree, but even as she tried to justify it as that alone, she knew she was kidding herself. This was more than lust. She'd pushed away the nagging suspicion before, convincing herself he was simply a man and she a succubus, but now, with his blood being absorbed into her very essence... *he cares.*

The thought shook through her being, rattling her confidence and stealing her lungs of air. She shook her head in denial. She was the monster. She wouldn't, couldn't let him ruin his life by being with her. And she would not let him steer her from her plans of revenge either. "Don't let some misguided savior complex confuse you. You don't want me."

His grip shifted to her arms, anger flaring in his bourbon gaze. "Don't tell me what I want."

"You want to bed one of the creatures responsible for Angeline's slaughter?" She forced a laugh even as acid churned in her gut. "The other Paladin are right. You really are sick, aren't you?"

He stiffened, the impassive expression that settled over his face not matched by the tense grip of his hands. But even if she hadn't been aware of the infinitesimal change in his grip, she would have known how much her words had hurt him. Valin was definitely stronger at projection than she'd suspected, because it felt like a knife had just been driven into her chest.

"What do you know of Angeline?" he asked softly. The words carried like deadly darts on the breeze.

Damnation. How could she be so stupid? No, not stupid, cruel. She twisted her head, unable to look him in the eyes. Why of all the cards she could have played had she tossed down that one?

"How do you know?" He shook her so hard her head rapped against the access door.

Knowing there was no escaping the ball of hot shame coating her innards, she lifted her chin. Cruel or not, the damage was already done. She could run and most likely face him and his questions later, or she could finish the job and ensure that he'd not only leave her alone but run so far and fast that she wouldn't have to worry about being the one doing so.

And why did that hurt so damn much?

Backbone, Gabby. You have one, use it.

"Christos told me," she said, striving to keep her voice even and unemotional, as if breaking his heart like this didn't affect her at all.

"Christos," he repeated.

She nodded. "He just loved reliving the details of the bloodbath, especially when I'd done something under-handed that would help one of you…Paladin." She sneered the word Paladin, injecting some of Christos's own hatred into her voice. After all, if it hadn't been for them, Gabby wouldn't be here to be breaking this man now. Or at least, without their blood running through her veins, perhaps she wouldn't have cared. "It was his crowning moment. The slaughter of so many, the turning of one of you do-good Paladin…oh yes, he loved describing every beseeching word, every bloodcurdling scream."

There was no hiding the emotions in his expression now. It was all there, plain as day: anger, misery, pain. Tears were openly running down his cheeks, the ache of his agony tearing at her own rib cage. The urge to reach out and comfort had every nerve in her body vibrating, but she had to stay strong if she was going to drive him off.

He swallowed, taking a deep breath. "How…how did she die?"

She stiffened in shock, her breath freezing in her lungs. He didn't know? How could he not know? From everything she'd been told she'd assumed he would have felt his mate die. Had Angeline somehow blocked the link between them? Had Christos? But even then, wouldn't Roland have told him?

His jaw tensed, his mouth thinning as if he could

sense her reluctance to answer, which couldn't be true; the blood bond was a one-way street when it came to reading another's thoughts and feelings. "What did he do to her, Gabby? You know, don't you?"

She shook her head, closing her eyes tight so she didn't have to look upon his misery-ridden face. No, she couldn't tell him that. To do so would be beyond the cruelty she'd already inflicted. To know the details of his mate's death would be...soul-consuming.

He smacked the door next to her head, scattering flaking paint chips and leaving a good-sized dent in it. "Damn you! You started this. Tell me how she fucking died!"

Gabby swallowed, sickened when the action brought with it the glorious aftertaste of his blood. She had started it. And if she had that backbone she claimed to have she'd finish it.

"He saved her for last. So Roland..." She swallowed, pushing away the vivid image her maker had painted of that fateful night and sticking to the facts that mattered. "So she'd die knowing what kind of monster her brother had been turned into and so Roland would know that his failure was at the cost of her life."

Air hissed in and out of his flared nostrils, his throat bobbing as he swallowed. "Do you know...was it quick?"

She could read the plea in his eyes. Knew he desperately wanted her to tell him it had been. But she couldn't, not without lying, not without showing him a compassion that would go against everything she hoped to accomplish when she started this cruel task of driving him away. Still, the next words she said seemed like the hardest ones she'd ever uttered in her life. More than any lie. More than anything Christos had ever forced her to do or say.

"No. She screamed for a very long time. But never for help; it was too late for that. She screamed for you. Prayed that you would be okay…and begged for you to save not herself, but her brother."

Chapter 10

THERE WASN'T ENOUGH SPACE ON THE FACE OF EARTH to run from the pain, so Valin resorted to the one other place he knew he could hide — the black and gray shadows of the shade embracing him into its bleakness. Not part of His realm of holy creation, nor part of the black chaos of Lucifer's evil workshop, the shade was a kind of neutral zone on the battlefield of good versus evil; a mixed motley of not quite good but not all bad where neither could comfortably tread. Valin didn't have such problems. He found a strange solace in the shades of gray between His light and complete darkness. He didn't have to be perfect here. Unlike the bathing radiance of heavenly light, in the shade there was no itch or subconscious need to squirm under the weight of his failures, nor was there room for such nagging things as extreme emotions.

At first he raced from shadow to shadow, hiding from reality. With the suffocating feelings of grief, loss, and impotence crashing over him, it had been all he could do not to strike out at the source of his renewed pain.

God, Gabby. He'd been so angry at her. She might not have been there to be part of the destruction of his life, but the fact that she'd known the details, had spoken of them so casually, heartlessly even…It had hit him low in the gut that he was mated to a coldblooded monster. But now, here in the gray shadows that took the edge off the sharpness of reality, he could look back on that moment and see more. The little movements that spoke of her discomfort, the tension in her body: She hadn't wanted to tell him about Angeline's death. Yes, she'd started the conversation, but he'd been the one to drag the details of Angeline's death from her, ignoring the nagging tickle from their bond that told him she hated herself for every word she uttered.

The truth was Gabby hadn't failed him by being who she was or knowing what she knew, but he sure as fuck had failed her by rubbing her nose in it.

Just like he'd failed Angeline all those years ago.

Save Roland. He hadn't. Instead he had hated Roland because he'd been there and not saved Angeline. Hated that while his family had been taken from him the vampire-Paladin had been granted a state of existence—no matter how horrible it may have been. Until Karissa, that is. Karissa had saved Roland. Karissa's love. Karissa's blood. Her blood had saved Gabriella too, which is why Gabby could tolerate the sun and wasn't killed last summer when Logan used His light to defeat the enemy. Yet Gabby seemed willing to throw that gift away by drinking the blood of her enemies, a slow-acting poison. The perfect way to self-destruct.

He'd be damned if he let her check out that easily. Life sucked. You moved on. And then you made something of it. He hadn't saved his child or Angeline. Hadn't honored Angeline's last wish by saving her brother. But there was one person he could save.

With a new goal in mind he shifted through the shade in a purposeful direction. It didn't take him long to reach his destination, and even less to find a crack in the seal around a window and wiggle his shadow-self through. He was definitely going to have to pick on Roland about his downgrade from his last fortress. But first things first.

Reforming in the middle of the room near where Roland was just about to settle down with a remote and a tumbler of scotch, he got a small thrill from seeing the vampire practically jump out of his skin. The moment was short-lived as the vampire collected himself, carefully setting both remote and tumbler down on the nearby end table and straightening to his full height, which was a good head taller than Valin. Bastard.

"Valin," the Paladin-turned-vampire said casually, as if having former mortal enemies appear in his living room wasn't an irregular occurrence.

"Roland," Valin replied similarly.

Roland lifted his brow, his gaze briefly flickering over Valin. "Think you could at least conjure up some clothes when you break and enter into a man's home?"

Valin smiled. "Now, Roland. That would require a measure of giving a fuck that we both know I don't have."

Roland shook his head, grumbling as he turned and popped open one of those ottoman storage units and began to rummage through it. A good twenty seconds of tap-foot later, he pulled from the very bottom an ugly-ass green throw that he promptly offered to Valin with a disdainful twist of his lip.

Stuffy, tight-ass, OCD bastard. And if the thought of Valin's naked jangles mixing with the air of his apartment set him off, how did he stand himself and his rather eccentric cravings? Blood was not exactly the cleanest of supplements. Especially when it came from the Red Cross discards pile.

Valin took the offered throw, wrapping it around his waist as he took stock of the apartment. Not nearly as nice as Roland's last digs. No voice-activated systems here. It was smaller too, though it looked like he'd managed to cram in all of the high-end furniture from his previous penthouse apartment. The place was cramped, though in a homey sort of way. It had all the extra touches that his last place hadn't had. Things like framed photos, bowls filled with smelly potpourri…throws. All things that spoke of a woman's touch. Speaking of which. "Where's Karissa?"

"It's her turn to sit with Logan."

Valin nodded, well aware of the babysitting detail. He'd taken his own share of turns the first few days after the loss of Logan's mate until duty had thankfully relieved him. The problem was not that he couldn't stand the Paladin's mopey silence, but that he could truly feel for the poor fucker. Even if Valin and Angelina had never been mate bonded, the severing of their pair bond had been like being degutted. The fact that he'd lost his best friend at the same time was almost like having his heart carved out of his chest cavity. Sometimes he still thought it had been. In fact, he would have sworn that was the case until four months ago when a cheeky little vampire had made it stutter back into rhythm.

And now she was trying to leave him too.

He worried the fringe of the throw wrapped around him. "I need the name of your supplier."

Roland smiled, his fangs flashing. "Why? You thinking of a lifestyle change? Want me to aid you in your transition?"

"You wish," Valin muttered with a shake of his head.

Roland felt about him about the same as Valin did about the vampire. Tolerable during times of need, but otherwise the world would be a better place without his presence. Still, he seriously doubted the vampire would actually turn him. Fangs aside, the excommunicated Paladin was still one of the most honorable bastards Valin had ever met. Which is why he was here; as much as it grated on his nerves, the Paladin cared about Gabby too. "It's not for me but rather a mutual friend that I happened to run into recently."

"Gabriella? She's alive?" Roland took a step forward, his eyes flashing crimson. Almost as quickly, he visibly checked himself, turning his head away. "Sorry. I'm used to the kid popping up all the time, so when she didn't, I assumed we were wrong and that she was dead. Or worse, that Ganelon had her."

Valin narrowed his eyes to study Roland's features. Squared-off jaw, high cheekbones, a heavy brow that shadowed… no fucking way. That was it: his eyes. There was something about how the wide-set orbs had framed the flash of crimson just now that set his gut to churning. It wasn't possible. Couldn't be, unless…

That night. Why would Christos use that night out of all the other massacres to torment Gabby?

Valin swore long and hard, his entire body itching to poof and zip away. He so didn't want to deal with this shit. Not on top of all the other crap.

"What? What is it? Does Ganelon have her?" Roland asked sharply, his eyes flaring red once more.

Valin shook his head, partly to assure Roland and partly because he wanted to deny what the logical part of his brain was telling him. Unfuckingbelievable. He'd just assumed Gabriella was a merker because that was the easiest explanation. And though, with any other Paladin he would have thought it damn odd for them to be mated to a merker, he figured being the "black" knight made it a moot point. Unlike his brothers, Valin had never thought twice about performing some of the...darker...tasks assigned to him—hence the name. Spying, lying, manipulation, killing...as long as the result was the desired one, it was no skin off his back. Hell, even if things didn't turn up daisies, he had no compunction shrugging it off and moving on. Just part of the job, right?

Oh yeah, he was far from pure as the driven snow. More like the muck kicked up from the plows after the salt, sand, and gutter slime had been mixed in. So when his often absent heart had made its presence known again at his first sight of the succubus/vampire, he'd just thought it fitting that she had been born from darkness. But Gabby had seemed truly offended when he suggested she could be at all related to Ganelon. Maybe part of it could be attributed to denial, not wanting to believe there could be more evil in her blood than what her succubus mother had already given her, especially given she'd been further cursed when Christos had turned her. But...what if she knew for sure she wasn't? What if she knew exactly who her father was and clung to the fact that he didn't have an ounce of evil blood in him?

A hand clamped around his throat and he found himself blinking into those damn crimson eyes again. "So help me, Valin, if you don't tell me where she is..."

"Ganelon doesn't have her," he said, wrenching the

hand from around his esophagus. He couldn't say she was all right. Not after he'd seen what she was doing to herself. Roland must have made the assumption though because he nodded, his breathing easing as he took a step back, the crimson fading from his pupils. The nearly black eyes that replaced those glowing coals were almost as harsh looking as the freaky red had been, but still…the shape, the tilt.

He cleared his throat, cringing mildly at the burn. Fucking bastard.

"How is she?" Roland asked.

Yeah, still not going there. "I never asked what happened that night."

Roland's brow furrowed. "What night?"

"The night you were turned."

It was kind of interesting watching the vampire shut down, his mouth cramping up into a hard line in his face. A knot of muscle rolled across his jaw, his teeth grinding once, twice, before he responded. "It's not something I share."

"Especially with motherfuckers like me, right?"

Roland's mouth quirked up, a self-deprecating chuckle rumbling in his chest. "Takes one to know one."

Hell yeah it did. And if what Gabby told Valin were true, then perhaps Roland's silence had been as much out of compassion as anything else. Valin sobered. "Tell me just this one thing."

Valin could see the tension pulsing through Roland's body simply by the stiff set of his shoulders, but somehow the ex-Paladin managed to grind out a, "What?"

"Was there a succubus involved? Maybe one with red hair?"

"What the fuck does that have to do with Gabriella…" Roland trailed off, his face paling as all sorts of light bulbs and connections flared to life in his brain. Oh, yeah, darkness was indeed bliss.

Valin rubbed a hand down his face. "Shit. I'd kind of hoped I was wrong. But damn if she doesn't have your eyes."

Roland stumbled back, grabbing the arm of the couch to find his way down.

Valin shook his head. Wasn't this fucking priceless? Gabby must know who her father was. And he was Paladin. The question was if she'd known, then why the hell hadn't she come to Roland for help instead of fucking over her own soul?

"Congrats, daddy." Valin slapped Roland's stiff shoulder, counting on the fact that the man was too shocked to say anything as Valin passed by him and dived into the innards of the rumbling fridge. In fact, Valin made it all the way to the door, the squeak of the ancient knob the thing that finally drew his former Paladin brother's attention.

"Where are you going?"

He hoisted up the sack of A-negative, the liquid squishing and slurping in his hand. "Going to go have a little talk with your daughter."

And then? Then he'd have her over his knee for a good spanking.

—◦◦◦—

Valin didn't get very far. He made it two feet down the hall before he was brought up short by a rather awkward obstacle: clothing, or rather the lack thereof. The need for something other than a puke-green wrap became obvious when he'd stepped out of Roland's apartment and been greeted with a shocked gasp. He'd spun around in time to see a pair of wide eyes topped by a towering white bun duck her head back into her apartment. Luckily the door to Roland's apartment had yet to close behind Valin, and a few moments later he tried the trip again armed with both the blood bag and an outfit that could be termed flasher-chic at best: a long dark duster…and nothing underneath.

He'd chaffed at the admittedly minimal amount of time taken up by the task of raiding a still-stunned Roland's hall closet. But worse was the sweltering cab ride that he'd suffered through smothered in the fully buttoned duster during more than a few blocks of clogged up cross-traffic. How did people stand to travel this way?

He'd finally made it back to the right end of town, and in another frustrating, but necessary, action had the cabby drop him off a few blocks away from the old school. When he was assured of no tail, he'd hastened to the base and managed to have a break of luck when the guard at the back door recognized him.

Once inside, it didn't take him long to track down Gabby in the old nurse's office. The place was amazingly quiet, the door propped open with one of those wooden triangles, and only two people in the room: Gabby and Aaron. She sat in one of those child-size chairs, her knees bent up uncomfortably as she leaned over an unconscious Aaron, both of her hands wrapped around his bandaged one, as if by holding tight enough she might keep him there.

Valin wasn't proud of the twist of jealousy that rose—the man looked like he was on death's door, for fuck sake—and ruthlessly squelched the mating instinct that all but screamed for him to go caveman and drag her away from Aaron.

"How is he?" he asked instead, folding his arms across his chest as he leaned against the doorframe.

Gabby jerked, swiveling in the chair to blink at him. As if she'd been dozing, that or crying, her eyes were suspiciously red and swollen. Either way it was equally obvious that she hadn't expected to see him again. If the shock on her face wasn't readable enough, then the zap of surprise he felt across their tentative link certainly was.

Or maybe it was the outfit. The dirty jeans, which he'd scooped up from the floor of his cramped room, didn't exactly add much to the ensemble other than to upgrade him from flasher to well, he wasn't sure what. With no shirt and the black duster jacket that—damn Roland's height—didn't so much as flare around him as drag on the floor, he probably looked like a kid playing dress-up in his parent's closet. Oh yeah, the outfit was damn comical in a how-sad kind of way.

Gabby recovered, dragging her gaze away from his exposed chest, and looked back down at her patient. "Oh, um. Better. Shae gave him enough painkillers to knock out a giant. She says as long as she can fend off any potential infections that he'll survive."

"And the burns? Will they scar?" he asked, flexing his own slowly healing arm. The ribs were coming along nicely, barely tender really, but something about fire—especially merker fire—seemed to resist the Paladins' innate healing capabilities.

She drew in a lungful of air, her shoulders shaking delicately as she let her breath back out. "Shae's powers aren't suited for burn therapy. She was able to start the healing process on the most life-threatening wounds but…" She trailed off, the misery on her face telling him all he needed to know. Poor fucker was going to look like a monster for the rest of his life.

"Would he be better off in a hospital with a good burn unit?" he asked gently.

She shook her head. "He's a power sink. If they hooked him up to anything electrical and he wasn't alert enough to control it, he'd automatically draw. Potentially he could black out the entire area."

"That makes things complicated, doesn't it?"

She nodded even though his question had been rhetorical. He fidgeted in the awkward silence that followed.

Gabby let out a sharp breath. "If you're wondering about your knife, the answer is yes, I grabbed it for you after you took off. It's in my room, as yours doesn't have a working lock and I figured you'd be pissed if someone came along and took the pretty magical relic hostage."

He blinked, glad the doorframe kept him from rocking back on his heels in shock. His knife? Crap. That just went to show how messed up he'd been that he hadn't even thought of the blade until now. Some Paladin he was. Not that he'd let on to Gabby how much their little encounter earlier had gone to fucking with his mind.

"Thank you. I'll grab it later," he said, trying for casual and cringing at the note of tension in his voice.

She twisted in the seat, her brow raised. "Don't tell me you need me to open my room for you. We both know you can get in anytime you want."

He had to work hard to stifle the obvious come-back that sprang to his tongue—*Is that an invitation, cookie?*—and said instead, "Actually, I was hoping for a minute of your time. Can I speak with you?"

The quiet stretched, long enough that Valin thought she might ignore his request, but she eventually cleared her throat. "No one's here. No one who's awake anyway."

He straightened from the doorframe, shifting uncom-fortably from one foot to the other. She was right, but for some reason having this conversation with her injured—albeit unconscious—puppy dog in the room wasn't how he'd envisioned it going down. She was sitting there waiting for him though, so he took a fortifying breath and blurted it out. "I got you something."

She tipped her head, her brow tugged down so she looked as much confused as inquisitive. He pulled out the bag of blood from one of the duster's many pockets and held it out to her like a peace offering. She recoiled.

"Take that away," she hissed, turning her back on him. She grasped onto the edge of Aaron's cot, her eyes pointedly fixed on the cabinets on the other side of the room, and her jaw working.

Take it away? After he'd gone through all those hoops to get it for her? Breaking and entering, having that oh-so-fun chat with her daddy, the old lady, the cab ride. Ungrateful, stubborn, little…He strode across the room, jerked her off the chair, and spun her around. Her hands instinctively settled on his chest as he pulled her tight against him.

"Goddamn it, Gabby. It's not like you're breaking some stupid-ass vow about drinking from a human vein. It's Red Cross discards, destined for the trash. Drinking this is not taking anything from anyone other than maybe some highly resourceful gutter rat, and that's assuming the blood isn't disposed of properly." He shook the bag at her, the contents sloshing. "Drink the damn blood!"

She averted her face, but that didn't stop him from seeing the tear streaming down her cheek. "I can't, I can't," she whispered, then repeating the refrain more firmly. "I can't."

Frustration settled like lead in his gut, making him want to scream. He wanted to kiss that tear, ease whatever pain and confusion she obviously felt. He settled for thumbing it away, the calloused pads stroking the tear across the fine line bracketing her mouth that he swore hadn't been there a day ago. Aging. Dying before his very eyes. "Can't or won't? Because from where I'm standing, refusing to feed is looking a lot like stubborn suicide."

She lifted her chin, the hands that had settled on his chest pushing him away. "You think I haven't tried? The first time I became positively desperate I broke into a blood bank and drank to my heart's content." She took a deep breath. "And then after, do you know what happened?"

He shook his head, desperate to understand. Desperate to help her.

"I could *hear* them. Every damn one of them was in my head. Even now, after diluting the blood with my other kills I can still hear them if I try. Worse, I know that because of what I am, if I really wanted to, I could tap into their thoughts and manipulate them." She shook her head, tears painting pale rivers in the smudged ash of her face. "I won't do that," she whispered.

Shock hit him first, followed by frustration, quickly tailed by weariness. This is why she hadn't gone to her father for help. She'd already known that how Roland fed wouldn't work for her. And since she was already convinced she was dying, sacrificial brat that she was, she probably didn't want to make Roland or his mate feel more sorry for her by asking for any other suggestions. Not that there were any others beyond the obvious one that he could see, and she'd already given her opinion on that. Still, he'd be damned if he gave up without the fight to end all fights.

"You won't manipulate me." He pushed his hair back from the side of his neck.

Satisfaction and something damn close to hope flourished when she licked her lips, her gaze fixated on the pulse at the base of his throat. She swayed, her head dipping forward, before she caught herself, her cheeks reddening as she twisted her face away. "Why do you even care?"

Fuck. It was a good question. Why did he care? Every interaction they'd had always ended in one of two ways: her running away or trying to push him away. Which, yeah, should have been a big fucking clue about what she thought of him, or rather the idea of him and her. Too bad for her, Valin had never been one to give a shit about underlying messages. Gabby was his. And he was too damn greedy to let her go. First step though was to stop her from the self-destructive spiral she was so bent on taking.

It was definitely time for an intervention. Only this makeshift ICU room was not the place for all the things they had to hash out.

He eyed the bandaged patient on the cot. Good bet Gabby wouldn't leave Aaron alone in here. With a sigh he stuffed the blood bag back in his duster and closed his eyes, taking a little mental look-see through the building and…

<<Bennett? I could use a hand here.>>

Gabby's eyes narrowed, her head tilting as if she were trying to catch the shielded projection. Not that he cared. Not that she'd given him any other options.

<<Mate… your timing… stellar as… always,>> came Bennett's grumbled reply. Valin frowned at how thin the mental thought was. Almost like the Paladin was projecting through static and cutting in and out.

<<I need you in the infirmary ASAP.>>

<<You okay?>> This thought was much sharper, as if the Paladin had moved away from the source of interference.

<<Just get here,>> he said and closed the connection, figuring if Bennett thought it was urgent he'd come quickly.

Gabby's eyes narrowed, her chin jutting up in that oh-so-adorable way that she liked to try and break others down with. "What do you think you're doing?"

He didn't respond, just waited. Sure enough, he caught the faint echoes of hurried footfalls from down the hall, though Valin was a bit surprised at the pitter-patter that sounded in the wake of Bennett's heavy thunder-boots. The question of who was clipping his heels was answered the moment Bennett burst through the door, a towering female stumbling to a stop behind him.

Amazon. Should have known it was her that had been causing the weak connection.

"What is it? Is there a change in his status?" Amazon asked breathlessly, clutching the doorframe.

"Valin?" Bennett asked in lieu of a real question, as he'd obviously already taken status of everyone in the room and checked it off as all is well.

"Just need someone to stay with him," Valin explained, almost sorry his lack of explanation in his request had spilled over onto Amazon, scaring her. He might have made it all the way to remorseful if her eyes hadn't narrowed as she came to her own conclusion that there was no emergency, a petulant you-made-me-run-for-nothing twisting her mouth into a scowl. Didn't take her long to realize the tactic wasn't going to work on him, and her gaze shifted to Gabby as if to point out the obvious: that someone was staying with Aaron.

"Gabriella is needed elsewhere," he told her.

As predicted, that idea didn't seem to go over too well with Gabby. She crossed her arms, looking like she was about to refuse. He leaned in close, lowering his voice as he spoke. "Unless you'd like to discuss your feeding habits with everyone here?"

She narrowed her eyes, a silent *you wouldn't*. He raised his brow, casting back his own *try me*.

She must have realized he was serious because she stepped away, turning to Amazon and addressing her. "Be sure to find me if there is any change."

"Of course, but…"

With a stiff nod, Gabby brushed past them, her boots clomping like thunderbolts as she stomped down the hall.

"If you'll excuse me," Valin said, making his own hasty exodus before Bennett—or worse, Amazon—could question him further.

Settling into step beside Gabby, he didn't make any move to alter her path. She was already heading in the direction of his choice: toward their quarters. Even so, she hesitated in front of her door, her brow knotted as if she was unsure, now that she'd led him here, that she really wanted to invite him into her personal space for their discussion.

He moved in behind her, angling over her shoulder so the heat of his chest brushed her shoulder blades, his breath feathering over the side of her face. "What's the matter, cookie—afraid of what you might do if you get me into the same room with a bed?"

She stiffened, the delicious curve of her throat lengthening as her chin lifted predictably in the air. He had to work hard to repress the smile when she determinedly reached out and twisted the knob, all but charging in ahead of him. He stepped in behind her, closing the door just as she spun on him, the flare of banked embers in her eyes giving away how angry she really was. Angry and sexy. Fuck, did her tits have to look so damn appealing heaving beneath that tank top?

"Okay. We're here. What did you want to discuss with me that you couldn't have done in the infirmary?"

"This." He shifted into her space, his hand slipping into the thick locks of fire at the base of her skull and pulling her toward him. Her eyes widened, air hissing between her lips as she read in his heated gaze exactly what he planned to do with her. If she'd objected, possibly he would have stopped, but then again, probably not, so it was a good thing she didn't.

His mouth touched hers, and like fire touching ice she melted, her lips parting to allow his intrusion. Her head

tipped back, sinking into the firm grip of his hand and
offering up more of herself to his plying tongue. A hand
settled on his shoulder, tentatively at first, but within
moments it had dug into the thick folds of the duster,
her other hand skipping across his rib cage as it found
its way beneath the material and clamped down hard on
his side—thankfully his good side, as the other was still
feeling tender.

Taking that as a sure sign saying *yes, more please*,
he wrapped his other hand around her waist and used it
to hold her steady as he pressed his body into hers. He
was rewarded by the most delicious sound of pleasure
from her, a rumbling moan at the back of her throat
that seemed to encompass both approval and a demand.
Happy to oblige, he delved lower, kneading the full
globe of her ass as he pulled her tighter against him.
She moaned and then blew his mind away when she
arched her back and rubbed her pelvis against the ridge
of his cock.

Fuck, he could smell her arousal. Worse for his
control was the throbbing need he could feel echoing
back across their growing bond. His cock wept with
joy, a shudder of anticipation driving up from his balls
through his body. God, he had to get into her pants,
now. Before he couldn't hold back anymore. And holy
hell, when did he have to fight the urge to come while
simply making out?

Needing a moment, he broke the seal of their lips,
though he couldn't bring himself to release his grip on
her. They stood there, bodies tight together, mouths
mere inches apart, their panting breaths mingling as
their eyes devoured one another's face.

"What the hell was that for?" she whispered, her body shaking with a mix of desire and confusion. As if, though she obviously wanted this, she couldn't fathom why he would.

Silly little fool still doesn't understand why I came back.

"You wanted to know why I care, right?" he asked, his thumb rubbing a circular path at the back of her neck. Damn but she had the softest skin. He wanted to touch every inch of it, brand it as his and his alone.

She nodded, though her brow was still pinched in confusion, her kiss-swollen lips clamped tight between her bottom teeth and one sweet little fang.

"The answer is simple, Gabby." He rubbed his hips against hers, letting her feel how much he ached for her. "You're mine."

Her eyes narrowed dangerously. "You're delusional."

"Must suck to belong to a delusional man," he said with a twisted smile, then crushed his mouth back down on hers.

Chapter 11

OKAY, SO MAYBE VALIN WASN'T THE ONLY ONE WHO was delusional, because whatever he was doing with his mouth on hers was crazy-ass good. And just like on that rooftop, she couldn't get enough.

Too many clothes. Or perhaps just too much…something. Since the clothes were more fathomable than whatever that something else might be, she went to work on them, her hands yanking at the oil-slicked material of the duster as she tried to pull it off his shoulders, though because he didn't seem to want to cooperate enough to release his grip on her, it got caught on his carved biceps. Stuck.

She made a mewling sound of frustration, her hands almost frantic as she tried to work the stiff material further down his arms. Most likely thinking she was trying to stop him, he growled, breaking the kiss long enough to pin his bourbon gaze on her.

She shuddered. Damn he was hot when he got all intense like this.

Breath skittering in and out of her lungs, she tried to explain. "Valin, let me…" She stomped her foot, frustrated by her loss of articulation. She finally managed to come out with, "your coat!" jerking on the offending piece of clothing as she did.

He blinked but nodded and began to help her. What ensued was a bit of a comedy of errors. Valin relented enough to release his possessive hold on her, but only one hand at a time, which might have been fine except that his skin had developed enough of a sheen of sweat that the thick fabric clung, kind of like when she tried to pull on her shirt after a shower when her skin was still damp, only the opposite. The result was a rather spectacular sight of Valin all but hissing and spitting as he spun in circles and fought with the coat that had ensnared him.

"Damn fucking Roland," he muttered.

Her eyebrows flew up, but whatever thoughts or questions she had about the man he was cursing fled her brain the moment he decided to solve the entire problem by dissolving into the shade, then reforming the moment both duster and jeans plopped on the floor.

Oh, my. Yes, she'd seen him naked on multiple occasions now, but never had the situation or the lighting given her the opportunity to drink in the sight of Valin in all his naked—erect—glory. And the only thought she could come up with now was that she'd been wrong, he and his jangles weren't just fine, they were spectacular.

"Like what you see, cookie?" he asked, his voice dripping with smugness.

She jerked her chin up, meeting his dancing gaze. Conceited bastard.

He chuckled and took a step forward. His gaze dragged over her, lingering on the curve of her hips, then her rising and falling breasts, before settling on her swollen lips.

"You are so gorgeous."

A shiver ran through her, but a good one, one that blended nicely with the heat pooling in her belly. He stopped just before her, his hands clenching and releasing at his sides, and waited. For what?

"Your turn, Gabby. I want to see every bit of that delicious body of yours, then I want to drag my tongue over every inch of exposed skin." His lips curled up into a Cheshire cat smile. "And I do mean every inch."

Heat rushed to her cheeks. There wasn't a thing, sexually, that she hadn't either used, been exposed to, or heard of, but somehow the way Valin spoke, and the implied savoring of such an act, brought with it a whole new world of possibilities. Possibilities that all started and ended with the words: mutual pleasure. As if there could be such a thing in sex.

Even as she tried to keep her mind from traveling down unwanted roads, a memory surfaced, bubbling up through her growing anticipation like a rotted cadaver rising back to the surface. She'd been given to Stephan as part of his reward for achieving status as second, though she would be damned if she didn't meet the challenge for supremacy with all she had. Winning wasn't even about who came away with a smile on their face but about maintaining control. Losing was to be subjected to the other's will—forever. Gabby was good at winning; her inner succubus was good at making men beg. For a moment she thought she'd gotten the upper hand, but then Christos had slipped into the room. All it had taken was that break in her concentration. Next thing she knew the vampire twisted a fistful of her hair around his hand and forced her down to her knees before him. And Christos…Christos was smiling as he leaned back against the door to watch.

Valin growled, shattering the memory with a good

shake of her shoulders. "Don't you fucking think about that. I'm not him. I'm not any of them."

"No?" she looked pointedly down at the hands bruising her upper arms.

He cursed, dropping his hands and fisting them at his sides. His throat worked as he spoke. "I'm sorry I gripped you so hard."

She didn't miss the implication that he was not sorry for trying to chase the memory away, but she nodded, rubbing her arms. The shudder that wracked through her body had nothing to do with the tender flesh, but a much deeper ache within her. Oh, how she wanted to believe in him, but the doubts…sex was for power. The only pleasure to be had was that of the control she held over the other player when the act was done.

"No, Gabby. That's not true," he said, his voice hoarse and uneven.

"Isn't it?"

He shook his head, his eyes darkening to a smoldering brown as he leaned close, his calloused fingers so comparatively gentle to his last touch as he traced a path through the tears on her face. And great, now she was fucking crying.

"Gabby, none of them cared enough to make you feel the things that I'm going to make you feel."

The quiet sincerity with which he spoke the words might have been enough to convince her to try, but it was nothing compared to the image he blasted her with next: him over her, his arms wrapped beneath her knees and his heated gaze locked with hers as he dragged his tongue across her clit, then dived in closer to suckle the juices dripping from her core. She knew it was just an image, a projected thought that he'd somehow managed to wrap up in a pretty bow of needy emotion and heady desire, but that didn't keep the gasp from escaping her lips, nor did it stop the tremble from skating along every neural pathway in her body until every inch of her skin tingled. Could it really be like that?

His eyes heated, his voice rough as gravel as he purred at her. "Yes, Gabby, it can be like that, but I'll only show you if you want me to."

Valin knew the moment she made her decision. There was that slight firming of her jaw, then the endearingly familiar tip of her chin. The problem was he didn't know what her decision was…until she crossed her arms over her belly, grabbed the base of her tank top, and pulled it over her head. Next came the sports bra, then her pants, followed by the most mind-blowing scrap of fabric that surely couldn't technically be called underwear. Finally she was standing before him completely naked, her lush curves begging him for his touch: a goddess, made for sex. And his. All fucking his.

Stop objectifying her, you ass!

He swallowed, jerking his gaze up to her face, and realized how much ground he'd lost. He should have noticed the stiffness in her frame while he'd been ogling her body, but bonehead that he was, he hadn't. He could see it now, along with the deep furrow of doubt in her brow, and the etched lines of worry around her pinched lips.

Damn those bastards. He was going to find them and tear every one of their goddamn dicks off.

Her eyes widened.

"Did you hear that?" he asked, sure he'd kept the thought tight behind his shields. He did not need her thinking about Christos and his fucking lackeys again. Not now. Not ever.

"Hear what?"

He shook his head and blew out a long gust of air, centering himself. They weren't fully bonded yet. She was probably just reacting to his physical cues, which were all over the place. Confident seducer, to Pavlovian dog, to murderous bastard in five seconds flat.

"So, uh…" She shifted uncomfortably from one foot to the other, her arms self-consciously rising to cover herself before she realized what she was doing and visibly forced them back down. He watched partly in amusement and partly with another emotion that he refused to give credence to as she raised her chin again, this time accompanying the movement with a cock of her hip and a hand planted upon it.

"So, uh, what?" he asked, trying to remembering what they'd been talking about before that little cold shower of a memory had fucked with their mojo.

She rolled her eyes, making a keep going motion with her hand as if to say *what's next.*

Damn good question. He suspected this was a bit of a test. Not that he thought she realized she was giving him one, but he wasn't fool enough to not know when he was in uncharted waters…near deadly hidden reefs.

Gabby was part succubus, but unlike any succubus he'd ever known, he didn't kid himself into thinking that she liked sex. Her nature might make her able to get past the type of circumstances that she'd doubtlessly faced and come away unbroken, it probably even made her crave the act to some extent, but abuse was still abuse, and just that brief glimpse he'd seen a few minutes ago told him that at best she considered sex a tool to maintain some slim measure of power over her jailors.

She'd never had sex for the pure enjoyment of doing so. She'd never allowed herself to be swept away in the sensations. Never released herself to the emotions inherent of the act. Which meant that he was going to have to show her how, but to do that she had to be comfortable with him first.

He reached down, cupping his balls. Her gaze followed, her mouth parting in the perfect little *O* as he completed the motion by stroking his fisted hand from the base of his cock up over the tip. "Next *you* touch me."

Her gaze snapped back up, one of her elegant eyebrows arched up. "I thought this was all about touching *me*."

"Oh, no, Gabby. You got it all wrong. That's not what this is about." He shifted closer, close enough to feel the heat radiating off her, close enough that it practically hurt not to drag her to him and devour. Instead he reached, placing his left hand on her right shoulder as if she were a skittish filly.

"Then what's it about?" she said, her words clipped, but he didn't miss the fact that she shuddered under his light tough…and that her gaze drifted down toward where his hand still cradled his cock. First victory. And hopefully many more to come.

"Oh Gabby, this is all about…" He stroked his cock while she watched, his other hand drifting inward across her collar bone, "…making sure…" continuing down the sweet valley between her rising and falling breasts,

"…you come…" and ended with a caress of his thumb across her peaked nipple.

She gasped, her head falling back slightly as she arched into the sensation, as if begging for more. So he did it again, and had to release his cock to steady her when she weaved on her feet. Holy fuck, she was responsive. Because it was him? Or was that the succubus coming out to play?

Does it matter?

Hell no.

He bent down, taking the nipple he wasn't touching into his mouth and suckling. She was sweet and soft and oh so perfect, and when he stroked the peaked nub with his tongue and she gasped, that was perfect too.

Shifting his grip, he switched his attentions to the other breast, determined to give it equal attention. By the time he'd feasted his fill she was breathless, her chest rising and falling, her limbs trembling as she stared uncertainly at him.

So beautiful. His cock kicked against her thigh, reminding him that he was skipping a good portion of his plan.

"Touch me, Gabby."

She sucked in a breath, going still. Determined to smooth over her uncertainty, he ran his hands down her sides, sliding them around to her ass and squeezing as he pressed his cock against the sweet softness at the juncture of her thighs. She gasped, her pelvis tipping toward him. He indulged himself by rubbing himself back and forth against her, coating his cock with the slick cream of her desire. Oh yeah, his Gabby was an inherently sexy creature—now if he could just convince her of it.

"Touch me," he commanded again, fitting his hands back on her hip bones as he opened up the space between them.

She made a noise of protest, trying to arch toward him, but he held her firm. She narrowed her eyes, glaring at him. "You're a greedy bastard, aren't you?"

"Oh, yeah I am." He leaned forward, claiming her lips in the gentlest of kisses, plying her lips as he spoke. "You make me throb with desire for you. I can't wait to be inside your sweet little body. I'm going to lap up every little moan you make. And then I'm going to hold you, watching your eyes go blank with mindless pleasure as you come."

Her eyes heated and her hand closed over his cock, the heavy weight pulsing in her slim grip. He groaned, then growled as she drew her hand down over the tip, her thumb delicately circling the rigid head as she collected his slick juices.

"God, Gabby."

"Like that?" she asked, spreading the juices down the length of his cock and fisting tight around the base. And that was too fucking good. No way would he last with her touching him. And since he had so much more planned…

"The bed," he said, leading her with his weight in the required direction. She seemed more than happy to oblige, her hand tightening on his cock and pulling, as if it were she who led him. Perhaps it was, because when they finally made it around the various obstacles to the cot, it was he who found himself being pressed down on it, her sweet little body climbing over top of him. Knowing it was going to be the end of him if she tried to ride him this way, he gripped her hips, lifting her off so he could shift onto his knees and face her. Her eyes flashed, a determined set squaring her jaw as she tried to push him back down again.

He cupped her face, running his thumb over her full lips, enjoying how her eyes softened at the simple touch.

"That's better."

"What's better?" she asked a little breathlessly, he thought.

"Part of making you come is not rushing things, cookie." Yeah, rushing was bad. Rushing meant he was as apt to lose his mind as make her lose hers. So he set out to seduce her using slow, featherlight caresses, gentle, teasing kisses.

The easier pace gave him the much-needed time to regroup. It also allowed him to truly tune back into her signals. She was still breathing hard and fast, despite the slower pace, and though, at first, he'd thought it was a measure of her own rising passion, he was beginning to seriously question his own reasoning. He was sure of it when she tried to press him down again, her eyes taking on a glint of determination that in no way matched the rapid thudding of her pulse.

She's trying to regain control.

He silently cursed, realizing he'd hit the nail on the head. She wasn't mindless with excitement, but trying to control her fear by controlling him. He understood her need, but fear had no place in their bed. Somehow he had to help her move beyond it.

"Lay down for me, Gabby. I'll stay here."

Her mouth twisted into a forced pout, another bit of bravado. "Going to be kind of hard to fuck me if we're at opposite ends of the bed."

He flinched at the crude word, not because he didn't use such words, and not because that wasn't exactly what he wanted to do to her, but because of what he suspected she meant by it. She'd stopped enjoying and fully expected this to only end one way: with him, the man, shooting his wad into a detached host.

Not fucking likely.

"Trust me, Gabby." And really that was what this was all about. Trust. She wasn't going to be able to accept his gift of pleasure, wasn't going to be able to embrace his love, unless she trusted him first.

This is insane. The thought came from her, and though he had to agree with her, he didn't like the fact that she'd been able to think it. But she did lay down, her brow arched in silent challenge.

"Do you ever masturbate?"

Her cheeks reddened, her gaze dropping down to his cock. "What does that—"

"Have you ever made yourself come?" he asked, secretly pleased with her reaction. He'd bet his knife she did, and that she'd thought of him at least once while doing so.

Her eyes narrowed. "I'm a succubus, remember?"

As if that meant anything in the grand scheme of all the crap that had happened to her, but he took it as the confirmation he'd wanted anyway.

"Touch yourself for me," he said, lowering his voice down to a husky whisper. "Show me what you like."

He wouldn't have been surprised if she refused, knew that he was counting on her stubbornness to win out. Sure enough it did, but not until after a good minute of bated moments where he wondered if he'd misjudged.

In a move that was so erotic it made his balls ache, she lifted her hand to her mouth, drawing first her index, then her middle finger into her mouth and coating them with moisture.

It seemed to take her forever to run those same fingers down over her body, stopping for a time at each nipple, before finally delving down between her thighs. She started out slowly, her legs curled up protectively around her hand so all he could tell was that she seemed to like to use these small circular movements, presumably with her fingers on her clit.

He dragged his gaze back over her body. Oh yeah, she had definitely masturbated before. Now that her initial shock at the suggestion had faded, she was thoroughly getting into it: eyes closed, back arched, her nipples raised in sweet little nubs as her chest rose and fell, and her lower lip gripped lightly between her teeth to hold back the most intriguing sounds.

He watched her pleasure mounting until she moaned, her body curling and arching as the movement of her hand got quicker. Oh, fuck yeah, that was hot.

"Open wider, Gabby. I want to see."

Her eyelids flicked open, her black pupils wide with arousal. She licked her swollen lips, swallowed, then took a deep breath and let her knees fall toward the bed.

It was his turn to close his eyes, for the sight of her, all flushed and swollen and slick beneath her hand, was surely enough to make him burst.

"God, you're so beautiful," he said and forced his eyes open again. She hadn't moved but was watching him, her hand splayed tentatively over her center as if she wasn't sure what to do now.

"Keep going, please," he said, settling one hand on her knee as if touching her on something so benign as her knee could ease the urge he had to fling himself over her and spear her with his cock.

She nodded, her fingers settling once more in that circular movement. At first he could tell she was uncertain of the exposure, her actions almost hesitant as she stroked her clit, but soon enough she lost her inhibitions, her pace climbing once more, her hips arching up against her hand as more of those delicious little noises rumbled in her throat.

He watched in fascination as her channel clenched, liquid weeping from the tight slit. "Are you going to come, Gabby?" he asked, surprised how hoarse he sounded.

She moaned, twisting her head back and forth on the pillow as she amped up the exquisite little circles she was making on her clit.

He couldn't help himself and slid the hand touching her knee down her inner thigh, intent on being part of it if she did find her release. Her eyes snapped open, her legs pulling together tightly. He stopped with his hand trapped midway down her thigh.

"Can't I touch you too?"

She sucked in a breath, her body quivering, heart racing, but then she let her legs drift back open. She didn't resume masturbating though; her delicate fingers held protectively still over her swollen clit.

He watched her carefully, measuring each movement of his hand against her reactions. There were no obvious rejections, and his fingers finally slid down over hers. He paused there, pressing gently with the same small circular motion that she had, and was rewarded when she licked her bottom lip, her fang catching slightly on the plump bit of flesh.

God, he could just imagine that hot little mouth around him. Just thinking of those full lips stretched thin to fit his width, that soft velvety tongue licking…even those sharp little fangs gently scrapping his iron-hard flesh made his cock dance in his lap.

Her eyes widened. There was a heart-stopping moment when he realized that he hadn't shielded that thought hard enough, but then the scent of her arousal feathered across his nostrils. Ah, fuck, she found the thought arousing. He was a goner—or at least his control was. Unable to help himself, he shifted his focus and gently pressed at the lips of her labia to expose the hot slickness of her core. Neither of them moved as he looked his fill.

"Beautiful." He brought his gaze up to align with hers. "You're so hot."

She shuddered, her breath releasing from her lungs as her eyes lowered in half-lidded surrender, and her hand fell away gently to her inner thigh.

Not going to get a clearer signal than that there, Don Juan.

Knowing it was now or never, he shifted between her legs, scooting around on the narrow mattress until he had perfect access to her most intimate places with both his mouth and hands.

He could all but feel the tension radiating off of her, but the moment his mouth touched, closing in the softest of kisses around that clit, all that tension exploded with a shudder of pleasure through her body that flowed right on through their link to his own.

Goddamn, if that was merely a precursor, she was going to kill him when she came.

He thought about rising up and taking her right then and there, counting on the fact that the bond was obviously growing, working, and that the feedback of his eagerness and pleasure would ensure her own, but he was too damn afraid to screw this up.

Any doubt that he hadn't made the right decision fled when he laid his mouth back down upon her for a second deeper kiss, and felt her hand tangle in the hair on top of his head.

<<You like that, Gabby?>>

Her fingers clenched tighter in his hair in answer, her grip urging him closer as she moaned.

Nerves vibrating, he responded, giving her everything he had, kissing her softly, then slightly harder, even interspersing the lightest of suckles and nips. And she kept on driving him on; her sweet little moans, the fingers that tightened to the point of that good sort of pain as she pulled the hairs along his scalp. He needed her. But first he wanted to give her everything. Shaking, he shifted, dragging his tongue over the delicious sweetness of her core. Her entire body clenched, more juices coating her center.

"Perfect." He swiped his index and middle fingers through the juices, pressing at the slit. She gasped as his fingers sank in, curling up to find that ultrasensitive spot just inside and behind her mons.

"Valin!" she cried, her hips bucking, her head flailing on the pillow as she sought for the next level.

"What, Gabby? What do you need?" He knew how close she was, could feel the rippling of her vagina walls.

"I don't...I can't..." She made a sound that could only be termed *frustration*, clenching her pelvic floor muscles, as if by doing so she could make herself come.

"Do you trust me?" he asked, pressing and stroking against the spot he knew would make her lose her mind—but only if she would let herself go.

"Yes, please, just..."

"Then come for me, Gabby," he said and closed his mouth around her clit once more.

Chapter 12

VALIN LAY WITH HIS HEAD RESTING ON GABBY'S BELLY as she sprawled listlessly across the bed. Holy fuck, he hadn't realized experiencing his mate's orgasm across their bond could be so…real. And though it should have been enough to bask in that pleasure while watching her relax like this, her muscles lax with satiation, her breathing drifting closer and closer to sleep, Valin *was* a greedy bastard. He had to have it all.

She was his mate. And he would claim her. Besides, there was so much else he wanted to show her. So many fantasies he wanted to share. So many dreams. But first he had to make her his in the most primitive and basic way. His cock, inside her. He needed to fuck his mate. Now. Before the afterglow of her pleasure wore off and she started questioning and analyzing what they were doing. He needed her completely lost in the pleasure. Not fighting him for control.

Then after, he'd go out and hunt down every one of the fuckers who'd hurt her.

Pushing the vengeful thoughts away, he hauled himself up, shifting over her body. She roused enough effort to tip her face forward and blink at him, the question of what next there but not fully formed in her furrowed brow.

Caging her face between his arms, he locked gazes with her. "You are so sexy, Gabby. Taste yourself on me."

Her eyes widened as he leaned down and pressed his mouth to hers. He needn't have feared she was too listless or embarrassed to respond; the moment his tongue plunged past her lips and touched hers she moaned and linked her arms around his neck.

Schooling himself on the need for restraint, he concentrated on rebuilding her passion, his hands drifting over her skin with not-quite touches until her body was taut with that good sort of tension.

"Valin…" She arched under his teasing hand, her soft breast pressing against his calloused palm as her sharp little nails dug into the flesh of his shoulder.

His cock throbbed against her pelvis, juices slickening their touching skin. Fuck, it was too much.

"Gabby, please, I need to be inside you."

She stilled beneath him, her pulse visibly fluttering at the base of her throat. Fear squeezed down on his rib cage. She was going to reject him. Worse, she wouldn't and he couldn't be what she needed.

She swallowed, her head dipping slightly then jutted back up in challenge. "Then what are you waiting for?"

"You have to open your legs for me."

Color rushed to her cheeks, but she complied. Determined not to fuck this up, he reigned in his randy cock, shifting his weight onto his right forearm and his knees so he could slide his left hand down between her thighs. Her eyes widened, a little pant of pleasure heaving out from between her lips as his fingers slid inside of her, the heel of his palm rubbing gently across the tender nub of her pleasure.

More color flooded to her cheeks, spreading down over her neck and chest. She made the most delicious little noise from behind her clamped lips, her pelvis arching and rotating beneath his administrations. She was so hot and slick, her channel gripping his fingers like a fucking glove or something. He wanted to kiss her again, lap up the taste of her pleasure, but his weeping cock reminded him that there were other needs that had to be taken care of.

He pumped his fingers inside of her as far as he could, dragging the pad of his thumb across her clit. Her head drifted back, her eyes closing as she bit off another moan.

It was now or never.

He pulled his fingers from within her, pausing just long enough to lick the luscious juices off. Beneath him Gabby made a little whimper of frustration, her hands fisting in the sheets beneath her as she arched her hips, as if seeking the lost sensations.

"Tease," she murmured.

He chuckled and settled over her. He was so fucking close. Close enough that the tip of his cock burned from the heat of her vagina. But she wasn't quite ready.

"Gabby, look at me."

"Oh, you're ready to do this now?" she said as her eyes opened lazily.

He ignored the jab, realizing the light banter was her way of dealing with the little twinges of doubt he still sensed she felt, and replied with all seriousness, "I can't wait to feel you come around my cock."

Her pupils flashed crimson before banking to coal-like embers. A slick rush of heat coated her vagina, teasing the tip of his cock and inviting him inside. It was too much. And before he could tell himself not to, he was thrusting inside her, all the way to the hilt.

She gasped, her hands instinctively clasping onto his shoulders. The thought that he might have hurt her crossed his mind, but not until *after* he had already slipped back and thrust into her again.

Stupid, fucking, idiotic bastard. You trying to fuck this up?

"Oh, yes..." she moaned, her leg curling around his calf as she arched against him.

Only, maybe not.

Still a bit unsure, he pulled back, this time sliding back into her on one long, languid stroke. She shook her head, making a sound in her throat that distinctly sounded like objection, then confirmed it with her next words. "No, I need...don't let me think."

Okay then. He resumed his intense pace, angling each heavy thrust to ensure that he'd stimulate that perfect spot he'd found along the front wall of her vagina as he slid in then out. Her eager response told him it was working and soon enough she was gasping beneath him, the slick walls of her channel clamping down on him like a vise.

Still she didn't come. And he wasn't going to last. Goddamn, he had to last.

"Come on, cookie. Let go," he urged, balancing his weight on one arm so that the other was free to reach between them and stroke the sensitive nub of her clit.

She arched beneath him, her fingers digging into his shoulders as she thrashed her head from side to side, and he could feel the grating rub of her frustration across their growing bond.

<<*Please... I need...*>> She flashed him with an image of her riding astride him. He faltered, torn with the

need to come after being blasted with the erotic thought and a sinking sensation in his gut. He knew why she wanted that. It was the whole control thing. If she was on top she wouldn't feel so vulnerable, so exposed. It about killed him that it was even an issue. He also worried that putting her completely in the driver seat would have her mind clicking into gear and ruin his chances of showing her how to accept the gift of pleasure. So he compromised—maybe they could both win this.

Sitting back on his heels he pulled her up with him until she was straddling his lap. Her eyes widened at the change of sensation, this angle and depth making it more about all the pleasurable little zones he could turn on rather than the overwhelming feeling of being possessed by one's lover. The Paladin instinct that demanded such caveman-like claiming grumbled a bit, but when he helped lift her, allowing her to wiggle back down on his cock just how she desired, the cave dweller settled back down, even purred. His mate was such a sexy little thing, and the wide-eyed look of astonishment she gave him as she wriggled up and down his shaft again? Fuck yeah.

Now if he could just hold out. Thankfully he didn't have to wait long. He felt the moment the orgasm took her, the shock of pleasure zapping like a bolt of static electricity between them. Her eyes widened in astonishment, but then she relaxed, arching up to take in more of the blissful sensations. He sucked in a breath, holding off his own orgasm as he watched her eyes drift close, then open, the black centers burning a smoldering crimson.

So fucking sexy. He couldn't resist thrusting into her, reveling at the tremor that rippled through her, though he tried hard to ignore his screaming balls. This wasn't over. Despite the fact that the pulsing grip of her vagina was beginning to ease, he sensed somehow there was something more, another level of pleasure that her body was striving to achieve. And given how elongated her fangs were...

"Do it." He turned his head, wrapping a hand in her hair and pulling her toward him. She needed this—no, they both did. Whether she wanted to admit it or not, she needed his blood to survive...and he fucking needed to give it to her. "Do it, Gabby. Bite me. I need to feel those pretty fangs under my skin."

Just like she was already under it. God, he couldn't lose her now. She was like the air in his lungs, the fire in his bloodstream, the other half of his soul.

I can't lose her. Not after all I've lost. Please, God. Let me be enough to save her.

Like a sweet answer to his prayer, he felt the sharp points of her fangs graze his skin. He tightened his hand on the back of her head, and a moment later she struck. He hissed at the sharp pain, but then the first pull of blood through the tight suction of her mouth had him exploding.

———

Christos squinted against the rising sun, his gaze honed in on the commotion down the street. Two blocks away he could just make out the figures scurrying to finish the last of the cleanup. Granted, there was no hiding that something had happened here—scorch marks were awfully hard to scrub away, even magically—but they were making a decent effort with the rest. And what a mess that was.

Ganelon thought him so stupid, an assumption Christos helped foster. But it was Ganelon who had lost this round. Evident by the three dead merkers currently being stuffed into black bags.

Christos knew what the problem was: Ganelon was risk averse. Oh, he might claim otherwise, but Christos had banked on the fact that under it all he hadn't changed. And typical of the general's MO, he'd delegated responsibility and sent his minions to sniff out the part-breeds, just like Christos had known he would when he mentioned the null. And what a great job those minions had done, too—until they died, of course. Definitely a bit of a kink in the Big General's plans. Not so much for Christos. Rather than waste his own resources, he'd simply kept track of Ganelon's merkers, figuring that eventually they'd uncover something interesting. And interesting is what they'd found.

His fingers ran across the dent in the rooftop door, his nostrils flaring as he drunk in the fading scent of magnolia, musk, and leather. Oh yes, that was his daughter's signature scent. And something…more.

There was no doubt in his mind that Gabby had been part of this fight. And if he was reading this right, the little bitch was shacking up with one of those Paladins too. He'd be pissed if it wasn't so rich. Gabby and a Paladin. And what seemed to be a rather impressive organization of part-breeds. All working together. Oh, the possibilities were endless. And if he did things right it would affirm his position at Lucifer's right hand.

All it would take was a plan.

His gaze settled on one of the soldiers. A tall but otherwise average looking youth of about twenty. Besides the fact that his gift barely pinged on Christos's radar, the way the youth hesitated before performing any given task said he was unsure of himself too, yet too self-conscious to ask for further direction. A quiet loner with no backbone. Oh yes, he'd be perfect for Christos's needs.

Christos smiled and stepped over to the edge of the roof. Day was breaking, and it was time to acquire some good help.

Chapter 13

"THAT'S RIGHT, KEEP IT STEADY," GABBY SAID, PUSHING lightly on the new recruit's shield to test its strength. Not bad, but far from perfect, and therefore not good enough.

"Easy for you to say," the woman grumbled, her brow beading with sweat. "I don't see how anyone could do this while in a fight."

"It's all about control. And stamina, of course." And okay, she shouldn't use those two words so closely together when one elicited thoughts of her lack thereof and the other thoughts of *him*.

Damn Valin, he just had to go and ruin everything. It had been bad enough when she'd gotten herself off thinking about him and all his fineness, but now? Masturbation was never going to be the same—and seeing how that was the only way she was going to orgasm again, that just plain sucked.

"Like this?" a voice rose from the other side of the gym.

She turned and walked across the scuffed floor, passing her ten other students to reach the other end of the line. Towering over her at a crane-her-neck six-five, Ryan had the type of lean musculature that made him always seem a bit…awkward, to put it kindly. The impression was made even worse today by the stark contrast of the tight-fitting black microfiber mock turtleneck he wore. Fashion plate he was not, nor was the young soldier particularly outgoing, both of which probably festered his inherent tendency to stay in the background. It was because of this that Gabby didn't know him that well, other than he was actually one of Jacob's first recruits. Normally he wouldn't even be in this sort of primer class, but the soldier didn't have a lot of power. Which meant he tended to throw all he had into a given task and peter out quickly; i.e., no stamina—*Ugh!* Now, however, Ryan's shields were pulsing softly with power, the protective mesh over his mind flexible but unbreakable. It was an excellent strategy, one that required more control than energy and would be effective against all but the most skilled of enemies.

"Very good." She gave him a sharp nod. "Those are the best shields I've ever seen you form."

"Thanks," he replied with a grin, his face pale against his sweat-drenched shirt.

Forcing her mouth into some semblance of a return smile, she moved on to the next recruit, correcting where needed and praising when correction wasn't necessary. Okay, maybe she didn't praise all that much. Today her students were going to have to be content with not being singled out. She was in a pisser of a mood *and* tired. Neither of which got better when a moment later she felt the tickle at the back of her mind announcing that Valin was waking.

She tried to ignore him, but her supposed proficiency at shielding aside, she couldn't fully block the emotions that fed across the blood bond she'd forged so thoroughly last night, which, ironically, was another thing she could blame on a certain unnamed individual. Goddamn egotistical, pushy bastard. He was such a *male*, not content until he had everything he wanted.

And holy crap, did she have to be exposed to this now, too? Like every other typical male out there, the jerk had awoken with an overenthusiastic hard-on and, dog that he was, was indulging in a bit of morning pleasure.

<<*Will you knock that off?*>> she cried, trying desperately to block the erotic little tingles that lapped at her through the blood bond. The fact that she'd rather be there, watching, was not relevant, because there was no way she could allow anything like last night to happen again.

<<*There's my woman,*>> he purred, eliciting an unwelcome shiver of delight at the touch of his mind on hers. She straightened, stiffening her spine—Lucifer knew she needed a steel one to deal with this man.

<<*Do you have to do that?*>>

<<*Yeah, kinda do, considering you're not here.*>> He paused, the sexual contentedness shifting easily over to annoyance. <<*Speaking of which, where are you, cookie?*>>

<<*Don't call me that,*>> she snapped back.

<<*In the building still,*>> he stated, probably basing the assumption on the bell-tone quality of her last projection. Still, she didn't need to respond. No way was she going to give him any help hunting her down, which is what he seemed determined to do. She sensed that he was up by the glimpses she caught of his thoughts as he rifled around the room looking for his jeans. And then his gaze must have fallen on the bed because the next thought had her gasping.

<<*Would you not do that?*>> she shrieked, viciously trying to scrub away the image of herself lying in bed, her legs wantonly parted while she vigorously stimulated her clit as he looked on.

<<*Why? You're so fucking sexy. And you have no idea how hungry I am for you. I crave your taste, your body... your screams. I can't wait to make you come again.*>>

She made a noise—half-growl, half-scream—even as she clenched her thighs together; her body was one duplicitous bitch.

"Uh, Gabriella?"

Heat flooded her cheeks as she spun around to meet the head-on gaze of a dozen astonished faces. Crap, she must look like an idiot, squirming and gasping like a sexed-up nymphomaniac. Which, sadly, is exactly what she was.

"You've all perfected your shields then?" she snapped at them. Eleven sets of eyes diverted their focus, all but one student. She frowned as Ryan continued to stare at her. For a painfully shy young man, he'd been making eye contact with her a lot today.

She started to take a step toward him when the gym's double doors banged open, slamming hard into the cement wall. She sucked in a breath, a delicious shiver running across her skin as a bare-chested Valin stopped just inside the entry, quickly scanning the room until his gaze honed in and locked on hers. The memory of how he'd looked at her just like that as he'd rocked her to orgasm had her body clenching—and her fangs throbbing—with need. A need she had no right ever feeding again. *Goddamn Valin.*

She was so busy drooling she forgot about her admirer until Valin's gaze flicked over her shoulder. She turned, her confidence in the young soldier's self-preservation instinct reassured when he had the good sense to look away this time.

She turned back to Valin. "Can I help you?"

"Why yes, you can. But do you want to help me here, or…" he smiled, his thumb hooking deceptively casually in his jeans, "somewhere else?"

"We're in the middle of a class." She was proud of how even and businesslike that came out, considering that she was panting like a bitch in heat. Damn her mother. If she could dig her up and wring her skeletal corpse for cursing her with these crappy genes, she would.

"Class just ended," he informed her, making a beeline for her.

She started to take a step back, then stopped herself, firmly planting her feet on the wooden floor. "I'm only going to ask you once to leave."

"Good, then I only have to say no once."

She narrowed her eyes, planting her hands on her hips. "Do I have to spell this out for you? Leave. Me. Alone. Valin."

"In your dreams, cookie."

And that was the problem. He'd already invaded those. And now, with his blood singing in her veins like a stubborn drug, no matter where she tried to hide he promised to be there too.

"Dismiss your class, Gabby," he said, his voice but a seductive rumble as he invaded her space, stopping just short of touching her.

She lifted her chin higher, making sure to clearly enunciate her response for the thickheaded bastard. "No."

His lids lowered to half-moon slits. "Ladies and gentlemen," he projected across the gym, "I'm afraid I need to steal your teacher. You'll have to resume class later."

She twisted to look over her shoulder, eyeing each and every one of her students. "Not one of you dare move."

The grin that split Valin's face when she looked back had her tensing. Jerk was up to something.

"What?" she asked sharply.

"I never figured you for an exhibitionist, but hey, I'm game."

"You're insane," she hissed in contrast to his still way-too-fucking-loud voice.

"Doesn't float your fancy?" He shrugged. "All right then." He stepped to the side, performing some sort of stupid little bow thingy to her students. "If you'll excuse us."

She swiveled on her heels toward him. "If you think I'm going to—"

He spun around, ducking even lower. She grunted as his shoulder hit her stomach, lifting her right off her feet. Next thing she knew she was balanced precariously on his shoulder, her head and feet dangling toward the ground on either side of him, and one of his hands clamped tightly across the backside of her upper thighs.

"Hey!" She hit him in the back, but all he did was grunt and keep on walking. "Valin," she squirmed, kicking out with her feet to try and knock him off balance, "you ass…"

"I like yours better." And then the jerk patted it.

She glared at her students, mortified that they were witnessing this. Only not a single one seemed to care; in fact, most had already started filing out of the room; only Ryan lingered, his lips pursed thoughtfully as he watched Valin go all caveman on her.

Fucking goddamn *males*.

She started thrashing, then hissed when her feet hit something solid—like the fricken wall, maybe? A moment later another door swung open and he squeezed them into the equipment room that also double-dutied as a makeshift office.

"Put me—"

The world tilted, the narrow window that was the room's only light source spinning by over her head as she landed with an unceremonious plop on a pile of rubber mats. She vaulted up, fists raised as she went for the bastard who'd manhandled her. He caught her wrists, his eyes dancing with mirth as his mouth pulled up into a smug grin.

"Conceited assho—"

He stopped her insult by crushing his mouth down on hers. Her body instantly responded, her nipples drawing tight and warmth pooling between her thighs. He tasted so good, like dark cocoa peppered with salt, copper, and just the slightest hint of *her*.

He released her wrists, freeing his hands to slide around the back of her neck to cup her head. Her own hands slid up his arms, circling the sculpted curves of his heavily muscled biceps.

"Jerk. I hate you," she panted as his mouth moved from hers and began a path of destruction across her jaw in a definite underhanded attempt to outmaneuver the last of her willpower.

"No you don't," he murmured, sucking on her earlobe. Her knees quaked, threatening to buckle, and she clutched his biceps tighter.

"You're an asshole," she gasped when she could catch her breath.

"So you've said," he growled, then brutally crushed his mouth to hers once more. She made a noise, one that she'd meant to sound like refusal but in reality sounded pitifully like surrender. And okay, so maybe she was protesting too much. She certainly could have stopped him from carrying her in here if she'd really wanted to. But she hadn't, which meant on some deep level—okay, not all that deep—she wanted this.

He's going to break your heart, Gabby... Or you'll break his.

A Paladin and a vampire-succubus, a true match made in hell.

Someone knocked on the door. They both stiffened. Before Gabby could decide if she was glad or pissed at the eruption—or make the effort to extract herself from the compromising position—the door tentatively cracked open, Annie's voice penetrating the dim interior. "Gabby? You in here? Valin's looking for you, he seems really..."

She trailed off as her gaze honed in on them. "Oh, ah..." Her eyes had begun to twinkle. "I see he's found you."

Gabby shot Annie a don't-you-fucking-say-a-thing glare, though what she really wanted to do was smack that oh-my-my grin off the girl's face.

"I'll just be going," Annie said, still smiling.

"Good idea," Valin said, never taking his eyes off Gabby as she watched the door click close. "That girl doesn't have a lick of timing, does she?"

Gabby shook her head. In general it was true, though this time the interruption was actually kind of opportune. *Now's your chance. Take it.*

She took a deep breath, her hands falling from Valin's arms. She expected him to object, so it was a surprise when he let her go and stepped away. Trying to process the rather foolish wave of disappointment caused by his capitulation, she watched him stride to the door—and flip the lock. Her heart started to race, her palms dampening as she fought with the inner imp in her that was dancing up and down yelling hurray and the Gabriella who'd survived more than her fair share of shit to get to this moment.

Nothing good could come from having sex with Valin again. Nothing other than falling for him. And yeah, falling in love with this man shouldn't have even been a factor (he was a conceited bastard and a real asshole most of the time), but then there were those other moments. Moments like that one in the cave when he'd laid his hand on her shoulder in comfort, or the way he'd stroked the tear off her cheek last night.

The heart hidden beneath the dark-humored shell. No wonder she was more than halfway lost to him.

Stupid, stupid, stupid.

"Undress for me, Gabby. I love to watch you uncover that delicious little body."

She trembled at his words knowing full well what that would lead to, even though she also knew she had to end this. Now. But when she went to take that step forward that would take her past him toward the door, she found she couldn't.

One time. What will one more time hurt? Consider it a good-bye.

Knowing that was the stupidest of excuses didn't stop her from doing what she did next. Keeping her gaze locked on his, she traced a finger across the neckline of her top, pulling at it teasingly so that it dipped enticingly across her breasts, while the other hand stretched the bottom hem upward. The fact that it was a serviceable tank rather than some frilly, pink negligee didn't seem to matter to Valin; he groaned, his own fingers fumbling at the buttons of his jeans. She held her breath as his erection sprang free, all long and hard and thick. As she watched, he took himself in hand, pumping once, then twice, again until a bead of moisture collected at the tip. Her eyes fixed on the evidence of his desire and she licked her lips.

"Are you going to take it off for me, Gabby?" he asked.

At first she thought that he meant for her to lick the glistening moisture from that intriguing little slit, but then she remembered that she'd been doing something. She nodded, wiggling a little as she pulled off the tank so that her breasts bounced freely as they popped out of the fabric. He stilled, his knuckles whitening around the thick base of his erection. "Fuck, you're not wearing a bra."

She shrugged. "I was in a hurry…and I didn't want to wake you fumbling around in the room."

"Damn considerate of you." His eyes took on a devilish glint. "Don't suppose you were considerate enough not to rummage around for your panties."

"Maybe…" She slipped her fingers into the waistband of her workout pants. "Want to find out?"

"Hell yes," he said as he chucked his own jeans in a move that was so fast he practically blurred. Had he actually pulled them off his legs or had he pulled his particle trick again?

"You better hurry if you don't want me ripping those off you," he warned.

She complied, not because he'd ordered her to, but because it suited with her desires as well. She was truly an addict. Just thinking about how good he felt as he pumped inside of her was making her heart race at a rate that couldn't be healthy.

Oh how far I've come in just one night. Sign me up for the next session, Doctor Valin. Right now.

She launched herself at him at the same time he moved for her. They met with a crash in the middle of the room. His mouth descended upon hers, hot and firm and demanding. His hands claimed her, his touch just shy of bruising as he tweaked and stroked every hot button he'd discovered upon her last night. As for her, she was a mindless animal, clawing and keening as she tried to wring all she could from him at the same time.

More.

Stay in control.

Had to have him. All of him.

And will you lose yourself when you do?

"No, no, nononono…" She shook her head, her hands fisting against his chest. She couldn't do this. Shouldn't have given over to the need in the first place.

"Bullshit," he growled and whirled her around, slamming her up against the door, his breath coming in short gasps as he pinned her there, his need readily evident against the soft dip of her lower stomach. "No is not an option for us anymore, Gabby."

"I just meant…" She swallowed, unable to voice her doubts sufficiently for him to understand.

That's assuming he'd care enough to hear.

She took a deep breath, trying to silence the doubts and needs that were splitting her in two. Valin stilled, his gaze searching as he looked for something in her face. "What did you mean, Gabby?"

"I meant..." She closed her eyes, leveraging her hands on his shoulders so she could wiggle her hips into the perfect position. She lifted her legs, linking her ankles behind his hips as she rubbed herself on the hot ridge of his erection.

He hissed, his body turning to hard iron. "Damnit, Gabby. First you say no, then you rub against me like a cat in heat. What are you trying to do to me?"

Nothing. Nothing to him. Though this would surely scar her.

Even knowing that wasn't enough to make her stop. The need was too great. The desire for this man too much to dismiss.

Just keep it simple. Him. You. Sex. We're all just animals, after all.

"I meant don't stop."

"Oh thank God," he said, the tension in his body transferring into a powerful thrust against her, his cock rubbing deliciously against her weeping folds. She clasped her lip between her teeth, barely catching the needy moan that bubbled from her throat in response.

"Do you like that, cookie?"

"Don't call me cookie," she responded automatically, but ruined the rebuff by trying to devour his mouth.

He chuckled around her tongue, breaking the lip-lock enough to murmur, "I'll take that as a yes."

"Bastard," she said, even as she ground her pelvis

against him. He was so hot against her slick core. So hard, if she could only angle her pelvis a bit more…

"Do you want more of me?" he teased, his hips rotating in sanity-breaking short motions against her clit.

"Yes, just…please."

"Please what?" he asked, shifting so that the tip of his cock barely slipped inside of her before pulling back out.

She whimpered, arching her back to follow his retreat, but was blocked from achieving her goal by the hand that clasped firmly down on her ass.

"Say it, Gabby."

She growled a sound, letting her head fall back against the door as she glared at him in frustration. "You want me to talk dirty to you?"

"I want you to tell me what you want."

"Fine." She gritted her teeth, then smiled and said with saccharine sweetness, "Please, Valin, oh man of all males, would you please fuck me?"

His jaw ticked, his pupils sharpening to dagger points. "Is that what you want?"

She nodded curtly. It was all she could have.

He growled, the noise rumbling deep in his chest. The sound, combined with the little power struggle they'd just had, dimmed her growing need enough that she finally clued in to his emotions. He was pissed, though whether pissed at her, her responses, or just that he wanted her at all she didn't know. She pressed against his shoulders with her hands, intent on telling him to forget this had ever happened, when he thrust, his cock piercing deep into the welcoming folds of her core.

She gasped, pleasure rippling from the overwhelming wash of sensations. Any thoughts of ending this drowned in the burning tidal wave of need that rode in on pleasure's tail.

Holy hell. How was she going to walk away from this man after this?

"Valin...I just...I want..."

"What do you want, Gabby? What do you need me to do?" he asked, his strokes almost brutal even as he eased into a pounding rhythm that she knew from experience would just drive her wilder.

Her nails dug into his shoulders. She was finding it difficult to draw in air as he seemed to be driving it all out of her. "More. I need...." She gasped on a particularly intense stroke, shuddering at the mind-numbing effect of their passion. "Yes, like that." No thoughts. No worries. Just sex. It's what she needed. And all she deserved.

He obliged, gritting his teeth as if maintaining the punishing rhythm was testing his willpower. She couldn't know for sure, not without opening herself to the glimpses of his other emotions and that...well, after the last lookey-see, she doubted she wanted to know. Especially when she was so close to coming apart.

She closed her eyes, straining against him, searching for the combination of sensations that would mean her release. Like the addict she was, she now craved the type of release that only he could give her.

"Is this what you want? Do you like me fucking you?" His voice broke her climb toward ecstasy, forcing her to cling to her current ledge.

"Yes, damn you, you know I do."

He slowed, drawing out the next stroke, then torment-
ing her with a long, languid rub back in. "How about
this? Can you like this?"

She writhed against him, her nerves screaming in
frustration. Just a couple more strokes and she would
have been there. Just a couple more moments until
that blissful moment of suspension where nothing
mattered—not her past, not her future, nothing but
right then.

"No, I need…Please, Valin, you're killing me!"

He leaned in, his hand wrapping in the hair at the
back of her neck as he pressed his lips against her forehead. The kiss was barely a whisper, no more than the
soft caress of air as he drew in a shaky breath. "I don't
want to kill you, Gabby. I want to love you."

Her eyes popped open, startled not only by his words
but by the small amount of moisture that sunk down
through the hair on top of her head. He was crying? She
shook her head, biting her lip. "Valin…I…"

"Don't! Don't say it." He tightened his grip around
her hair, yanking her head back so that she had to look
at him. His face was angry, nostrils pinched tight, mouth
but a thin line, and, angels help her, tears glistening in
his eyes.

What had she done to him? How could she…He
thrust into her with such force that she gasped, leaving
her no breath to speak.

"Don't say a fucking thing, just…God, Gabby. I need
this. I need to make love to you. I need you." He pressed
another kiss to her forehead, closing his eyes as he resumed his pace of long seductive strokes.

Her heart melted. The one she wasn't really sure she

had. How could she? She seduced for power, fed off evil. How could she ever be worthy of this man?

You fought. You fight still. Now get some fucking backbone and fight for him.

Courage. Until now it was the one thing she would have said she didn't lack. But it seemed, with Valin, it was most possibly her weakest trait.

Not anymore, she told herself firmly and then did the bravest thing ever. She relaxed, giving over to the seductive pleasure he wooed her with, laying her head on his shoulder.

"I need you too. I just can't…can't say…I don't dare…" She choked on something. Something hard and achy that stole away her words and threatened to boil up into tears.

"Shhh…That's enough. Has to be. Because I can't fucking let you go again."

Then don't. Oh, please love me, Valin. Love me as much as I love you.

As if he'd heard her words, he drew her closer, kissing her lightly as he slowly rocked her toward a pleasure she'd never known.

Chapter 14

BENNETT PUSHED OPEN THE CAFETERIA DOORS, LEAVING behind the raucous din of the midday diners as he turned right down the hall. He wasn't surprised he hadn't found Valin there—the man liked dark, out-of-the-way corners—but Bennett was beginning to run out of places to look and becoming increasingly frustrated.

He and Valin needed to come up with a strategy to convince Jacob to open a dialogue with the Paladin council. These men and women needed help, whether they wanted it or not. The only reason they'd survived so far was because they'd basically gone unnoticed by their enemies. But how long could that last?

With three dead merkers after the pyro attack, Ganelon would have to put some time and effort into a serious investigation. And these people were sitting ducks.

Benett rounded the corner, his mood picking up a bit when he saw Annie walking toward him. She kept *very* close tabs on her mentor, Gabby. And where Gabby was…well, Valin was sure to have followed.

She caught sight of him, her eyes lighting up and her hand lifting in a little hi-ya wave. He couldn't help but smile a bit in return as he felt the influence of her gift surround him, cutting out the constant chaos of emotions that prickled at his skin. Too bad the effect was almost immediately countered by a coiling of his nerves.

He knew that Valin called her an Amazon, but he

didn't see it. Yes, she was tall, her lean body carved with long, smooth muscle, but there was something decidedly fragile about her too. Perhaps it was just the double-edged curse of her gift. Being a null might seem like a great weapon to strip your opponents of their magical powers, but a little time with her had shown him just what sort of handicap her gift really was. The complete absence of magical energy that was a side effect of her gift made her a virtual beacon to all things that could sense the ebbs and flow of power. It also made her a walking bomb to anything and anyone relying on magic—a weapon that, unfortunately, could be yielded by friend or foe.

And Bennett had no idea what to do about it.

He knew what he wanted to do: wrap her up and tuck her far away from anywhere Ganelon might think to look. But he'd spent enough time with her to know that doing so would kill her spirit. It was bad enough that she was a virtual prisoner here in this base, and this cell was forged with love. He'd seen her watch the patrols come and go and all he could think of when he did was of a caged bird. Her heart urged her to fly forth into battle with the rest of the warriors, but she couldn't even test her wings within the confines of her cage. The result was a cranky and often sullen young woman, though damn, she looked content enough right now.

"Hey, Bennett. It's a beautiful day, isn't it?" She beamed at him.

He closed his eyes, taking a deep breath. If she'd been outside again, he didn't want to know. Not only would it put him in the position of keeping her secret—or not—but he simply didn't want to think of the risk she was taking when she did such things.

"Something wrong?"

He opened his eyes, rolling his shoulders to relieve some of the ever-increasing tension. "Have you seen Valin?"

"Um, actually…" She glanced over her shoulder toward the double doors at the end of the hall.

"He's in the gym?" He started to brush by her, but she caught his arm, dragging him to a halt.

"I don't think you want to go in there just now."

His stomach tightened. Ballocks, what had the Paladin done now?

"Actually the gym is safe, but I wouldn't go into the equipment room if I were you." Her grin widened, and she did this wiggly thing with her brow that made absolutely no sense to him.

Unless she caught Valin naked again. And bloody hell, why did that piss him off? "Care to tell me why?"

"Let's just say he and Gabby are having a long overdue…um…discussion."

He blew out a breath, rubbing his forehead. "Hell."

Annie elbowed him. "What's your problem? This is a good thing."

He grunted, not able to muster the obvious happiness that Annie felt about them finally getting together. Sure, he wished Valin the best, but given the obstacles, Bennett didn't hold too much hope for a happy ending. His brothers were dropping like flies. Love, the obvious poison. Thank the maker he had yet to be cursed with that affliction.

Annie tipped her head to the side, nibbling her lip as

if unsure whether she should speak. He raised his brow. "You look tense," she said.

"I guess I am a bit."

"You want to spar?"

Actually, the idea sounded rather appealing but…"I thought you said the gym was occupied." Or rather the equipment room, but if things were progressing how Annie seemed to assume they were, he frankly didn't want to be anywhere nearby. Rather not overhear that, thank you very much.

"I have another place in mind."

"Lead the way," he said, figuring he had at least an hour or two to kill, if not more. A smart man did not come between a Paladin and his mate during bonding, and Bennett was nothing if not smart. Besides, there was no way he was going to risk interrupting…that… for fear of having some rather unwanted images burned into his retinas.

He followed Annie back down the hall, then up the central stairs. Needing diversion from the reason he followed her, he indulged in watching her backside as she climbed the cement steps ahead of him. The woman had a fine arse, and those legs…they went on forever and brought to mind thoughts of what they'd feel like wrapped around him.

She smiled over her shoulder, then, as if she knew just what he was thinking, took the last few stairs with an exaggerated sway to her steps.

"Tease," he accused.

She laughed, linking her hand with his as she turned left down the hall. He didn't try and take his hand away. It felt good in hers and he was sick of denying himself.

He was interested. She was obviously interested. What did he care about her big bad daddy, especially when the idiot refused to listen to him anyway?

She led him about halfway down the hall, pushing open the door to an old classroom tucked back in a corner. It was easy enough to tell it had been the art room. If the rows of cabinetry with its towering rack of faded colored butcher paper next to it hadn't given it away, the various works of art, both framed classics and classroom examples, hanging on the other wall would have.

It was also obvious that this wasn't the room's current purpose. Someone had dragged over enough mats from the gym that the floor was completely covered. That, along with the heavy-duty punching bag and small rack of free weights at one end, screamed personal gym. Almost too personal, because damn if that wasn't a cot tucked into the corner by the free weights.

"This your room?" he asked casually, all the while trying to ignore the overeager organ in his pants. To go from hand-holding to tossing her on that cot might be a little fast even for him.

"Like it?" she asked, walking over to the cabinets. He pulled his eyes away from the cot as she popped open the cabinet doors, revealing a virtual arsenal of hand-to-hand combat weapons.

He moved to stand beside her, the soft scent of her shampoo tickling his nose as he studied her collection. Brass knuckles, tiger claws, escrima sticks, nunchucks, sai, throwing stars and knives, regular knives, a manriki chain, and even fighting fans—all well worn and lovingly cared for.

"I like these." He reached out to test the tip of the

sai—not a practice instrument, at least not with a live partner. Of course, even the escrima sticks could be deadly if yielded with skill. "Do you know how to use all these?"

"Of course," she scoffed.

"Who was your instructor?"

"Mostly my dad, but whenever we get a new recruit who has an expertise I normally charm some lessons out of them."

His groin tightened, his imagination running away with the thought of her charming some lessons out of him too—though the lessons he would want to provide had nothing to do with the contents of that cabinet and everything to do with that cot in the corner.

"So, what's your poison?" she asked.

The knife, but he wasn't about to play around with a sharp object with her, and she didn't appear to have any sparring weaponry besides the escrima that didn't threaten stitches, and those were far from his favorite. "You don't appear to have any staffs."

"Ah!" She moved down to a tall cabinet at the end and yanked it open. "Ta-da!" She waved her hands in a Vanna White imitation at the contents, which were, sure enough, a variety of fighting staffs.

His fingers began to itch. It had been a while since he'd had the time to devote to simple sparring. But he also didn't think he had the patience to play teacher tonight either. "You any good with them?"

"I'm good with all my weapons," she replied and tossed a staff to him.

He snapped it out of the air, twisting it around a couple times to get a feel for its balance and weight. Perfect.

She smiled, grabbing her own staff and whirling it around in a pattern that suggested she wasn't too shabby with the weapon either.

Wanting to ensure that her proficiency extended to sparring, he moved into an easy pattern of strikes and jabs to test her skill at blocking that any student should know. She didn't disappoint, meeting each movement with its countermove and often following through with her own attack.

Their pace quickened, running through more complicated maneuvers, and soon enough he found that he was defending as much as attacking.

"You're good," he said after one particularly powerful clash of their staffs, the vibration of the block running up his arm.

She wiggled her brow. "I know."

He chuckled and, stepping back from the lock, quickly swung the staff around the other way. She blocked that too, countering with her own blow, which barely missed his side.

Oh, this is going to be bloody fun, he thought, and stopped holding back.

They sparred for what seemed like forever but was really only a couple hours, still long enough to turn his muscles to liquid. Her stamina, like her skill with the staff, was amazing. She was amazing. And just plain comfortable to hang out with. Which was good considering they both were laying on the mats now panting like exhausted dogs.

"I think you could come teach some of my brothers a thing or two," he said when he'd caught his breath enough to speak. Even as he suggested it, he didn't like the thought of bringing her anywhere near his brothers. There was no doubt that with her gift, they'd see her either as a weak link to be eliminated or almost as bad, a potential mate. Neither of which sat well with him.

"Hmmm…but what would I get in return?"

"You expect compensation?"

She rolled over onto her side, propping herself up with her elbow as she smiled down at him. "I always collect my payment."

He stilled, his entire body tensing as she blatantly ogled his body. Predictably Mr. Thomas decided to put on a good showing, straining against his trousers.

She raised her gaze back to his face, her eyes twinkling. "Hmmm…and here I thought I'd worn you out too much for that."

"I'm not at death's door yet."

"So it's not just my amazing gift at revival?"

"That's a gift?"

She pulled off her top, then arched like a stretching cat on the mat as she slowly drew her arms up over her head and kept them there. "Isn't it?"

He groaned and, with an amazing burst of newfound energy, shifted over her. She was right; she did have a gift, because right now the heavy thud of his racing heart had nothing to do with exhaustion and everything to do with the woman staring expectantly up at him out of her golden eyes.

Damn, she was sexy. Her short spiky hair glowed like a sunset, framing the dramatic features of her face. Her nose might be considered a bit too long, her jaw too square, her lips a bit thin, though wide and nicely shaped. Possibly even her wide-set eyes could be considered almost eerie with their unnatural golden hue. But for him everything matched, melding together into a combination fit to inspire the most gifted of poets. Too bad he wasn't one. Though he could worship each and every one of her features in turn, first, though, he had to pay homage to the offerings she'd so generously given up to him.

Holding her gaze, he slid his hand up her torso to cup her breast. He'd known she didn't have much up top, but he was surprised how much he seemed to like the slight weight against the palm of his hand. She'd never get saggy, or need a bra, and the thought of her going around without one sent his heat levels to raging. And her nipples, the sweetest little nubs of pink against her creamy skin. He had to taste them.

Lowering his head, he pulled one of the rosy pink disks into his mouth, gently flicking the pebbled tip with his tongue. She gasped, lacing her fingers through his hair and digging into his scalp with her short little nails.

He shuddered, his pulse quickening at the evidence of her increasing desire. The fact that she had to communicate her need through such actions made it all the more exciting for him. To be able to concentrate on the sensations, to kiss her like this because *he* enjoyed doing so and not because of some twisted feedback loop his gift created from her pleasure. Not that he didn't want to please her—he did—but he knew, for once, that the trembling in his muscles that came with rising need was his, *all* his.

"Woman, you drive me mad."

"Ditto," she replied and wrapped her long legs around him. Oh lord, they fit just how he'd imagined, her ankles crossed behind his back, her heel digging into the cleft of his arse, and his erection grinding against that sweet, sweet juncture of bliss. And then she proceeded to rub herself against him in a way that had him practically weeping.

Can't take it. Have to be inside her now.

He pulled back, breaking the lock of her legs as he stood.

"What?" she asked, pulling herself from her unceremonious sprawl up onto her elbows.

"Too many damn clothes," he growled, pulling his T-shirt off.

She licked her lips, then got with the program, wiggling out of her sweats on the mat as he shucked the rest of his clothing. She was gorgeous, all lean muscles and slight curves...except for those hips. They flared out from her narrow waist into the most spectacular arse he'd ever seen. He'd always thought himself a boob man, but he'd been watching that fine bum for days now and knew that he just had never seen one as perfect as hers. The desire to flip her over, pull her back on her knees, and then drive into her from behind just so he could see that wonderful arse while he banged her was like a vicious monster in his system. But he wasn't a complete bastard, so that would wait—until the second time they'd had each other at least.

He reached down for her. At the same time she sat up, reaching for him. They collided with a resounding smack, her nose to his jaw.

"Ow, shit..." She fell back down, clutching her nose.

"Are you okay?" he asked anxiously as he knelt beside her.

She chuckled, though the sound was laced with tears. If her nose felt anything like his jaw it was no wonder.

"Sorry, that was…smooth." She gingerly wiggled her nose, sniffled. "Can you tell I've never done this before?"

His heart thudded behind his ribs, which all of a sudden seemed way too tight. She couldn't possibly mean…"Wait. Done this as in attacked your partner or done *this* this?"

She lowered her hand, her lips pressed tight together and her eyes wary as she met his gaze.

"Bloody hell." He drew back, sitting on his heels as he regarded her. She'd seemed so sure of herself he'd just assumed…but she was innocent and he was…well, a man-whore. And though he didn't have many scruples, one rule was inviolate: He didn't have sex with virgins. With Annie that rule had the added weight of her heritage. She deserved to have the option of giving her innocence to her mate. He wouldn't take that from her. He liked her, genuinely liked her, and sometimes he thought maybe…but even he had to admit much of his fascination with her could simply be her gift's ability to calm his beast. With her he could be alone in his own head. No one else's emotions messing with him. He could be as selfish as he bloody wanted and not consider her emotions at all. Which was just plain fucking wrong. If she was his mate, then wouldn't her feelings be all that mattered?

"I think I better go." He stood, grabbing up his trousers from the floor, and began pulling them on. Behind him, Annie leapt up, laying a hand on his arm.

"Wait! Does this have anything to do with my father?"

"You don't think Jacob wouldn't kill me if he came

in here and found us like this?" He found that he was breathing heavily, not because he was really worried about what Jacob might do, but because of what he'd almost done. He'd almost stolen something precious and meaningful to her—worse, he would have done it simply to satisfy some damn curiosity of what sex without his gift could be like.

She folded her arms across her breasts, her legs crossed awkwardly as if that might protect her too. "I'm of age. By more than a few years, too."

"You're a virgin!" Taking a deep breath, he closed his eyes. Thank God he couldn't read her. This was damn hard enough as it was. "Get some clothes on, Annie."

"I thought…"

"You thought what?" he asked, though he knew exactly what she thought. She thought what almost happened here meant something. She thought maybe… *Don't go there, you bloke. Way too fucking complicated. We like simple, remember?*

He heaved out a frustrated breath. "Annie, let me teach you a little something about men and sex."

Her lips pulled in tight, her eyes turning wary, but she gave him a subtle nod.

"Men are men and sex is sex. Don't confuse it with being something more."

"But you won't have sex with me," she said, her voice but a whisper in the supercharged air. It wasn't hard to read the underlying question there: Why? Why if men were the dogs he claimed wouldn't he have sex with her? He knew she was trying to read more into his actions, which was dangerous, for both of them. She wanted more than a player like him could ever give, but he knew, just knew that if she offered more of the heaven she'd just given him a glimpse of he wouldn't be able to refuse. Which meant he needed to ensure that she never did.

"I don't fuck virgins. It's as plain and simple as that," he said and took himself from the room.

Chapter 15

ANNIE STARED AT THE OPEN DOOR, HALF-EXPECTING Bennett to come back through. That couldn't be it. She couldn't be that wrong, could she? He was her mate, wasn't he? But as the minutes stretched out and he still didn't return, she had to face one glaringly depressing fact: obviously he didn't think so.

Numbly she turned from the empty doorway and stepped back onto the center of the mat where her world had just fallen apart. How sad that her life could be reduced to a pile of rumpled clothing and a whole bunch of could have beens that now wouldn't be.

She'd been a fool. The flirting, the hand-holding, the way he'd held her, letting her cry on his shoulder when Aaron was hurt, the wide smile that had become his standard expression when he saw her…obviously it had meant a hell of a lot more to her than him. *Stupid, stupid, stupid*. Bennett wasn't her mate, nor was he her savior. He couldn't help her escape herself, and how did she ever believe that he, a warrior, could find a partner in her? She was cursed. She couldn't even leave the building without drawing enemies to them. Anyone who loved her would be in constant danger. And that's not what mates were supposed to be. Mates were partners in mind, body, and soul—that's what her father had told her. She should have seen that past the sweaty palms and racing heart. She could not be the other half of Bennett's team. She was a handicap that she couldn't blame him for not wanting to be saddled with.

But that hadn't stopped her from hoping. Hadn't stopped her from dreaming, and planning, and...falling. She'd fallen in love. He hadn't. And now she didn't know what she was supposed to do next.

I should get dressed.

She bent down and retrieved her sweats, carefully pulling them on one leg then the other. Her T-shirt was a few feet away. She shuffled toward it, listing slightly as she plucked it from the floor.

Once it was on she turned back toward the open door, figuring she should close it or something before someone else came along and saw...what?

Me crying.

She cursed, swiping at her eyes, but the tears kept on coming. She swallowed, the tears catching in her jagged throat as she frantically looked for something to plug the waterworks with. There, on the floor.

She swooped down and grabbed the camo-green T-shirt and buried her face in it. His scent flooded her nostrils. She gasped, pulling the shirt away and staring down at it.

Bennett's shirt. In here. Her room. What a cruel, cruel knife to the gut.

She sucked in a breath, then another, unable to get enough air into her lungs. It felt like the walls were crushing in around her.

Have to get out. Have to escape.

Tossing the T-shirt down like it was a bundle of hot coals, she bolted out of the room, her bare feet slapping on the hard floor. It wasn't until she reached the stairs, the echo of voices drifting up through the chimney-like area, that she realized she had nowhere to go. As a compromise for not having a constant guard, her father had assigned round-the-clock double watches to all the exits, and there was no place to go inside the walls that wouldn't result in personal contact with another. She couldn't go back to her room. Not when…not with…

The lights dimmed, the floor tilting under her feet. Instinctively she reached out to grab the railing. She clung to it, sucking in deep breaths before she realized it wasn't some sort of freaky attack, but her.

God, Annie, you're pitiful.

That she was. She was also an idiot. There was one place she could go. It was just she hadn't been there in so long she'd almost forgotten.

Calmer now that she had a destination, she released the railing and moved over to the window that framed the stairwell. She could reach it from this window; all she had to do was lace her fingers under the edge of the sill and coax it…

The window slid open with far more ease than she remembered. Some rather bored, or possibly just a type-A, industrious person must have oiled the frame.

She lowered it back down until the gap was only eight inches—better to not attract attention—then with a furtive glance over her shoulder to make sure no one had either come up the stairs or exited one of the class-rooms, she slithered out through the window. It wasn't a far drop, just a touch over five feet, and her toes touched down on the gritty coating of the rubber matting.

Barely noticing the prick to the bottoms of her bare

feet she stood up, drawing in a deep breath of cool evening air. Oh yes, this is what she needed.

Aware of how easily she could gash up her feet, she gingerly eased a few feet to the side and settled down with her back to the building, the roof of the cafeteria stretched out in front of her. She knew from experience that no one could see her here in this corner so, as long as she didn't stay out here long enough for her father to get worried and send someone after her, she should be able to steal a few minutes of peace. Besides, it wasn't like she was truly disobeying the outside rule. She was still physically in contact with the building, after all.

She tipped her head back, gazing longingly up into the sky. When was the last time she'd stargazed? She used to love it. It wasn't dark enough yet, and truly never would be here in the city to see them, but she found herself searching anyway.

Back when she was a young child she and her dad and Aaron would take trips out to her father's childhood home. His parents weren't alive anymore but he'd wanted to give Annie the chance to run and roam and enjoy her youth—something she couldn't do here in the city. They hadn't been back in years, not since that horrible night, but she hadn't forgotten the stories he'd told her.

Maybe she'd romanticized all those stories about her grandparents. What was it he'd said Grandma had told him? That meeting one's mate was like having the stars suddenly, miraculously align and everything in the universe unexpectedly make sense. So when she met Bennett and that little spot deep inside of her went click, she'd thought she'd found her little miracle.

Turns out she was just a really big wisher.

She closed her eyes, biting back the chest-rattling sob that threatened to erupt. How could the connection have felt so real? She knew she was all over the board emotionally—a really fucking late and frustratingly drawn puberty, her father told her, thanks to their family genetics that appeared to include longevity—but she also wasn't a fool. She thought she knew the difference between hormones and real feelings. It was that edge of emptiness that accompanied them. That feeling like you were standing inside your own body and saying whoa, what's your problem even as your mouth continued to spout off. She'd been experiencing tons of those moments over the last half-dozen years and had gotten to recognize the signs. But with Bennett? There had been none of that. When she was around him she felt solid. Like her head, heart, and body were all in accord: He made her stars align.

Yeah? Then how come nothing makes sense right now?

"Oh, excuse me."

She whirled, automatically shifting into a crouch that would allow for her to meet the emanate threat. Only this young soldier, standing awkwardly with one arm still clutching the window ledge, wasn't a threat, but another escapee like her.

And right. Way to top her humiliation but to be caught in a crying jag. Nice.

She stood up, brushing off the butt of her sweats. "It's okay. I was just, uh, leaving."

"No, no, please don't…" He waved his hand at her, then let it drop, shrugging a bit self-consciously as he gave her a sympathetic grin. "Looks like you could use the solace as much as me."

What followed was an awkward silence. A really awkward one. The fact that he could tell meant that her face must look like a puffed up marshmallow—with blotchy pink paint flecks added, of course.

"I didn't think anyone came here," he said, glancing back at the half-open window. One guess who had oiled the window.

"I haven't been out here in a while."

"Well," he moved over closer and sat, draping his wrists casually across his raised knees as he looked up at her, "I won't tell if you won't."

"Thanks." She folded her arms awkwardly across her breasts, very aware of what the cool evening air was doing to her nipples.

"You can sit with me, if you'd like." He patted the roof beside him, smiling up at her. "I promise I won't bite."

Okay, and he was definitely flirting with her. Considering what a fright she must look like he was either really desperate or just being kind. Not that it mattered. She wasn't at all interested. Nope, only assholes with golden god complexes turned her on.

Still, he was being nice, and she really didn't want to go in yet.

She folded her legs, settling back down. He flashed her a grin, but quickly turned his gaze forward, looking out of the dusky cityscape—or rather what they could see from here, which included the roof, a cracked and pitted playground, and the backside of the adjacent buildings.

They sat in silence, which she appreciated. It was nice to just sit and breathe in the simplicity of the night, though it was getting downright chilly as the breeze picked up. Clouds for the promised night rain were rolling in. She shuddered, wrapping her arms around herself. So much for her stars.

"You look cold."

"A bit," she admitted, even as she tried to repress the shivers.

"Here." He wiggled out of his jacket, his shoulders bunching and bulging as he worked it off his back. "Take it," he said, holding it out to her.

She shook her head. "I couldn't."

"Sure you can. I'm hot right now anyway." As if to prove his point he set the jacket down between them, leaning indifferently against the cold brick wall.

She reached, hesitated, then grabbed up the warm material and pulled the jacket on. Warmth immediately surrounded her and a shudder ran through her body, though this one had nothing to do with being cold and everything to do with her tight nerves releasing.

See? Men were not all dogs. Now she just had to convince herself that she would be better off without one *particular* dog.

Angling her head unobtrusively, she studied the man sitting next to her. She knew him, she just couldn't place him. Despite the fact that he was taller than her and had the type of hair that itched to be played with, he was actually pretty average looking. She frowned, dissecting each of his features. It wasn't until he glanced her way, then quickly averted his gaze, that she figured it out.

"That's where I've seen you before! Shielding class. Ryan, right?" He always stood in the back, never drew attention to himself, and had trouble meeting anyone's eyes.

"Yeah." He shifted uncomfortably, exhibiting some of the self-consciousness issues she remembered. "I'm not very good at shielding."

She chuckled. "Me either, obviously."

He cocked his head to the side. "You weren't there this morning."

"Oh, um…" She fiddled with the tie on her sweatpants, picking at the loose threads. "No. I was with my uncle in the infirmary."

"I'm sorry." His voice was sincere, his eyes soft with sympathy. As if he were offering condolences or something, which just made her mad. Aaron wasn't dead. "It's all right. He's going to be okay, just…"

She gulped, blinking to clear her vision. What was she saying? He wasn't going to be okay. He was going to be scarred permanently because of what had happened, worse than her father's scars, even. And like before, this was all her fault too. True, no one had said it, but after the dressing down both Gabby and her father had given her the other day, it didn't take major math skills to figure out that her little excursion so closely followed by this attack…

I led them here. Me and my cursed gift. Just like it was my gift that led them to me and Daddy that first time.

Memories surfaced. The dark night. The man who wasn't a man stalking a much younger Annie as she ran through the woods. And the dogs. No, not dogs, creatures that resembled them but with bloodied fangs, scaly gray skin, and oily black eyes. She'd been cornered, climbed a tree. The dog-creatures snapping at the base. The man had stopped behind them, his head tipped oddly as he lifted his head to stare at her. She'd wanted to scream, but couldn't find her breath. Until she'd heard her father's frantic calls in the distance. Too far. She'd known he was too far. But the storm that had rolled in wasn't.

"Annie?"

She leapt up. "I need to go inside."

"Oh…all right." He stood too, blocking her way.

Of course, he wanted his coat.

She shrugged out of the jacket, offering it to him.

He took it, pulling it on, then stood there with his hands planted on his utility belt.

"It was nice talking to you, Annie." He glanced over his shoulder at the window, then concentrated his gaze on her again, his mouth twisted up almost wistfully as he added, "It's too bad we didn't have more time."

"More time? We'll see each other again next class, remember?"

He just nodded, that same wistful smile on his face.

Weird. She shook her head, shifting so as to get around him. He twisted, his gaze still locked on her. The movement brought him in line with the light casting out from the window and she gasped, reaching for him.

"Ryan, what happened to your neck?" she asked, pushing back his jacket to get a better look at the vicious looking wound.

"You know, it's a funny story." His smile slipped, his features closing down, though his eyes never left her.

Her gut sunk, warning bells skittering up her spine. *Hunter. Prey.*

"Too bad I don't have time to tell you about it."

She barely heard the whisper of sound above his words, just the click and scrape of a blade sliding out of its holster. She drew in a breath to scream even as she struck her arms out in a cross defensive motion. One arm met air, but the other caught his wrist, and the knife meant for her throat skidded by her ear, a near miss. Unfortunately she hadn't seen the second attack. Before she could scream or run or do anything else, something hit her in her right side. Pain ripped through her, her body crumpling onto the roof as she began to convulse. Through the haze of agony she heard her captor laugh, his voice rolling through the night in multiple layers.

Chapter 16

VALIN LAY AS STILL AS HE COULD BENEATH A SLEEPING Gabby, staring at the crooked and chipped tiles of her ceiling as he siphoned through the volatile emotions riding him like a ghost horse. He hadn't bargained for this, though damn if he could figure out what this was.

After rejecting his own declaration of love, her silent plea for him to love her had torn his heart. Not only did he sense she didn't believe herself worthy of that love, but the overshadowing fear of being hurt had left him wanting to lash out at someone. But who was there to do so? Her mother was long buried, her maker Christos dead too. And though a mere glimpse at some of her memories showed dozens more worthy of his wrath, to seek them out for the sole purpose of revenge would teach Gabby nothing of moving on and letting go of the past.

So he'd concentrated on loving her. And as the day had worn on, turning to night, she'd opened to him. Her body, her mind, her soul. The uninhibited intensity with which she'd showed him her unspoken love had outdone him.

He should be happy. If nothing else he should be purring with satisfaction by the number of times she'd come undone in his arms. But he wasn't. Something was off. Something that had his heart palpitating and his nerves riding on edge. What was it?

He'd thought at first it was simply a sense of incompleteness. He hadn't asked her to complete the mate bond with him yet, but that would only account for a sense of nervousness...not this soul-consuming sense of dread. It was like his soul knew something his mind was unable or unwilling to grasp.

He glanced down at Gabby's hair spread out over his torso, her head resting on his chest, and her hand tucked in tight to his armpit. She looked tired. And though he supposed he should expect that after a long night and subsequent day of lovemaking, they had certainly taken more than their share of naps between their marathons of sex.

And that was it, the long night then subsequent day of lovemaking had done nothing to ease the lines around her eyes, and worse, despite the number of times she drank from his vein, there was no change on the darkness that stained her soul.

You're going to lose her, just like you lost Angeline.

He swallowed, closing his eyes against the brutal barrage of images. Another time, another bed, only it was Angeline lying beside him, his hand tucked possessively at the base of her distended belly. They'd woken together, laughing at Peanut's antics in the womb and enjoyed a few moments of happy bliss before he'd risen to start his day. It had been the last morning they'd had together.

He hadn't been able to save Angeline then and now here lay Gabby, still aging, dying with each breath she took secure in his arms. His veins iced over, his breathing becoming ragged with thoughts of the long cold years of darkness that had followed Angeline's death. He

couldn't relive that. He would not, could not fail again.
Yet here he was, holding Gabby, and he couldn't…Shit.
Shit! He couldn't breathe for the tightness in his chest.
There was only one way to escape such pain. One place.
There he could regroup. There he could forget. If only
for a little while.

Taking a deep breath, he closed his eyes, shifting into
the soothing darkness of the shade.

—⁓—

Gabby lay motionless upon the cot, the only movement
that of her hand fisting in the cooling sheets beneath
them. Valin was gone. She'd woken, alarmed, at the racing of his heart beneath her ear, then before she could
react she'd been blindsided by his turbulent thoughts
of his lost mate. Angeline. Oh, how she wished she
could have shut his memories of that woman off, but
she couldn't, not after feeding from him so many times.
Five to be exact, if you counted the little taste on the
rooftop the other night. The last had been after he carried her back to her room and proceeded to teach her
that sex—at least with him—could be the best, most
perfect, and yes, erotic, thing in the world. To let go
like that, acting purely on instinct and need…His blood
had tasted so good, and she'd reveled in the bloom of
connection between them that came with each drop that
hit her tongue. She knew she couldn't do it again anytime soon. Accelerated healing or not, even his Paladin
blood couldn't sustain her indefinitely. Not without
weakening himself. And given the type of constant
danger he threw himself at, that was not something she
was willing to risk.

Of course, looked like that wasn't really going to be an issue. Valin had finally wised up and been the first to run away. Why wouldn't he after having slept with one of the monsters that killed his mate? The thrall of her succubus heritage had finally worn off and Valin had woken, the repetitive thought in his mind of Angeline, his unborn child, and how he'd failed to save them from Christos and his bloodthirsty vampires.

Because of her. Because her mother had been a power hungry bitch and Christos had believed her conception to be the key to some prophecy.

But all she could claim was being the key to pain.

She'd lain on Valin's chest, commanding her body to be still even as her ribs tightened, crushing her heart. She'd forced herself to keep breathing, to pretend she wasn't awake. *Don't say anything; it will be easier on him if you don't make him confront the face of his shame.* Thankfully she hadn't had to pretend long.

Valin was gone, and in his place was an empty hole in her heart to match the still-cooling spot on her bed.

Are you really going to lay here and weep? Last I knew there were still vampires to stake and merkers to exsanguinate.

Heaving herself out of the cot, she took a few minutes for a hasty freshening before pulling on her leather pants, tank top, and her favorite set of throwing knives. If her eyes drifted to the carved blade of the knife Valin had yet to remove from her room, she didn't let them linger. Tonight she'd track down Bennett and ask him to get it back to Valin, but today she would extend her patrol area; make sure there was no new activity after the merkers' attack the other night. First, though, she'd go and find Jacob. She needed to talk to him about what happened as she'd yet to get a full rundown on the exact details. On the way she'd stop in to see Aaron. She'd like the distraction if he was awake and if he wasn't, then she could at least talk to Shae about when he might be.

She opened the door, stepping out into the hall…and almost got run over by a soldier as he skidded to a halt just short of the door.

"Yes?" she asked when he continued to stand before her, his hand half-raised as if he'd been about ready to go a round with her door.

The soldier straightened. "Jacob needs you."

Her heart performed a heavy pound behind her ribs. "Aaron?"

He shook his head. "Annie's missing."

Crap. This is not what she needed today of all days.

She brushed by the soldier, heading down the hall away from the infirmary. She'd have to check in on Aaron later, after the current crisis was past. It was probably another case of Annie deciding she was sick of being "trapped," but even so she couldn't deny the unease that was pooling in her gut.

Why would Annie risk going out? Especially after what happened to her uncle two nights ago?

Her unease did not lessen when she pushed through the door into Jacob's planning room to find him bent over his "war" map, his face pale.

Determined not to add to his anxiety by showing her own unease, she squared her shoulders and walked by the handful of soldiers in the room to stand beside Jacob. Already the map was all but obscured with the pushpins—devoid of the actual pins—that represented his soldiers' distribution through the surrounding area.

"How did she get by all the guards?" she asked. Jacob had virtually closed down the base after their unexpected houseguest's arrival a week ago, and tightened it even further after Aaron's attack. It was this that had been the basis for his agreeing to call off the constant shadow-guards around Annie, and Gabby had encouraged it, figuring a semblance of freedom within the walls might go a long way to easing the girl's sense of claustrophobia. Guess not.

He sighed, rubbing the back of his neck. "We assume via the window at the top of the second floor stairs. We found a scrap of her T-shirt on the cafeteria roof below."

Jacob hit the table, the pins jumped, many of them tumbling down on their sides. "How in the hell could she be so stupid? I thought Aaron's injuries had finally impressed upon her how dangerous it was out there. What could she possibly be thinking?"

"Obviously she's not," Gabby mumbled, shaking her head in frustration. The cafeteria was the only part of the structure that wasn't two or more stories high. Granted, it was still pretty tall, with its soaring ceilings, but it was possible Annie had managed to lower herself over the edge then drop the rest of the way without getting hurt. But even Gabby found it hard to believe that Annie would be desperate—or stupid enough—to try it.

Someone cleared their throat. Gabby swiveled to see Bennett over near the door.

"I, um, may have something to do with that," he said.

Silence descended in the room; everyone stared at the

Paladin expectantly, but for once, the Paladin who went around touting communication didn't speak.

"Oh? And how is that?" she asked.

"First, can I ask, do you know how long she's been missing?"

Gabby looked at Jacob, who shook his head. "We're not sure. Though given the fact that the stairwell landing was covered in a good amount of water when people came and went from their shift change early this morning, we're assuming it was before the storms blew in last night."

"So before midnight." He closed his eyes, his hands fisting at his sides. "Bloody hell."

"What do you know?" Jacob asked with icy calmness, sending off all kinds of uh-oh alarms in Gabby's brain. Jacob was his most dangerous when he got like this. First the calm, and then the storm. Literally.

"Jacob…" She laid a gentle hand on his arm, simultaneously sending a silent, cautionary jab at the Paladin, the mental equivalent of think-hard-before-you-open-your-trap. But the big, blond idiot must have missed the class where they taught projective thought nuances, that or he was too hung up on the whole one-must-be-truthful thing because with little more than a quick glance at her he opened his big mouth.

"I fear she was quite upset when I left her quarters last evening. She must have misinterpreted—" Bennett never got to finish, let alone blink before Jacob was on him.

Gabby leapt after him, cursing that she'd gone for the gentle touch rather than the iron grip. Jacob's hands were locked around Bennett's throat in a death grip. And as Bennett's face turned red, then purple, his eyes beginning to bulge, all Gabby could think was: Thank God Jacob hadn't used his gift.

She was, however, beginning to seriously worry about her ability to stop Jacob from killing Bennett through natural means. She also wondered why in the hell the Paladin did nothing to fight back. Unless…

Ah, crap. Stupid, idiotic fucknut. He did *not* have sex with Annie. For a moment, a brief moment, Gabby thought of switching the pressure of her hands from pulling on Jacob's to aiding the angry father, but no, that wouldn't be right. And it was possible this was just a misunderstanding. Surely there were a zillion other reasons why he'd be leaving Annie's rooms.

Yeah, right.

"Jacob! Let go," she said firmly, tightening her hands around his wrists. Much tighter and she was going to break his damn arm. She was beginning to think she might have to when the door banged open and a breathless soldier ran in, his face pale and what looked like a Taser gripped in his hand.

"Commander!" He skidded to a halt, his eyes uncertain as he took in the scene.

Finally, finally, Jacob released his hold on Bennett's throat, the Paladin doubled up and gasping for air as Jacob turned—all businesslike—to face the soldier. "Yes, Tyler?"

"Sir! Me and Will were searching our grid when we stumbled upon, a…uh…"

Bennett started coughing, the grating hoarseness rather painful sounding. Tyler's gaze darted briefly to Bennett, but a quick clearing of Jacob's throat commandeered his attention, though he still seemed unable to spit out his tale.

"What did you find, Tyler?"

His throat bobbed nervously, but then he croaked. "A body."

"A body...not...Annie?" Jacob's voice cracked, his hand reaching out as if he needed steadying. Gabby moved to hold him up, but he stepped away, his fear transferring to an uncontrollable tremor of his hands.

"What?" The soldier blinked. "Oh, no...Not Annie." He shifted uncomfortably, obviously distraught that he'd upset the commander. "We're actually not sure of the man's name, but both Will and I are sure we've seen him around. He tends to keep to himself though and—"

"How did he die?" Jacob asked with a firmer voice this time, folding his still-shaking hands together behind his back.

"Vampire, sir. At first we weren't sure because his throat was practically ripped out, but Will, he, uh, got a closer look and said he could make out the original bite."

Jacob's jaw worked. He nodded down at the Taser gripped in the soldier's hand. "And that?"

"We found it next to the body. Holding down the note."

"The note?"

Tyler nodded, his throat bobbing. "I have it right here, sir." He dug into his pocket, pulling out a crumpled envelope. "Only..." He lifted the seemingly innocuous paper, his gaze fixed on Gabby as he said, "It's addressed to you."

Chapter 17

"It's obviously a trap," Bennett said, clipping Gabby's heels as he followed her into her room.

"I'm aware." She swiped up a set of throwing knifes from the table, shifting things around on her utility belt to make room to clip them on.

"I would not advise playing into it."

"And I appreciate your advice." She opened the drawer, grabbed the gun, checked the ammo, and stuffed it into the back of her pants.

"You have a plan?"

"Yeah, I do." A stake, slim and reinforced with a core of metal slipped into her boot.

His brow rose.

"Give them exactly what they want."

He grabbed her arm, yanking her to a stop. "Are you daft? You go out there alone and walk into a trap, it's going to be a bloodbath."

She smiled, flashing fang. "That's the idea."

"I meant the blood would be yours." He shook her, rattling her teeth. "Vengeance alone will not fuel you in this fight. You think going out there and killing everything in sight until they kill you is the answer? You think Valin could stand for that?"

She jerked her arm away, hissing at him. He had no right to bring up Valin, no right to judge her. Her methods may be bloody, their actions rooted in evil, but it was *her* life. Her vengeance. Her choice. Her sacrifice.

Some sacrifice. Think Lucifer will be happy with it? One scrawny vampire in exchange for an army of men and women's souls.

"You have a better idea?" she asked, grabbing up another stake. There would be no time to indulge. Get in quick, hit them hard. If she were lucky, real lucky, she could have Annie out by sunset.

And then the real hunt would begin.

"Aye, I do. Let me contact the council. They can authorize my brothers' aid."

"Why? So they can help rescue Annie, then turn around and lock her up themselves? Annie would be just head over heels grateful to you for coming up with a plan like that."

"I don't give a bloody damn about what her opinion might be if it means she's alive to have it!"

Her eyes widened as she staggered back from the emotions pouring off of him. Holy crap, misinterpreted indeed. The Paladin was scared to death right now, and she didn't think it was because of some sort of deep-seated sense of guilt for taking advantage of Jacob's daughter. He cared about her. A lot. And was about going out of his mind worrying for Annie right now.

"I'll get her back, Bennett," she vowed.

"You and what army?"

She glared at him, drawing on all her mommy-born and stepdaughter-taught skills to make him back off and let her do her thing, but all he did was raise his brow.

She huffed out a breath, her gaze locking on her thigh

holster and knife. "Wonder if that's a trait He instilled or if that's the human in the mix," she muttered as she snatched them up.

"What are you talking about?"

She jerked the laces, securing the holster, and slid the knife home. She was talking about Valin in all his lovable stubborn-ass male glory. God, she missed him already.

He'll be better off. They all will.

She shook her head, moving to the door. "Valin's knife is on the shelf over my bed. Tell him…" She paused, her sweaty palm slick around the door handle. Of all the times to be scared. "Tell him I'm sorry. For everything," she said and walked out the door, Bennett's curses echoing down the hall behind her.

Frankly, she didn't care if he went and tattled to his brothers or not. From what she'd heard and seen of the councils' responses, it would take a bit to convince them to lift a finger for anyone who wasn't part of their little club. And by then she would have done what she needed to do.

Jacob was still ranting as she passed by his war room. Gathering soldiers, planning their attack—as if throwing enough lives away would save the one he wanted.

The front door guard, wrapped up in a frayed trench coat as part of his disguise, glanced up when she pushed open the metal door, his mouth gaping in his dirt-smudged face when he saw the rather conspicuous arsenal of weaponry she wore.

Hmmm. Good point.

"Give me the coat." She made a hurry-up motion with her hand.

He blinked, but set down the rifle he'd stuffed in the trench coat's folds and scrambled to his feet, shrugging out of the material to reveal his faded fatigues and long-sleeve undershirt he'd been wearing beneath. He handed her the coat, then stood there, his gaze drifting uncertainly to the rifle by his feet.

"Probably better keep that out of sight," she offered helpfully as she pulled the itchy coat around her shoulders. It dragged a bit on the ground, but at least it was cleaner than it appeared—i.e., it didn't smell.

"Uh…" He eyed the coat she'd just commandeered, then looked at the door behind them.

"Keep your eyes sharp." Confident he'd figure something out, she started down the stairs. Besides, she didn't really expect trouble until nightfall, but that didn't mean they shouldn't be prepared. Contents of the note aside, she couldn't dismiss the merker attack the other night. Yes, it could be a coincidence, but maybe not. Just because Christos's methods had generally been to go in alone didn't mean that the current vampire king wouldn't be willing to work with Lucifer's general. In fact, it was rather likely.

Stephan might have been known for his sadistic viciousness, but when push came to shove he was actually weak-spined. If Ganelon had somehow caught wind about a budding army of part-bloods, he'd be interested, and not at all averse to using Stephan and his coven to flush Jacob's army out. And that was the real purpose for kidnapping Annie. Taunts and ransom notes aside, she knew that Stephan didn't really want her, and she doubted Ganelon cared much either. It was just that Gabby had been the most visible with her personal eradication of her former comrades. They probably thought that she was the leader here and just didn't realize that she wasn't actually in charge of things.

Well, they were in for a surprise. They were likely counting on it taking a while for her to organize her troops. If she was fast enough, struck quickly enough, maybe she could pull this off.

She paused at the entrance to the subway, her gaze inadvertently drawn back to the building three blocks behind her. It might be the last time she laid eyes on it. Chances were this was a one-way trip. Even if she didn't bite the big one in this fight, she knew she couldn't come back here.

When had that run-down building become home? Her residency had never been meant to be more than a temporary layover. But sometime between training Jacob's inept newbies, butting heads with Annie, and fencing with Valin, she'd forgotten that. Despite her end-of-game plans, there were enough people she'd been…invested in that she'd wanted to make sure things turned out all right. She'd never meant to stay. Never meant to get attached.

Never meant to fall in love.

She swallowed, choking down the bitter tears that threatened as she descended into the dim subway interior. She'd already shed too many of the damn things. Now was the time for action, not regrets. She'd get Annie back, kill the fuckers who'd hurt Aaron, and ensure Valin never had to look in the face of his shame again.

The trip on the subway passed in a blur as she worked to purge her mind of distractions. Annie, Jacob, Aaron,

Valin…they didn't need the woman right now, they needed the monster.

Her stop came, the last on the 1 line. Only her and a handful of others exited here, and each one took off briskly heading to their own destinations with not so much as a glance to their fellow travelers. She made her way through the gothic Victorian station down to the street, using her gift to scan and dismiss the various minds in the area.

No one was paying her any mind; even so, she pulled about her a don't-look-at-me shield and made her way to the center of the vampire's NYC powerbase. Tucked between the affluent neighborhood of Fielding and Manhattan College, the coven's primary estate was a one-acre slice of easy-to-disappear-in heaven for a vamp. Large trees, overgrown gardens, and a shroud of evil even the least sensitive human would have run away from marked the edges of the grounds. It even had the prerequisite fog thing going on today.

She knew she was taking a bit of a gamble by coming here rather than to any of the other vampire safe houses sprinkled around the city. There were certainly more appropriate ones to hold captive and definitely ones better suited for an attention-drawing battle if Gabby or the others managed to see past the tease of a meeting place the note had laid out and gone searching, but this is where Gabby knew Stephan to be, and if he was anything like she remembered, he'd want to keep his newest prize close at hand to play with at his leisure.

Over my dead body.

She took a deep breath, releasing some of the anger. It would serve to motivate her when needed, but too much could blind her as well. What would also blind her? Keeping her shields clamped down tight as she'd been doing.

Carefully she lessened them, just enough to get an imprint of any thoughts or minds in the vicinity. There should have been nothing, what with the vamps in residence snug as a bug in their thick-walled mansion, but something poked her back, a sick, twisted mind that could only mean one thing: demon.

She slammed her shields back up, cringing at the sharp throbbing of her bruised brain. Crap and hell. So much for sneaking in while everyone was sleeping. Where there was one demon, there was bound to be more.

She'd really been hoping Ganelon wasn't involved in this.

Think of it as having all seven courses of the meal at once. Too bad she wasn't all that hungry.

"How did I know you'd be alone?" a low baritone voice rolled over her from behind.

She spun, automatically plucking a throwing knife from her belt as she zeroed in on the source of the voice, but saw nothing other than the twisted growth of the overgrown grounds. Lots of places to hide.

"Who says I'm alone?" she stalled, her eyes keen for any bit of movement.

"Oh, come now, Gabriella, don't lie."

She spun again, following the shift of sound that had moved by her and deeper into the overgrown garden.

"My question is," the voice rumbled again, to her left this time, "do you really think you have a chance of killing me?"

"I don't have to kill you; I just have to send you

back to hell." Which, admittedly, wasn't an easy thing. She'd been practicing banishing spells but had yet to have the opportunity to test them. There was always the old standard though: inflict enough pain on the demon's earthly body so it decided hell's fires were the better option.

The man chuckled, the sound eerie in the shadowed garden. "Ah…still the same old Gabby. You always did have trouble with displaying respect."

A shiver ran down her spine, unease at the use of her nickname off the vile creature's tongue.

"But you will for me."

"Will what?" she spun again, sure the voice had been closer that time.

"Kneel, Gabby." The command crashed into her shields, ripping and shredding the solid weave of power as if her barriers were nothing but newspaper. Stumbling back, she poured more energy into an ever-flowing river of power that the demon's attack would ripple off of. Only it didn't.

She screamed, her knees buckling beneath the force of the creature's will. The moment her knees hit the ground the oppressive pressure lifted, leaving her entire body aching and her lungs gulping for breath.

What the hell? Only one person had ever been able to invade her mind like that.

Panting, she held her head, trying to fight back the tunneling vision.

Sitting duck. Vulnerable.

She lurched to her feet, her hand shaking as she pulled her gun. If she could wing the thing, she could possibly distract him enough to break his concentration.

"Come out and show yourself, you chicken-shit bas-tard!" she yelled, cursing her still-fuzzy vision. For all she knew he was standing right in front of her.

"As you wish, Gabriella." Movement to her right had her spinning around, gun raised. The outline of a man stepped out of the shadows, sending her heart racing. She'd been wrong. The creature was not a demon, un-less he'd stolen a body—albeit an impressive one. Not that it mattered. Whatever or whoever this was, he was pure evil.

But she'd faced evil before. And she'd face it this time too.

She lifted the gun, her eyes narrowing on her target. Then gasped as pain spliced into her mind. Her vision blurred as she watched her fingers fall from the gun's grip. It landed with a thud upon the ground.

"How?" She staggered back, her hands shaking as she lifted them before her eyes.

"Sorry, it just seemed rather tacky accessory for our reunion."

Reunion? She'd never met him before, was sure of it.

He smiled, his lips curling up in a manner that made every muscle in her body scream at her to run. "What? You don't recognize me, Gabby?"

Her gut sunk, a hole opening up beneath her feet. *Not possible.* Not. Possible.

"Ah, how I've missed you, Gabriella." He held out his hand, the king's ring glinting in a stray ray from the overcast sun. "Come now, let me bring you home, daughter…"

———

Valin shifted, wincing at the scrape of the bark against his skin. What a loser he was, sitting up here in the branches of some tree in Central Park getting pine sap on his ass. The park had been one of Angeline's favorite places to go. She'd love to come and people watch, especially when they set the ice rink up in the winter and the families came out to laugh and play. Frankly, all that bubbling happiness made Valin squirm. Give him a dark, dank alley any day. Throw in a merker to kill and he was more than content.

And didn't that sum up the difference between them in a nutshell. Angeline had been all light and smiles and happiness, and he'd been a grumpy bastard.

Memories filtered through his mind, but this time he was able to smile now by the gentle way they wrapped around him. It had been good. She'd balanced his sullen nature, kept him from drifting too far into the dark. But as much as he'd love her, she hadn't been meant to be his forever.

Gabby. Just thinking about her twisted him up in knots, both the good and bad kind. He loved her so much, would worship the very ground she walked on if she'd let him, but the thought of losing her was driving him mad.

He'd known he was bonding with Gabby. Known it was the real deal. Had thought he'd accepted that eventually his feelings for his mate would hit him on a level that, as much as he may have wished otherwise, he could never have experienced with Angeline. The compatible pair bond that he and Angeline had formed shadowed in contrast to what he felt for Gabby. He thought that would feel wrong, but it didn't. Angeline and their unborn child would always hold a place in his heart, but Gabby was his heart *and* soul. And he knew Angeline would understand.

She would also have been the first one to tell him to stop being stupid and get off his sticky backside and go claim his mate.

He'd run this morning. Those chronic feelings of impotence raising their ugly head again as he realized that loving her was not going to be the cure-all to the darkness that had shadowed her life. Which was damn ironic considering how often he danced with the dark shadows of morality. Maybe it wasn't about him saving her. Maybe it was about them saving each other.

But first he had to get back to the base and convince her to take on his sorry ass as a mate. They'd figure what they needed to do together.

More at ease than he'd been in a long time, he shifted, willing himself along the currents toward the base. He made it most of the way when something hit him: a feeling—terror—that ripped him right out of the shade and sent him smacking into pavement. He groaned, then screamed, arching as a darkness far different from the shade's welcoming solace swelled around him.

"Dude, you all right?"

The darkness eased. Chest heaving, he lifted his head and stared through blurry eyes at the alarmed face of a disheveled teen and his two buddies hovering a couple feet behind him.

Not an attack. Not on him. But that meant...

<<*Gabby!*>> He struggled to rise, his thoughts far from here and the confused trio of teens, but with his mate who was not where he'd left her. <<*Gabby, where—*>>

For a moment they connected, a brief moment where her terror grabbed for him and clung like he was her lifeline. And then she was gone. Ripped away. The very pulse of her essence winking out as if it had never existed. Valin staggered, the stunning impact of loss curling around his heart and squeezing so hard he swore it stopped.

Not yours, hers. Told you this would happen…told you…

"Gabby, no!" He clawed at his chest, as if he could reach in and pump the organ back to life again. Only it wasn't his…

"Gabby…" He'd lost her. Lost. Gabby.

His legs buckled. Someone grabbed him, helping him down to his knees. "Dude…you having a heart attack…"

Whatever else the boy said was drowned out as Valin began to scream.

Chapter 18

VALIN MATERIALIZED IN HIS ROOM, HIS MOVEMENTS quick and efficient as he gathered what he would need. Too long had passed since he'd fallen. He wasn't sure how much time, just that the street had been empty when Valin finally screamed his vocal cords raw, the eerie silence suggesting that the teens and anyone else unlucky enough to be in the area had fled in fear from the crazy naked guy in the street. Probably best. When he'd lost the ability to express his grief, his emotions had switched to the next best thing: anger. It had fueled him on the journey back to the base, his only thought to find and kill the bastard who'd taken Gabby from him.

Clothes, shoes...his knife. Fuck, where was his goddamn knife?

Gabby's room. He'd never gotten it from her after the merker attack that night.

Gabby, oh God, Gabby. He sucked a deep breath into his tight chest, bracing his hands on his knees to keep from hitting the floor with his already abused knees. He would scream again if he could, but since he didn't think his vocal chords would respond, the only recourse he had left was to weep. He couldn't do that now. Not until after he'd found her. And he would find her. She was alive. She had to be. The other option was not acceptable.

It had occurred to him when he'd come to his senses

in that empty street that there were other reasons why their connection could have been severed, the most logical being that she'd lost consciousness and had simply yet to wake. Wasn't that what happened to Roland when Karissa had been taken?

But he'd had the blood bond, so he knew and could find her. You have nothing.

No, not nothing. He knew approximately where she'd been. And whether he had to move heaven and hell to do it, he *would* find her, because if he didn't?

Don't go there. That was the road to insanity and a sure one-way trip to absolute darkness. If Gabby was truly gone then he would not be able to find his way back, and God help anyone near him if he were to reach that journey's end.

Determined not to waste any more time, he sent out a general ping through the base for Bennett. Almost immediately he got Bennett's absentminded return ping. He followed the response back to Jacob's planning room, then stood in the doorway as he watched the two men face off amongst a handful of other soldiers.

Though a couple of Jacob's soldiers noticed his presence, neither Jacob nor Bennett did, and since they were discussing something that, turns out, Valin was eager to hear, he settled in against the doorframe to listen.

It didn't take him long to pick up the bits and pieces of the story he'd been missing. Annie had somehow disappeared, a ransom note delivered: Gabby for Annie. For a moment he saw red, his anger flaring and burning as it found a new source: *Fucking selfish brat, if it hadn't been for her...*

He took a deep breath, focusing on the conversation

again. Jacob, besides sending scouts out and a smattering of patrols to defend the area, had also sent out the
command to prep everyone—new recruits included—
for war. Bennett was arguing the wastefulness of such
actions, demanding instead that they contact the Paladin
council and ask for their aid.

"We can't involve the council," Valin said in a voice
that sounded far calmer than he felt.

Bennett spun toward the door, fixing him with a lethal
glare. "Why the bloody hell not? They may be our only
chance of getting Annie out of there alive…wherever
there is." He mumbled the last under his breath.

"There is somewhere on the north edge of the city."
He pushed off the doorframe and walked over to the table
the men had been facing off over, glancing down at the
smattering of tack-heads on the map. The greatest concentration was near Prospect Park. "You're not even in
the ballpark if you're concentrating your efforts there."

"That's where the note called for the exchange."

He would have rolled his eyes if he could have mus-
tered the effort, but he just fucking didn't feel like it.
"Yeah, and I'm sure that's where they're holding Annie."

"Why do you think she's being held at the northern
end?" Bennett asked.

"Because that's the approximate location of where
Gabby was when I lost…" His breath hitched, unable to
go on against the remembered despair of that moment
when Gabby's essence had been cut from his senses.

Bennett's eyes widened. He reached out, clasping
Valin's shoulder in silent support. "Valin…I'm s—"

"She's alive," he growled, cutting the Paladin off before he could say the irreversible word. "I lost connection

with her, that's all. There are a million reasons why that might have happened." And only one very probable one that would mean the end of his world.

She's alive. She has to be alive.

Bennett nodded, dropping his hand. "If you think she's been taken too, then the direness of the situation is even worse than I believed."

Valin knew what he was getting at and didn't give a shit. "And bringing the council into this will make that worse, not better."

Bennett's mouth thinned, the muscle along the length of his jaw twitching as he ground his molars to bite back the words he obviously wanted to say.

Not. Dead. Because if she was his world was on a free fall to destruction and there was a good chance he just might take the rest of humanity with him.

Jacob tapped the table, nodding his head curtly as if they'd made a decision. "I need to finish gathering my soldiers and we need to leave. Now. Too many hours have passed since Annie was first missing."

Valin shook his head. On this he and Bennett saw eye to eye. "No offense, but we need more of a strategy than running off in a vaguely northerly direction and hoping not to be ambushed when we draw near."

"And I suppose you have a plan?" the man asked in a deadly low voice.

"Does anyone have a phone on them?" Valin asked the room in general.

Jacob blinked, but crossed the room, grabbing up a cell from his desk at the back.

"Who do you plan to call?" Bennett asked, his eyes narrowed speculatively.

"The one Paladin I can trust to care about saving
Annie *and* Gabby."

Bennett tipped his head to the side. "You think
maybe Alexander?"

With how closely Senior was probably keeping the
aider and abettor? Valin shook his head, twisting his
mouth up in a semblance of a smile. "Nope. I'm going
to call Gabby's father."

⚬⚬⚬

The phone slipped from Roland's loose grip, the beep
signaling that the call had been ended sounding on its
fall to the wool rug. He couldn't move, couldn't think;
the shocks were hitting him too fast.

Roland had hardly had time to come to grips with the
thought that Gabby was in fact okay, then further had
the shock that he was her dad laid at his feet. After the
events of his turning he'd been too angry to accept, too
self-centered in his own misery to connect the dots and
come to the same conclusion himself, but now, with the
slick sweat of fear coating him, the crunching sensation
in his chest, he knew without a doubt that what Valin
had suggested was true: Gabriella was his daughter. And
if she had been taken by their enemies, there was a damn
good chance he'd never get to tell her how glad he was.

He looked up at the sound of the bedroom door
creaking open. Karissa shuffled down the hall, yawning
even as her eyes locked on him with concern. "Roland?
What's wrong?"

He cleared his throat, shaking his head. "I'm sorry. I
didn't mean to wake you."

She'd come in late last night after spending almost

forty-eight hours straight at her brother's side. Roland had been itching to talk to her about Valin's visit the day before, but one look at the circles under her eyes had him sending her to bed instead. After all, he'd gone almost ninety-four years without even knowing he had a daughter; what was another few hours before sharing the shocking news with his mate?

Too long. You waited too fucking long.

"Roland?" Karissa crossed to him, her brow knotted with worry as she slid her arms around his waist and looked up at him expectantly. "Why are you blocking me? Correction, why have you *been* blocking the bond?"

"I'm sorry, I didn't even realize…" He took a deep breath, trying to release some of his tension in the comfort of her embrace, simultaneously letting go of the walls he'd built around his turbulent thoughts. He couldn't project, but Karissa could read him anyway, merely one of the miracles of being her bond mate.

"Valin found Gabby," he told her to clarify the most pertinent of what must have been an avalanche of turbulent thoughts.

Her eyes widened, relief spreading across her features before her brow furrowed again, marring her face with confusion. "But this is good. Why are you so upset?"

"Do you remember how I was turned? How I said there was a woman? A succubus."

She nodded, pulling her bottom lip through her teeth as he watched her mind tumble toward the obvious conclusion. "Roland, does that mean…"

"There's a chance, a good one, that Gabby might be mine."

"Oh Roland…That's wonderful." A smile spread

across her lovely face, her grip tightening around him in
a hug. "You didn't think I'd be mad, did you? You know
I would love someone to talk girl-talk with."

"You unman me." He closed his eyes, his love for
her, for her acceptance, overwhelming him. He knew
what this cost her. Knew that she wanted children of her
own, but given what she was, what he'd made her, she'd
never have them. He felt so deficient in the fact that he
couldn't provide her heart's desire, had half-feared she
would feel awkward that he had a child by another, so
her obvious happiness, the bright love for his child that
streamed across their bond, was almost enough to have
him crying tears of joy. Except for one thing.

"Roland?" she asked again, her happiness dimming
as his misery fed back across their link. She stepped
back, searching out his face for an answer.

"She's missing. Valin thinks she might have tried to
trade herself for the null that broke into Haven."

Her hand lifted to her mouth, his fear, her terror eating up the air in the room. "Oh no…" A second later she
was pushing away that fear, her shoulders straightening
as her face set with determination. "Do we have a plan
yet for getting her back?"

And that's why he loved this woman. Fear, hopeless
odds, neither ever stopped her when it came to fighting
for someone she loved.

"Not yet, but we will," he said, taking her hand.

~~~

Christos stopped inside the dimly lit room, waiting
for his eyes to adjust. It had taken him longer than he
thought it might to subdue his prodigal daughter enough

to leave her unattended, and he worried that his men might have become…creative…in their torture of the null without him there to provide instruction. He was a bit surprised to find only two bodies in the room. One the unconscious form of the null stretched out on the bed, the other his chief surgeon who was currently tying off his last suture.

"Where is Stephan?" Christos asked, having detected his heavy residual scent in the room.

Cyrus shrugged, setting the thread and needle on the steel tray on the nightstand as he stood to face his master and king. "I don't know. He got frustrated and left."

"Frustrated?"

Cyrus jerked his head toward the bed. "She doesn't respond to a thrall."

"Ah…." And Stephan was such an egotistical bastard that he probably took that as a failure. "And you? What do you think of her gift's resistance?"

"Me?" Cyrus lifted his brow, his mouth curving up into a smile. "I consider her a welcome challenge."

Christos grunted, moving over to the bed to study Cyrus's work so far. The ravaged neck that Cyrus had just finished stitching would have been Stephan, and he made a mental note to speak to his second about risking the commodity's life. The rest? Well, he had to admit that Cyrus had a skill for the type of pain that wouldn't actually kill, but would make the recipient wish he would. Results had proved Cyrus's method highly effective in breaking the spirit, but also time-consuming.

"You might not have as much time as you normally do," he warned. The moment Ganelon got wind that Christos had captured the null, he could be assured that the bastard would be breaking down his door. And no way was he going to hand her over—or his other ace in the hole for that matter—without making sure that no matter where they were, they'd answer to him first.

"Hmmm. That does make things more difficult." Cyrus looked at him with glowing red eyes. "How far did you want me to take this, my king?"

"However far you need in order to make her break. Just don't kill her." Christos's gaze flicked up toward the ceiling and the present that waited for him on the top floor of the other wing. "And keep her in a state that she won't interfere with my other project, of course."

"Of course," Cyrus agreed, sweeping his arm in a wide arc as he tipped his torso toward the floor.

Christos swept by the bowing vampire, his blood already churning with anticipation on how next to break his daughter. Oh yes, Gabriella was indeed proving to be the best welcome-back-to-the-living gift a minion of his Lord Lucifer could hope for.

Chapter 19

GABBY WAS BACK IN THE CORNER OF HER ROOM, THE one that she'd spent way too much time curled up in during her seventy-nine-year sojourn here. She hurt, her entire body groaning with the mammoth effort it took to breathe. But it was her spirit that was bleeding out.

Christos was alive. And though the body may have changed, the evil core had not. From the moment she'd been turned at the age of fourteen until her escape four months ago, she'd fought and resisted, clinging to the remnants of her humanity, etching out the barest of an existence from beneath the whims of his will. She didn't kid herself into thinking that she'd just been that strong. She'd survived then because he'd had other things to do...and because, she suspected, he found her amusing and enjoyed playing with her. She didn't fool herself into thinking she'd be afforded such luxuries again.

She was going to die here. Soon. Today even. Because the alternative was unthinkable.

He means to break you, another her whispered from deep within her mind, the one born of blood and darkness, the one who'd taken her pain and molded it into an angry determination to never, ever yield.

I know, she replied, her gut clenching at the visual aids offered from her own memories.

We can't let him.

I won't, she promised.

A pause. *He'll go after those you've helped next.*

Warm tears coursed over the bridge of her nose, combined, then trickled across her temple toward the cold floor. No heat here. Not that vampires needed the warmth. No electricity either, though not because they wouldn't have enjoyed such luxuries but because they relied so heavily on magic for their wards. To keep the unwanteds away…and to keep their prisoners within.

Magic and electricity didn't mix well. And this entire place pulsed with the first. Which meant that she had failed before she'd even had a chance to succeed.

Annie was either dead, dying…or they were keeping her someplace else. Regardless, her coming here had played right into Christos's plans.

The door swung open. Even knowing it was useless, desperation made her lunge toward the opening. The predictable lash to her mind cracked like a whip on her fraying shreds of hope. She moaned. Her brain muddled with pain. Her limbs unresponsive as rough hands grabbed her under her armpits, dragging her up. It was as if her body wasn't her own, and all she could do was watch as another tied her wrists and looped them over the hook that hung in lieu of the light fixture from the ceiling.

Not Christos—the coward. After subduing her and stuffing her behind the magical bars of her current prison, he'd yet to come himself. Only the others. Her kin. Her torturers. Christos would use them to peel away every layer of resistance she possessed before coming himself.

She closed her eyes, willing her mind to another place as the hands roamed her body. She hardly cringed as fangs pierced her skin, lapping, suckling, before moving on.

It doesn't matter. They can do what they want to your body, just protect your soul.

She tried to laugh but choked on the sound. Soul? She still wasn't sure she had one. But even if she did, mental vacations could not help her. She was living her nightmare. And no matter how she fought against the sweeping tide of horror, she knew it was only a matter of time until she succumbed to the onslaught and drowned.

Think of Valin. Close the connection between your brain and body and think of how full your heart felt when he held you in his arms.

She swallowed tears. Yes. Valin had held her. He'd made love to her again and again, his gaze burning as he made her unravel in his arms. Until the morning. When he left.

<<*Because that's what they do. Use and betray. The only reason he ever touched you was to have his revenge.*>>

She moaned, shaking her head against the sibilant whisper that threatened to sever her last lifeline.

<<*What other reason could there be for him sleeping with you? You killed his mate, remember? It was your conception that caused his ultimate suffering.*>>

He made love to me. He kissed me. He...

<<*He was playing you. Using you for his revenge.*>>

No...

<<*Deny all you want, Gabby. But you know. Unloved. Unwanted... except by me.*>>

Don't listen... Don't listen...

Fangs pierced her throat, their weight suffocating

against her windpipe as her attacker pulled directly from the carotid. Her limbs went heavy, clammy sweat beading on her skin and chilling her. Her ears began to ring, her limbs shaking involuntarily.

Holy crap. He's going to drain me dry. Her brain screamed at her to struggle, though her limbs still refused to respond under the lock Christos had placed upon her. *Draining me dry. Going to die.*

Valin... God, Valin!

<<*They're right. Something different about you. Your taste... it's...*>> Her attacker pulled away, his tongue swiping across the tender wound to start the healing. How sweet.

She opened her eyes to glare at the asshole that had made her realize how very unprepared she really was to die. Her eyes widened, her breath catching in her bruised throat as she stared at the man fondling her breast: Christos.

She forced herself to swallow her horror. She'd survived before and would again.

"So you finally decided to come face me yourself?" she asked, inserting every bit of bravado she could muster into her voice. "A girl could almost feel loved."

"Ah, Gabby, how I've missed the sweet lash of your tongue." He ducked down, his tongue darting out to cleanse a path of still-moist blood that dripped down between her breasts before moving on to lap at a still-oozing wound below her nipple.

Hate boiled in her veins, her body shaking with the need to respond despite the bonds upon her will. Those bonds would fail, had to, because somehow, someway she would kill him. Sink her fangs in him and drain him dry. And with his blood she could kill every one of the fuckers who'd touched her.

Careful. Remember what he wants. Don't let him win.

Hands cupped possessively beneath her breasts, Christos lifted his head, his eyes filled with crimson fire as he breathed deeply of the pulse point at her throat. "It's no wonder your Paladin was able to fuck you. Monster or not, you are one sweet bit of ass."

And just like that, the bonds snapped. She lunged, her fangs sinking deep in his neck. The first heady mouthful of warmth slid down the back of her tongue. He stiffened, but then sank a hand into her hair, pulling her closer so she had to swallow hard and fast to keep from drowning on his blood.

"Yes, my daughter. Drink. Let my blood heal all your pains."

No! He tricks you! He poisons your soul with his evil.

For one heady second she continued to drink before the truth caught up with her battered and bruised mind that had been locked in nightmarish reality. She gagged and jerked away, her throat working convulsively around the last drop of toxin coating it. What had she done? Son of Lilith, favored child of Lucifer, Christos had been evil before the abomination of his hell-born resurrection, but now?

Pure evil. And you've invited him into your body with his blood.

She screamed, but no sound came from her lips. Only in the distant recesses of her mind could her death cry be heard. For it was not her body that died, but something far worse. She, the Gabby she might have been, the child she'd fought to protect for seventy-nine long horrid years, was dying with each pulse that distributed Christos's poison blood in her veins.

Above the sound of her own silent screams came another—a malevolent chuckle that in no way matched the tenderness of the hands lowering her to the floor. "Ah, Gabby, Gabby, Gabby. Where is your savior now?"

—∿∿—

Christos twisted his head to the side, studying his child as she arched her wet dream of a body up toward his hovering hand. It mattered not to him that her action was an unconscious one driven by the call of like to like as his blood forged a path through her system, completely and irrevocably binding her to him.

Finally, he thought as he allowed himself the pleasure of caressing the full swell of her offered breasts. His cock immediately sprung to attention, need pulsing through his groin and echoing in the throb of his fangs. Remarkable. He'd touched her before, but never had it elicited such a reaction. Possibly because she'd been nothing but a task to him them. A work in progress to be shaped and molded. But now that he'd achieved his goal?

Is this what Lucifer felt at my own rebirth? The pride that comes with knowing you've created perfection?

Christos had been like a harbinger of evil before, but now? Now he was a plague. One drop of his blood and he'd achieved in Gabby what years of transfusions had failed to do. Gabby was his. Her body. Her mind... her soul.

The door creaked open behind him, the coppery scent of the null's dried-on blood announcing the man's identity. "My king?"

"Cyrus, is our guest properly indisposed?"

"Yes, my king. I doubt she will wake for hours yet."

"Very good then," he replied absently, his attention fixated once more on Gabriella and the writhing convulsions her body had started going through. How long would they last? How long before she woke?

"My king?"

"What is it?" he snapped, eager to be rid of the voyeur. He couldn't even count the number of years he'd waited for this. Centuries he'd worked to set up the situation in which the conception of a child of light and dark could occur. And decades more before he'd finally found the key to her conversion. But he'd done it. And Gabriella would be the one to earn him his rightful place to the right of his father's throne. That joke of a general, Ganelon, was wrong. Gabriella *was* the prophecy. They'd simply misinterpreted the signs before. But the prophecy was now on the eve of its fulfillment. Fueled by the potency of his blood and the gift of her Paladin heritage, Gabriella could walk into the depths of Haven and begin the spread of the contagion that would burn like a swath of evil through their ranks. The child of *his* blood. His soon-to-be lover. His future queen.

He touched her cheek, undisturbed by the grayish cast to her face. The blood of the master that ran through his veins would now run through hers as well. *<<Hurry, my love. I've waited long enough to find one worthy enough to be my queen.>>*

"They approach," Cyrus said, dousing Christos's good mood.

They'd found them more quickly than he anticipated.

He sighed, reluctantly removing his hand. The

consummation of the binding would have to wait until later. After she'd fulfilled her purpose. She would come to him then, having bathed in their blood: the perfect match to his evil soul.

"You may lead those I've chosen through the tunnel."

"And the others?"

His mouth twisted up at the corners, his fangs scraping more flecks of Gabriella's drying blood from his bottom lip. The others: those that had readily embraced Stephan's leadership and even now would prefer to align themselves with his second. They would never get the chance to share his blood. They were unworthy. Unless…"I think, perhaps, it is time for them to prove the mettle of their faith, don't you?"

"My king?"

"Yes, they shall stay. Martyrs for our cause."

Reluctantly he stood, his eyes dragging one last time over the yellowing bruises and already scabbed wounds covering his bride-to-be's luscious curves. <<*Wake, my love. Then stand. Stand and fight and kill the bastards who did this to you. Kill them all…*>>

Chapter 20

VALIN SHIFTED FROM ONE LEG TO THE OTHER, FIGHTING back the lethargy that threatened his muscles. He was tired of waiting. Weary of staring at the eerily still exterior of the run-down mansion. And sick to death of the endless strategizing going on around him. He'd already put in his opinion: Barge in through those thick wood doors, let loose on any fuckers in his way, and get his mate back. But the others insisted they needed some _sort_ of plan of action. As if killing vampires was really all that difficult.

Crouched by him on his right, Karissa reached over, placing a hand on his forearm. "It's okay, Valin. Bennett, Jacob, and their team are almost in place."

Valin nodded at Karissa to show that he heard her, though he personally considered the flanking technique a waste of time. Both his own scouting and Karissa and Bennett's radar screens had shown no one outside, which meant the chances of a merker force being present were pretty damn slim. First, those factions didn't normally hang together and second, if they were, then why wouldn't the merkers be out here monitoring the property for potential breaches?

Unless Lucifer's minions were really so egotistical as to believe they would not be attacked in their own home.

Or if getting your asses inside is part of the trap.

Valin grunted, figuring that was the most likely.

Either way, the action was all going to occur on the inside, not out here, which meant all the sneaking around
to the back Bennett, Jacob, and his team had done was
nothing more than a waste of time. No merkers to alert
outside and no vampires were running out the back door
on this one. Not with the sun breaking through the low-
lying fog.

"Do you know what this place is?" Roland asked
from his other side, breaking into his thoughts.

"You mean besides a coven's stronghold?" he answered with the obvious, figuring that, like his mate
Karissa, Roland was trying to distract Valin enough to
curb his impatience. Yeah, good luck with that.

"Yes," Roland drew out the word, as if Valin was
being particularly dense. "But do you know whose
stronghold specifically?"

"Should I?"

"This was Christos's power base. There are dozens
of other vampire safe houses around the city, but this
is where the bastard lived." He hesitated. "Gabby too."

Valin turned his gaze back to the home of Gabby's
youth. The place where for seventy-nine years she'd
been subjected to whatever forms of torture Christos
could think up in his attempt to break her. And though
he wanted to personally dig up the bastard's body and
decapitate him again, Valin couldn't help but be proud of
his mate because Christos had never succeeded. Gabby
had fought, slithering countless times from his grasp of
evil, bending but never breaking beneath his will. She'd
persevered and eventually clawed her way free.

*But she's back in there now. And you know what
they'll be doing to her. You've seen it in her memories.*

He shook his head, unwilling to go down that road. He'd helped her move beyond the horrors of her past before and he'd do so again if need be. The important thing now was getting her the heck out of there. As quickly as fucking possible.

"I'm a great fucking father, aren't I? Leaving her there."

Valin turned to look at Roland. Realized the vampire-Paladin must be referring to past mistakes rather than discussing strategies of the present. Good thing, too, as Valin would have cut off the man's balls before he let him walk away. Furthermore, he really couldn't argue with Roland's self-assessment of his former stellarness. Though in all fairness, Roland had a shitload on his plate back then, and hadn't actually known Gabby was his. From snippets around the Paladin water cooler, Valin heard that Roland had tried to help her where and when he could. That, added to the fact Roland was here now, risking both his and his mate's life on a potentially already doomed rescue mission?

"You're not the shittiest father of the year."

"Gee, thanks," Roland muttered, eliciting another pull at the corners of Valin's mouth. The fact of the matter was Roland was here, by Valin's side, ready to fight. And Gabby was in there waiting to be rescued, which they were going to do in *mucho más rápido* fashion—as soon as Bennett and his buddies got their asses in gear, that is.

Valin cleared his throat, his eyes fixed firmly ahead. While he was waiting, there was no time like the present to kill…or be killed, right? "I'd ask you for her hand so that when we get her out of here…you know…but frankly I don't give a damn if you approve or not."

Roland shifted, and damn if Valin couldn't feel the weight of his crimson gaze on him. "That's okay. I don't care if you want my blessing or not." He paused, leaning in closer to whisper, "Just know that if you ever hurt her, if you ever cause her so much as one tear, I'll fucking kill you."

"Roland!" Karissa gasped, but Valin ignored her, turning his head to meet Roland's red eyes.

"I would never do that," he vowed.

Roland lifted his brow, a blatant not-buying-it-bastard.

"She's my mate." Emphasis on the *she is*, not *was*. She had to be in there. In there and alive.

Roland's eyes narrowed, the crimson subsiding as he glanced past Valin to meet Karissa's gaze. Valin felt the soft brush of their silent communication. Roland's probably asking *WTF, does he actually believe that shit?* and Karissa's own perplexed *believe so.*

"Yeah, unfuckingbelievable, right?" Valin cracked his neck first one way, then the other. "Bands of misfits, vampire-Paladin who walk in the sun, freaks of darkness like me. Makes you wonder if He's even still up there or not."

"He is," Karissa said, her voice soft yet filled with conviction. "And He has a plan."

Valin's brow furrowed as he turned to stare at her, wondering when she'd grown two heads. "Then why the fuck is Gabby in there?"

It was Roland who answered, his hand gripping Valin's shoulder to draw his attention back to him. "Have you forgotten it's our duty to make sure His plan comes to fruition? Annie, Karissa, Gabriella...they are as much His warriors as the rest of the Paladin. You know as well as I that being one of His soldiers often comes with hardship."

Valin chewed on that, not liking the thought that Gabby, if truly one of His warriors, would be called upon to place herself in danger. If they got her out of there—no, *when* they got her out of there—he wanted to carry her away, wrap her up in silk, and stuff her as far away from Lucifer's hordes as he possibly could. But if she was His, then Valin wouldn't be able to do that, nor would she let him.

He squirmed, thinking his ability to play in the gray area between good and evil could be part of some grand plan, that he might be as beloved as someone like Logan or Alexander—it just felt odd and somehow blasphemous. "You really think that what I am, what I can do, is really part of His plan?"

"No, I don't know what the fuck you are, you freak." The quip was delivered with such indifference that Valin had to chuckle.

"Takes one to know one, huh?"

"Damn straight." Roland sobered, his face grim as he met Valin's gaze. "I don't presume to understand how we fit into His greater purpose. But I know one thing. If you're my daughter's mate, then you're not half as bad as I or even you think you are."

"Thanks. I think."

"Don't thank me." He looked back at the shuttered mansion. "Just help me get Gabriella out of there."

<hr />

Unloved. Unwanted. Evil... Monster.

Gabby lay on the floor, her body twisting and

contorting to escape the horrific truth seeping through her veins. Like black oil, the dark poison eating at her caught and flared, burning away the agony of her loss until she didn't even remember what that loss was. All she knew was the fire's blistering heat had come, consumed, and obliterated everything but the last command her master had given her.

Stand. Stand and fight.

Breathing through the smoldering heat in her lungs, Gabby pulled herself up to her feet. Not sensing anyone nearby to actually fight, she surveyed the room. The dark paneled walls stained darker by their gaslights, the floor sticky with blood, the hook in the ceiling, and the coil of rope tossed negligently in the corner. Something about it all struck a deeply buried chord of familiarity. She tested the connection, automatically recoiling from the images that swept over her, before she forced herself to stand before the onslaught.

That's right. That had been her life. Though no longer. Now she had but one purpose. One reason for being here: revenge.

Stand and fight. Kill all the bastards who've done this to you.

Good idea. Now all she had to do was find them.

She moved out into the hall, making her way on some sort of subconscious memory toward the main stairs. The place seemed strangely empty. As if there had been a mass exodus by its occupants. As if they knew she came and thought it prudent to vacate the building. Wise, but it did nothing to ease her hunger.

Blood. Death. Destruction. Nothing else would feed her need for revenge.

She neared the central landing. Movement caught the corner of her eye, someone making his way down the last curve of twisting stairs. She edged forward toward the banister, twisting her head. The soft hiss of arguing voices rose like sweet music to her ears from the hall below.

"...said to remain here," said a man sitting in the largest leather armchair centrally placed in the spacious foyer. The sour taste of bitter memories had her stomach churning even as saliva pooled in the back of her mouth. Oh, he was definitely one of the ones she would kill, this vampire with his superior sneer.

"You expect me to sit and wait patiently like a lamb for the slaughter!" replied another, presumably the vampire descending the stair. She recognized him now too. His voice at least, and decided he was a fit companion for the impending bloodbath.

She began edging down the stairs, far enough back from the edge to be hidden in shadow, but not so far that she couldn't keep an eye on her quarry. There were almost a dozen of them there, but only the man in the armchair and the man she followed down seemed to be close enough in status to quarrel.

The vampire sitting in the armchair pulled back his lip, revealing fangs that he had to have forcefully elongated. "Are you so weak that you fear a handful of part-bloods?" he addressed the latecomer.

"Not weak. Wise. Though it's not the part-bloods I fear, but who comes with them." He stopped before the vampire Gabby presumed held the higher rank based on the uncomfortable silence that surrounded them. Cowards, all of them. Cowardly enough to torture and

abuse, but only when the victim in question was tied up
and already weakened.

Kill them. Kill them all.

"Who?"

The other vampire smiled, folding his hands. "Roland."

Gabby tripped, her hands grabbing for the banister.
Somehow she managed to grasp the grime-covered oak
without making any noise but for her thudding heart...
surely they could hear her heart.

That name. It meant something...

Unloved. Unwanted. Evil... Monster.

She sucked in air, trying to fill the hole that had
opened in her chest with great gulps of air. Why the
name would cause her such pain, she couldn't fathom,
but it was there, drilling through her like her insides
were a cavity that needed to be eradicated.

<< He abandoned you... remember?>>

That's right. That was right. He left her. Abandoning
her to the type of monsters who gathered on the marble
below her now.

"Cyrus said nothing about Roland being with the
part-bloods."

"Because Cyrus knows how to pander to your ego,
you fool. And saying the name of your executioner
might even make *you* balk."

Gabby didn't see him move from his chair. One
second he was there, the next he was across the room
pinning the other vampire to the wall by the throat so
that his feet dangled well above the floor.

"Don't call me a fool," Armchair sneered, the
violence of his action centering her enough that she
was able to resume her progress down the stairs. The

situation was so intense no one noticed her, even though she'd stopped trying to hide her approach. She made it all the way down, her hand resting on the finial before a single one of the vampires in the room looked over at her.

<<*Because you're nothing to them. A toy. A slave. But not a threat.*>>

Bull. Shit. She could make them hurt as much as they'd hurt her. If not for the fact she was too damn impatient.

"Gabriella?" a vampire from across the room asked, his eyes wide as he stared at her. His clothing was coated in dried blood. The scent? Her own.

And what do you know…he'd just volunteered to die first.

Gabby leapt across the room.

———

Annie woke to the adrenaline-pumping sound of a dying scream. She stumbled out of bed, her legs collapsing beneath her, sending her smacking onto the floor. Pain hit her, firing across every nerve in her body and stealing her breath. For long precious moments she lay there silently gasping for air, her hands clawing desperately at the damp carpet.

It was the second scream that seemed to open the block on her windpipe. Another surge of adrenaline doing for her what she could not do herself. She had to get up. Had to figure out what was going on.

Where was she?
Don't know.
What happened?
You don't want to know.

She believed that and decided she'd worry about those things later. Right now she needed to make sure that if the danger out there crossed her threshold, she'd be able to do something about it.

Panting against the pain, she pushed herself up onto her hands and knees. She cringed at the sticky dampness of the rug beneath her, her nostrils quivering at the strange scent. What was that...blood?

Sickened, she scooted back onto her knees, her hand clutching for the nearby nightstand. Using the heavy oak antique for support, she dragged herself up, first one leg, then the other, until she was sure they could hold her.

More precious seconds slipped past as she waited for her vision to clear, the dark edges that had funneled down around her sight eventually receding. The room was dimly lit, only the gas-powered lamp on the nightstand next to her seemed to be working. Even so, she could tell that it was a large room, though apparently sparsely furnished with only the nightstand and the dim outline of the bed behind her.

She looked down at the nightstand, her brow bunching as she spotted the surgical tray precariously balanced on the back corner. Sutures, clamps, needles...a scalpel. She picked up the scalpel, careful to avoid the bloodstained blade. Why would this be here?

Don't look. You don't want to look.

Closing her eyes, she pressed her fingers against one pulsing point of pain across her torso, her fingers trembling as she followed the stitched cut across her body. Had she been in some sort of accident? Had her dad...

Her breath came in great gasps as she forced herself

to glance behind her and take in the bloodstained bed, her hand rising shakily to touch her throbbing face.

Long, jagged welts, buckled up with stitches.

A noise much like a keen rose in her throat as snapshots of remembered consciousness, nightmares really, filtered across the mental block in her mind. A block she must have put in place to protect herself. Her knees collapsed under the weight of the horrific images. Only the bed, that vile, disgusting bed, saved her from completely falling as she caught it on the way down.

Ryan…the bites on his neck. He used a Taser on her and then…then…

Get it together, Annie. You need to move. Get out. No one is going to save you but you.

Her entire body trembling, she forced herself to make her way toward the end of the bed, pausing to pant when she finally reached the footboard. It had been a long time since the last scream; maybe the danger was past, maybe…

The door creaked. Annie's grip tightened on the scalpel, even as she leaned heavily on the corner post. A figure stood in the doorframe, barely taller than a child but obviously a woman, her curves caressed by the hall's shadows, her long hair hanging in matted locks around her model-worthy face.

"Gabby? Oh, God, Gabby, thank God…" Annie took a stumbling step forward, her legs trembling beneath her weight, then stumbled to a stop, reaching back for the bed once more. Gabby was in no state to help her. Like Annie, the only thing Gabby wore was the evidence of her own abuses. Half-healed wounds, yellowed blotches upon her gray skin, and her eyes…

Annie shifted back just as Gabby took a step forward, her crimson gaze fixed firmly on Annie. Annie sobbed, shaking her head in denial. She'd only seen Gabby lost to a killing craze once before and had hoped to never see the results again. But there was no escape from this room, and nowhere to hide.

"No…Gabby, no, it's me," she tried, even as she twisted to keep the scalpel in her hand hidden.

"You're one of them," Gabby said, her voice cold, mechanical as if reciting something from rote.

"No…It's Annie. You remember me, right?"

Gabby nodded, taking another step forward. "You brought me here."

"No. I'm your friend!"

"Friend?" Gabby cocked her head to the side, her red eyes narrowing to slits.

Annie nodded. "I was tricked, betrayed by one of our own."

"Ah…" Gabby paused thoughtfully. For a moment Annie harbored hope that her reasoning had broken through, her grip loosening infinitesimally on the scalpel, but then Gabby lunged. Annie raised her arm but Gabby was quicker, her hand tightening around Annie's wrist and squeezing tighter and tighter until the bones popped, the scalpel falling uselessly to the floor.

"That's the thing: They. Always. Betray," Gabby hissed, eyes smoldering as she visually caressed Annie's neck. "But never again. Never again will they betray me."

Annie's eyes widened, her cry of disbelief muffled beneath the sudden pressure of Gabby's fangs as they bore down on her throat.

Chapter 21

VALIN BOLTED FOR THE DOOR AT THE FIRST SCREAM, ignoring Roland's curses as he and Karissa struggled to catch up. Valin might have completely outrun them—regardless of their vamp strength—except he was ten feet from the door when he smacked up against the wards surrounding the mansion.

"Not a good sign for the null," Roland said behind him as Valin cursed and stumbled back to his feet. "You guys thought her powers would negate the ward, right?"

"Fuck." Valin shook his head, not wanting to think about what it meant if Annie wasn't in there. "I'm shifting," Valin said, knowing he could cross the wards that way—the shade didn't play by the same rules.

"Valin, wait!" Karissa grabbed his arm. "We can take this down if you work with us. And your knife alone will be worth the cost of time."

Valin's hand closed instinctively over the blade. His knife, the one Gabby had given Bennett with instructions to return to him. If she'd kept it, brought it with her, instead of sending it with a fucking I'm-so-sorry message, would she be in there now?

Now who's wasting time?

"One minute," Valin growled, knowing Karissa was right. Fighting hand-to-hand took time, but since he *did* have his knife, he could cut through a horde of vampires as if they were nothing more than tissue paper.

She nodded, slipping her hand into his and reaching across for Roland's, like they were at some sort of kumbaya jamboree or something. Not that he gave a shit how corny it looked as long as it got the results.

He took a deep breath, easing back on his shields until he felt the heady mix of her light and Roland's power. Beyond was her link to Bennett and the echoing support of Jacob's soldiers lending their aid. That was good; a double-fronted attack on the wards should weaken them quicker.

They began chanting, the spell to dissolve the wards no more than a banishing spell. Unlike the various wards the Paladins used to keep baddies out of their home, these wards were formed from evil, their power coming from decades of blood spilled. Just touching them with the edge of his power made him feel sick to his stomach, but it also gave him the incentive to put his all behind it. This had to end now. No more pain. No more suffering. The bastards who'd made this place were going to crawl back into the hellhole from which they came.

The ward fell. Valin dropped Karissa's hand and launched himself at the door. Cocky bastards hadn't even locked it, let alone barred it, so it was a short trip into the front hall of horrors where he drew up short. Bodies and blood. The destruction was so ultimate he had to pause and really look to assure himself that one of the bodies wasn't Gabby. Someone must have been in a real pisser of a mood to mete out such violence. And though he could appreciate the poetic nature of these monsters ending their existence this way, he sincerely worried for the mental state of the person doling out this kind of justice.

"She's not here," Roland said, even as he moved past Valin and bent to inspect one of the corpses.

"Yeah, got that." Valin breathed deeply through his nose, then cringed. Death was never pretty and it normally smelled worse than it looked. A half-dozen bodies, and unless his mojo was completely shot, not another soul in the place. "The question is, where is everyone else?"

Roland didn't respond, his focus on his examination of the corpses.

"I don't sense anyone either." Karissa drew up beside him. "Well, other than…" She jerked her chin toward the doors at the back of the cavernous foyer. Bennett, Jacob, and their team pushed through, their attention immediately catching on the rather morbid attempt at decoration the last living party in the room had done.

Bennett was the first to recover, his gaze lifting to meet Valin's. "I'm getting a whole lot of nothing—you?"

"Not a thing."

"It's possible the others took the hidden tunnel out, but…" Roland trailed off, moving on to another dead vampire.

"Hidden tunnel?" Jacob asked sharply.

"But what?" Valin prompted, figuring the tunnel was the least important part of that statement.

Roland sighed, twisting the vampire's head to the side and exposing the relatively intact bite marks flanking the ripped out throat. "Fang marks are kind of like a primitive form of fingerprinting. I can't definitively tell who bit whom, but I can tell you that all these," he gestured around the room, "seem to match."

"What are you saying?

"I'm saying whoever killed them was one person. And I have to wonder, why would a coven numbering close to a hundred flee from just one little vampire?"

Little vampire. "You think Gabby did this?"

"I do." He stood, his face pulled tight as he averted his gaze from the corpse. "Which leaves us with one question."

"Why?" Bennett ventured.

Roland turned his hard gaze on the Paladin. "No, I know why. The question is where is she now?"

They didn't have to wait for the answer. A second later, from deeper in the house came the most bloodcurdling scream Valin had ever heard.

Bennett jerked as if he'd been hit with a live wire. The next second he was bolting past the closest soldier and running headlong down the nearby hall. Never had such a short distance seemed so long. Bennett knew it was Annie who'd screamed. Not because it was truly discernible from any other female in distress, but because he hadn't sensed another soul in the mansion. She was alive—though only barely to not have broken the wards—and in immediate danger.

His gut, already twisted and cramped, churned. Acid pooled at the base of his throat. Whether the unprecedented chink in his composure was from guilt or something more, he didn't bloody know. All he knew was the annoying organ in his chest that was pounding like it was on its last leg might as well just give up the ghost if he couldn't get to her in time.

He reached the end of the hall, the pure absence of power announcing he was at the correct room. The others were behind him, but he didn't wait, setting his shoulder to the door with all the force of his rage behind the assault. Hinges and bolts groaned and gave, the old hardwood cracking and tearing free from the frame. The door burst in, Bennett right on top of it. And there she was: his Annie.

All doubts that she *wasn't* his were answered. Because there was no way he could stay detached after seeing the ruin of her body. And no way the creature sucking the life out of her was going to leave this room alive.

With a roar, Bennett drew his knife and launched himself across the room.

———

Valin had almost caught up to Bennett when the Paladin went all commando and burst through the bedroom door. He'd made it inside the room as far as the Paladin's heels when the warrior roared. And because of the shock that Valin, too, experienced when he saw what was in that room, it was still almost too far away to stop what happened next.

Bennett drew his knife and lunged; Valin had no doubt he truly meant to kill with the blade.

Terror displaced shock and he dove after the warrior, tackling him around the waist and bringing him down just feet from where Gabby was stretched over Annie lapping at the jagged wound at the base of her neck. He needed to go to her, needed to stop this madness, needed to…fuck, he didn't know. But he couldn't do anything until he'd knocked some reason into Bennett.

"Bennett, wait—" An elbow jabbed into his side, taking away his breath and anything else he might have said. From there, their struggle devolved into a whole lot of hitting, rolling, scrambling, and cursing. Precious moments slipped by, fear spiking anew when someone leapt over them.

"Don't hurt her!" he yelled, even as he slammed Bennett's arm with the knife into the floor. Bennett swore, trying to roll, but Valin latched onto his wrist, twisting the arm behind him as he ground his knee into the Paladin's back. From the other side of the room rose an enraged scream. A second later Gabby's slight form went sailing across the bed and landed in a heap in the far corner.

Valin glanced up in time to see Roland leap over the bed, his feet barely making noise as he landed and began stalking across the floor after her, his eyes boiling a deep crimson as he cowed her into the corner of the room.

"Annie!" Jacob yelled and rushed by toward the crumpled form of his daughter.

"Back off!" Bennett growled from beneath Valin, straining against Valin's hold.

"You won't go after Gabby," he told the Paladin, though he saved his glare for the handful of soldiers who were piling up behind the five-foot-six barrier named Karissa who blocked the ragged doorframe.

"How can you defend that thing?" Bennett asked.

"She's not herself," Valin said from between clenched teeth.

"She's a rabid dog!" Bennett yelled, then closed his eyes, taking a long breath. "Just let me up."

Stiffly, Valin rose to his feet, his body tense and ready, but all Bennett did was rush over and kneel next to Jacob, who was quickly and efficiently binding his daughter's wound.

"Her pulse is lower than I'd like but steady," Jacob told Bennett. "The wound was already stitched once. Looks like it was only reopened."

A rumble rose from Bennett's throat, but all he did was nod as he carefully began checking her over for signs of injuries beyond the visible obvious, which, shit, numbered a whole hell of a lot.

"Gabriella, stop this!" Roland barked, snapping Valin out of the surreal haze he'd been watching events unfold through. Annie fighting for her life, Gabby reduced to little more than a rabid animal. This was wrong. A nightmare.

Now if only I could wake up.

Valin eased over behind Roland, his focus completely on the snarling and spitting creature crouched in the corner that looked so very much, and so very little, like the woman he loved. After seeing the destruction in the hall, he half-wondered why she hadn't ripped them all to shreds yet, but then he realized that she'd de-evolved even further since that bloodbath and was acting purely on instinct. Thank God Roland was the more dominant vampire; otherwise he might not be getting this chance to bring her back.

"Gabby…" Reaching for her, he stepped past Roland, but stopped when she lifted her head, her lips parted as she panted through her blooded fangs. There was positively no sign of recognition in her crimson eyes. Not even the most tentative thread of connection between them. The only thing he felt emitting out of those crimson eyes was pure, unadulterated hate.

Hollow horror settled around his heart, his lungs clamping down on the soiled air he breathed as the reality of his nightmare hit home. Gabby stood before him, her body painted in blood, her hair matted, her eyes red, and he couldn't see one bit of the woman he'd made love to just hours ago. His Gabby was already gone.

You failed, again.

In his mind he fell to his knees, crushed beneath the impotence that seemed to be his curse. Why could he never be enough? As little more than a second-class Paladin he hadn't been powerful enough to save Angeline, hadn't been the protector of their child. And now...Gabby...

Not her too.

The world twisted, scents and colors becoming too sharp, the air like jagged blades sawing in and out of his lungs. Something snapped in his mind, sanity slipping askew as he tried to make sense of this reality. What did you do when there was nothing left to be done?

Rabid dog. What do you do to a rabid dog?

No! He wasn't strong enough...he couldn't...he wouldn't survive...shouldn't survive...

Then go with her.

A calm eased over him, a hidden pathway opening up before him. This wasn't the end. He'd do what he must but they'd be together after, even if he had to follow her into hell.

"—all I can do for her. The sealant properties should help, but you still need to get her to a hospital." Karissa's voice, soothing, yet matter-of-fact as she spoke with the others over Annie, brought him back. That's right; there would be witnesses to his fall unless he got them to leave.

Gabby's gaze kept on shifting between the others and

him, or more specifically the others and the hand he held on his knife. In fact, he sensed that knife was the only thing that kept her from attacking.

"Get Annie out of here," he commanded, his eyes tracking Gabby's own. She hissed as he switched the blade from his right to his left as if she knew it was his killing hand, which would suggest a state of memory and awareness that wasn't evident in her crazed eyes. More likely she just didn't like any sort of movement involving the knife.

He knew the moment Bennett, Jacob, and his team got Annie down the hall by the comfortable weight of the shade filtering back into those gaps in reality and easing the sharp focus of colors back out. Good—when he'd done what he needed to do, that is where he'd go. Only this time he wasn't coming back.

"Valin," Roland growled from behind him, alerting him to the fact that not everyone had left. "What the fuck are you doing?"

Guess Roland had, at one point, seen him fight with his knife in battle.

Despite the surreal sense of detachment, it was still difficult to draw enough breath to speak and even more painful to put the knowledge of necessity into words, so it was amazing to him when his voice came out steady and strong. "You know who Gabby was in her heart, Roland. Tell me, would she want to live like this?"

"Fuck…FUCK!" Roland roared, his own pain and loss exponentially fanning Valin's. Valin clenched his teeth, trying to tone out Roland's explosion.

Rabid dog. Put her down. You'd want her to do the same for you.

"Look at me, Roland. I need you to look at me," Karissa said, her voice alone like a soothing bit of cool-headedness in a room burning with misery.

Roland growled again. Valin spared the briefest of glances to see Karissa wrapping her arms around her mate. It was only a split second, but long enough that their eyes met, a silent moment of understanding passing between them before she looked away and flickered out, pulling Roland along with her as she teleported.

And then it was just him and Gabby, though not really. Without the balancing effect of Karissa's inherent light, he could feel the evil seeping out from every molecule in the room, the dark magic that had sunk into and sustained this house of horrors for so long like a living entity breathing for the house itself.

Karissa's silent demand to make sure, as well as his own need, had him pushing his awareness out into that dark ether, grasping once more for the lost connection between him and Gabby, even though he feared what he knew he would find. The mate bond was truly gone; either her hatred was too strong or it had been irreversibly severed by the evil she'd been exposed to here.

"Fuck, Gabby, what did they do to you?"

Not every bit of blood on her body was from her mindless massacre back in that foyer. Beneath the drying blood and the more recent sticky paths of red she'd drawn from Annie were patches of brown surrounding still-healing wounds and yellow-black bruises.

They'd hurt her. Again. And for that alone he wished he could go back, revive them, and then tear them apart again for her. Maybe he'd even join her in her madness because he knew, just knew, that when he'd done what he needed he'd be there anyway.

His hand flexed around his knife. *Strike to the heart. Quick and easy.*

No, never easy. Not when it was Gabby. Even if it was just the shell of her body and not *his* Gabby. With sinking comprehension he realized he couldn't do it. He couldn't kill her. Couldn't end her misery. Only obviously she could end his.

Her mouth twisted into a snarling smile as she bent down, grabbing up a scalpel he hadn't noticed before. Not a very good weapon but...She lunged. His arm automatically came up to block, her puny knife skittering uselessly off his blade, but he'd underestimated her. Claws slashed deep across his side, tearing through his shirt and ripping parallel tracks of flesh from muscle.

He stumbled back, putting distance between them as he tested the wound. Not by any stretch of the imagination fatal, but shit, it stung. "Hey, cookie, I know you like it kinda rough, but don't you think that's—"

She screeched and charged, and crazed as she was didn't bother to watch his knife this time. All he had to do was follow through on instinct and take the strike, but again he failed, instead twisting out of the way.

"Stop it, Gabby. This isn't you. You don't want to do this."

She narrowed her eyes, likely because she was pissed at missing and regrouping, but he couldn't help but...

"Do you remember me, Gabby?"

"I don't need to remember you. You're one of them."

"Who're them?" he asked automatically, his mind reeling at the fact that she'd actually spoken.

"The ones that betrayed me," she hissed.

He sucked in a breath. That was it. Just that simple stream of conscious thought, even if twisted, sent his hope soaring. He took a deep breath, passing his knife back to his other hand. Her pupils widened, a hiss of disbelief slipping from between her teeth.

"I'm never giving up on you, Gabby. Not while there is breath in my body," he told her, knowing in the depths of his heart it was true. If there was a mind beyond the instinct then somewhere in there was a soul. And he would not let that soul be won by darkness.

"Let's see if we can fix that then," she said and threw the scalpel at his face.

He ducked before it speared him through the eye, though he lost a good swath of hair in the process.

Useless. Your Gabby is gone. You know she's gone.

No, she wasn't. Not if she could reason. He just had to help her find the right ones. So he spoke to her, his voice hoarse from the desperate effort he put into trying to bring her back as he blocked and evaded each of her attacks. She was completely enraged, her assaults no more than senseless charges in response to each memory he tried to restore to her. But it wasn't until he mentioned Roland and the caves that something flickered in her eyes, a momentary banking of the crimson fires.

"I told him, you know," he said, leaping on the chance that this was the key. "I told Roland he was your father. He came here tonight. To save you. Put both himself and his mate in danger to do so."

"You lie! You lie!" she shrieked, not even bothering to attack him this time but held her fists over her ears like a child.

"Why? Why do you think I lie?"

<<Unloved. Unwanted. Alone. Betrayed.>>

He sucked in a breath, both elated and torn anew at the misery-laden thought she'd unwittingly projected. "Oh, Gabby, no. That's not true. That's the lie."

He moved forward, reaching for her. She screamed, leaping at him, fangs bared. He didn't try and strike her, but her sudden forward movement as he was reaching brought his knife into contact with her upper arm.

She hissed and retreated, her eyes glazed and confused as she clamped her hand down on the wound. For a moment she looked just like the scared vampire he'd found chained up inside the dilapidated building back in that coal mine; a helpless child, hiding behind bravado, though she couldn't fathom why she'd been left for dead. She hadn't been helpless, of course, nor had she been the child he'd first thought, but she had been betrayed by her maker and left for a crack in the cloud cover.

And you promised never to use your knife on her.

"Shit...Gabby, you moved and I..." He reached for the bond again, and this time he swore he felt something, only it was immediately severed by a blast of evil so strong it left his head ringing and his knees threatening to crumble.

<<See? Even now he seeks to end you. This bastard Paladin who has as little blood as you do. Why should he be accepted when you aren't?>>

Valin gulped in deep breaths, trying to draw his shields back around him even as his mind whirled. He knew the feel of that mind voice. But it was impossible, he'd watched the man, or rather vampire, die in a cave by Roland's blade four months ago.

"Who is it, Gabby? How did they convince you to believe these lies?" Valin asked as he sheathed his knife. This battle was no longer a physical one, but one for his mate's soul. She was still in there. But whoever that was whispering lies into her head had somehow sunk his black claws into her, smothering her true self beneath his pall of evil.

How, though? How did they so completely and absolutely obliterate her will when years of Christos's tortures didn't before?

Gabby straightened, the lick of her cold fury lapping the edges of Valin's shields. She dropped her hand, her fingers flexing as she stared him down. Valin sucked in a breath, his own gaze fixated on the blood trickling from the split in her gray-cast skin. It was black. Thick and oily. Like some sort of poison coating her veins.

Being careful not to open himself fully, Valin reached out with his senses. He could feel the lingering evil of horrors past permeating the air, but it was the sucking chasm of evil that he associated with Lucifer himself that he sensed seeping out of the blood weeping from her wounds.

"Blood tie." He shook his head. It was the only explanation for how deeply and completely the evil had invaded her soul. Somehow Lucifer had managed to poison her very essence with his evil, the blood that sustained her eroding the lightness within her soul, *his* Gabby's soul, with each beat of her heart.

No, not Lucifer, one of his minions. Someone who knew just how to break her too...

"Fuck, Gabby. He's still alive, isn't he?" No, not still alive, resurrected. Somehow Lucifer had brought

Christos back, only now he was more than a pawn of evil, but evil himself.

And his blood runs in Gabby now.

He took a step forward. "You have to fight him, Gabby. You beat him before, remember? In the cave? You broke the bond then. I watched you do it."

She hissed, grabbing for the knife that he'd thought-lessly left unprotected in its sheath. He managed to grab her wrists before she could use it. The contact of their skin meeting, the burn between them, had some of the twisted hatred fading from her gaze, a flash of green flickering like a stuttering light in the crimson depths.

<<*Kill him! Kill him!*>>

The green burned out under the crimson flare, her arm with the knife straining against his hold.

Can't fight a blood tie. Not like this.

No, but perhaps he could another way…

"Not that way, cookie." He turned his neck, pur-posely exposing his throat. "If you're going to kill me, then you'll have to do it this way."

He shouldn't have been shocked when her fangs pierced his skin, blood flowing from his jugular into her stomach carved empty by hatred, but he was, his body stiffening with a surge of adrenaline. Instinct screamed for him to fight her. Instead he closed his eyes and forced himself to relax. Three pulls, six, his life was pumping out of him into her, but still he didn't give in to the urge to stop her. The way to fight the evil holding her was not to raise a hand, but to accept, to love unconditionally.

Letting go of her wrists, he slid his hand up her arm to cup the back of her head. "That's right, Gabby. Drink from me. Let me sustain you."

There was a breathless moment when she hesitated, then her arms tightened around him, his own blade sinking into his shoulder as she gripped him tight. He growled then accepted the pain, calling forth from the blade His light. The itch that always came with the touch of such pureness made him want to scream, but he pulled that light into him, calling it through the wound into his very bloodstream. Perhaps it would be enough. Perhaps it could break through the evil that held her. Perhaps the sacrifice of his blood, now infused with His purifying light, would save her. And if not, then perhaps as she drank the last of the life from him, so too would He see to her end…and then see them together afterward.

Valin trembled, his limbs going weightless with weakness, yet for the first time it didn't hurt to be in His light. Because he was going to die with the one he loved.

The sucking lull of her swallowing stopped, a growl rumbling in her throat. He felt the rejection of his thoughts. Holding his breath he stretched out his consciousness, practically weeping as he felt a ghostly trickle of their bond stretching tentatively between them.

<<*Kill him! Kill him!*>> Christos's voice rung through her mind, smashing at the fragile bond.

Not fucking going to work. Gabby was his and his alone. The blood tie. Had. To. Go.

Arm shaking with numb fatigue, he tightened his hand in her hair, pulling her closer as if his presence alone could push back the evil trying to take her from him. Chanting in the back of his constricted throat, Valin began the ceremony that would make Gabby his. All the while he prayed, bargained really, that if He would just see fit to grant him this one wish—save Gabby—he'd trade anything, his life, even his soul to see her returned to herself.

The air pulsed with Christos's rage, but Valin held strong, chanting faster, pushing power behind his words. All that was left were the words.

"Gabby." He stroked his thumb across her cheek, his voice barely a hoarse whisper as he gave her his last promise. "My heart, my life, my soul for yours."

And as if He had actually heard, Valin felt the shift of power. A scream of denial rose in the darkness surrounding them to be cut off a split second later as Gabby tore her mouth away.

Silence descended, the only sound her rapid breathing...and the thudding pulse of his slowing heart.

"Valin?" Her voice, clear and unfettered by the evil blanket, was like a ray of sun after an endless winter, but even the wonder of hearing his name from her lips once more couldn't fight the cold that had taken him.

Teeth chattering, he smiled at her, wanting to give her this last thing. "I love you, Gabby."

Her mouth opened in an *O* of wonder. "I love you too..."

Valin closed his eyes, swallowing. Oh God, how he'd longed to hear those words. Too bad it was too late to enjoy the moment: It was time to pay up.

Chapter 22

Everything came back to Gabriella in an avalanche of denial and horror. The memories, the torture, the things she'd done after she'd given over to fear and hate. She knew deep in her heart that she would never have made it back from that on her own. But Valin had come, they'd fought, and he'd...done something. She stared at him. He still smiled though his eyes had closed. And as she drew back she saw that his entire front was covered with blood, the source evident by the dripping pathway of red that led to two ragged holes at the base of his throat.

Horror clenched in her gut as she recollected the words he'd chanted as she'd drawn the life-giving blood from his veins, the bargain he'd made. "Oh God, Valin, no..." She grasped his head between her hands, twisting it to the side. "Let me seal the wound."

She dragged her tongue over the wound, then did it again, cursing when the skin stubbornly refused to knit.

Too late...

"No!" she cried as what was left of Valin's strength seemed to fade, his body becoming deadweight in her arms. He slipped in her grip, his body sliding to the floor. She slid down with him, managing to keep his head from cracking on the floor, and shifted him just enough that his head lay cradled in her lap.

"Valin...don't you dare die on me. Don't..." She

choked back a sob, her fingers tightening in his thick hair. No way. No way in *hell* was this happening. She couldn't, wouldn't, let him die for her.

Her eyes fell on the knife. She knew the Paladin could use the blade to call His light. Perhaps if she were to…She grabbed up the knife, bracing the tip against her breast as she closed her eyes. Valin wasn't the only one who could bargain.

"Please save him. My life to spare his. Please!" Even if the answer was no then she could at least use the thing to end her own miserable existence. Because Lucifer knew there was no life for her without him.

"Do you really think so?"

Gabby sucked in a breath, her eyelids fluttering against the bright light flooding the room. It was so bright she had to shield her face, turning her head away.

When the light finally eased she lowered her arm, tentatively turning her head back. A woman with fair, shining gold hair in locks down her back stood before them, white gown flowing, and holy shit, were those wings or just a trick of the light that glowed like a fricken supernova around her?

Gabby swallowed, noticing the woman wasn't looking at her but down upon Valin's face, her mouth curled into a fond smile.

"He never did believe in himself enough," the woman said, her voice invoking thoughts of angelic choirs and other such nonsense. And wasn't it rather tacky to be thinking that right now?

The woman lifted her eyes to Gabby, the full of her heavenly-blue gaze bearing down on Gabby's tainted soul. "Until you. You are his light and he is yours."

And okay, the Big Guy was obviously a bit out of touch with reality. Only, yeah, this just as obviously wasn't *Him*. Not that Gabby bought hook, line, and sinker into the whole God is a man thing, or even that He had a gender that could be specified, but, though this woman's presence was powerful, it just wasn't…enough.

I wouldn't be conscious if He were truly here.

She didn't know how she knew this, just that it was true. God's company would be too much for an earthly embodied soul to comprehend. But this woman, no, this *angel* seemed to be under some misinformation if she thought—

The woman chuckled, shaking her head. "Perhaps it is a match made in heaven. I honestly didn't think I'd ever meet anyone who could be as stubbornly foolish as he."

"Angeline?" Gabby gasped, her brain finally snapping into gear.

Angeline tipped her head, kind of a confirmation and a hello. "He told you about me, I take it."

Gabby nodded, easier than saying it was really Christos who'd educated her on Valin's lost mate. Who was standing here. Now. In the same room. Gabby jerked her gaze away, feeling tainted, like the *other* woman simply for holding Valin's lifeless body. Though she'd be damned if she set his head back on the bloodied floor.

"He misses you." She couldn't say missed. Despite the fact it had been almost a minute since she'd picked up the sound of his heartbeat, she couldn't, wouldn't…

Still time. You can still bring him back. Fight for him!

Her gaze dropped to the knife still gripped in her left

hand. Was this woman who she was supposed to bargain with? If so, He had played a cruel trick. His mate, the mother of his child, would of course want him to come home into her embrace.

"I miss him too." Angeline sighed, the light around her rippling. "However, it is not as much as he shall miss you."

Gabby's fist clenched tighter around the knife, her lungs seizing. She understood what Angeline was saying. If she went ahead with this and took her own life, even as part of a bargain, it would not be to go into His realm. Which meant that Valin would be irreversibly lost to her.

"If that is what it takes," Gabby vowed, pleased her lungs cooperated enough to let her calmly agree to the bargain.

Angeline chuckled again, her amusement like a cheese grater on Gabby's effort to be calm and dignified when all she really wanted to do was yell and scream and plead and…yes…break and kill. Starting with this woman who was—Fucking. Laughing. At. Her. Loss.

"Oh, yes, definitely a pair."

Gabby's head snapped up, her eyes narrowing. Angeline tilted her head to the side, her blond curls dancing as she shook her head in the slightest of movements. "What? You think he isn't up there right now trying to make the same bargain?"

A chill ran down Gabby's spine, fear gripping her heart. Between herself and Valin, he had more clout, and though the Grand Poobah might rather keep Valin in the fight, it seemed that Angeline was part of this decision, and so far Gabby hadn't been doing the most spectacular job of endearing herself to the angel.

Gabby shook her head, not sure what she should say to convince Angeline.

"Try the truth," Angeline suggested, her voice strangely gentle after the grating laughter.

The truth was…"It is he who should live, not me. I'm just…" She looked down at her bloodstained skin. Valin's blood, Annie's blood. Oh what had she done?

Unloved. Unwanted. Evil… Monster.

A hand touched her chin, tipping her head. Angeline had sobered completely, her blue eyes darker as if her light had been diminished. "And you have even less belief in yourself than he, don't you?"

Gabby met her gaze, sure that the haunts of her past and how they'd tainted her would be visible to the angel. "I'm a succubus. A vampire. And I killed him. I killed the man I love."

"Love, is it?"

Gabriella flushed, seeing immediately the blasphemy of such a statement in the face of what she'd done.

"He would say he gave his life to spare yours."

Gabby shook her head vehemently. "No! I don't want that. I would not ask that of him."

Angeline pursed her lips, her finger tapping lightly on Gabby's chin. "Hmm. Then I guess there is really only one choice now, isn't there?"

"What?" Gabby all but leapt on her, just barely stopping herself from grabbing her arm. "Tell me, please, what can I do?"

"Will you still give your life for his?" Angeline asked, straightening.

"Yes. YES! I'd give anything." Her life. Her soul. Her very existence—oh, yes, she'd gladly give that. To wipe out the past, to erase all the pain she'd caused?

Angeline nodded, smiling sadly as she gazed once more at Valin. "Then I guess it's time for good-byes."

Gabby blinked down at Valin, her vision blurring, or at least it must have been because he was but a smudge of light before her.

This is it. Say it quickly...

"I love you, Valin. Forgive me." She bent to kiss him, momentarily confused by the salty wetness on her lips as she licked them in preparation. Her tears. Of course. Gently she pressed her mouth to his, needing this one last touch to seal the bargain. Her eyes widened, surprised at the warmth of his lips. She drew back just as the room blazed. Like a star exploding, the power rocked through her, ripping her from her body. And then came the pain. Endless, unfathomable pain as the purging of His light tore through what she guessed was her soul. And God, how could she have been so foolish as to think that being wiped from existence would be the easier path? It went on and on and on and all she wanted to do was scream though she had no earthly body to house such misery.

And then it stopped.

She floated. The light, which had burned before like a raging inferno, now soothed like a balm. It tugged her gently from here to there, touching on everything that was good or even remotely happy in her life, oftentimes showing her things in a way she'd never thought to look at them. She wanted to cry again, though this time her tears would be of joy, as something Logan had once said

to her drifted through her thoughts: *He's a merciful God.*
The truth rang through her being like a cymbal crash,
and she began to think that perhaps, just perhaps He was
merciful enough to hold her here in His planes. And if
that were the case then maybe, someday, she might possibly see Valin again. Even if it would simply be another
good-bye as he passed on to the woman he truly loved.
The mother of his unborn child.

"You little fool. How could you even think I would
pass you by?" The gruff voice pulled her like a bungee
jumper who'd reached the end of her cord, snapping her
back into her body.

She blinked, trying to figure out what the heck had
just happened by opening her eyes. She was still sitting
on her heels in that horrid room only…holy crap…

"Valin?" she choked, reaching for him, only she
couldn't because he was already holding her, his hands
tight on her biceps as he glared at her out of perfectly
alert, perfectly lively eyes. No, make that livid.

She frowned, her body tensing as she waited for the
one-two sucker punch. Bloody room, check. In the coven's house, check. But that was most definitely a very
alive Valin sitting on his heels before her.

Careful, nightmares never end like this.

Oh how well she knew. They got far, far worse than
a little glaring from the man she loved.

Valin gave her a good shake, an imprinted memory
telling her it wasn't the first one in recent moments.
"How dare you try and trade your life for mine."

"What do you mean, how dare I?" She punched him
in the gut, eliciting a satisfying oomph that still did nothing to ease all the pent up anger and horror and fear

she'd felt when she'd first snapped free of Christos's evil influence and realized what she'd done. No, what *he'd* done—selfish bastard! Of course, she ruined her anger by throwing herself at him. He gave another oomph, but caught her, his arms linking with a reassuring tightness around her shoulders.

"Oh, God, you're alive. I can't believe..." Sobs chocked the rest of her words in her throat. Valin's hands slid into her hair, his lips pressing against her forehead as he murmured reassurances. Words like "it's okay" and "I'm here now" and all sorts of crap that didn't change the facts at all and had her heart racing with fear that this was just a horrible, horrible nightmare that would end with her waking and having to relive the eviscerating moment of Valin dying in her arms all over again.

She pulled back, searching out every feature, and finding no telltale inaccuracy, shook her head. "You were dying. And then Angeline came and offered a bargain for your life if I were to give my own."

"I know. And I'm royally pissed that you would even think to take such a bargain."

She stilled, wondering if this was the sign that this was not at all real: He'd given no flicker of pain at the mention of Angeline's name.

A Paladin never stops grieving for a lost mate.

She pressed out tentatively with her mind. Nothing in the room. Nor the mansion. Besides, wouldn't she feel if Christos had any control on her still? Even he had difficulty hiding the evil within the lie.

"I don't understand," she said carefully, still not convinced this wasn't some sort of sick joke.

Valin shook his head, making a garbled noise that sounded like a combination of frustration and disbelief. "She was right; you are as much a stubborn fool as I am."

"What are you—" she started to question, but he cut her off.

"*You're* my bond mate, Gabby. Angeline was only my pair mate."

"Pair mate?"

He nodded. "Compatibility pairing. Friends. Best friends even. And I do miss Angeline, shall always miss her and my unborn child. But you are of my heart. The soul to complete my own. And though I may miss them, it's you I need."

Her mind reeled, hope trying to blossom through the thick fog of disbelief. "But the bargain?"

"You're not the only one who can bargain."

No shit, but if those in charge had gone with his, then why was he here? Not that she'd argue, but…She narrowed her eyes. "What did you bargain for?"

"I just pointed out that He needs warriors. But I also told him I wouldn't come back without my mate. Of course, my mate had already stupidly bargained away her own life so there was only one thing to do."

Her heart hammered. Here it was, the sucker punch. "What's that?"

He tipped his head, stroking her cheek. "How do you feel, Gabby?"

She thought about it, mentally checking each part of her body. Relatively whole, considering she'd been blasted with His light. In fact, she didn't even ache much and…she glanced down, gasping at the sight of the white gown that clung to her clean skin. No blood, no wounds; in fact, the only thing to mar its smooth lines was the bulge along one of her thighs.

"How?" Feeling as if she were poking at a scorpion, she gingerly fingered the lump through the thin material—her hand closing around the object she already knew was there.

"This can't be right." She lifted her gaze to Valin's, her heart thumping again at the simple pleasure of seeing the familiar mischievous glint in his eyes.

"Oh it's right. Welcome to the club, cookie."

She shook her head, unable to comprehend or believe. How could she know this was real?

"Go ahead, test it out."

Well, she supposed that was one way.

Taking a deep breath she pulled the knife from the holder on her thigh, lifting the jewel-encrusted weapon before her face. It was a curved blade, symbols etched into the blade itself. And when she blew out a breath, thinking of the serenity that had embraced her after the purging, energy throbbed through the blade, the glow of His light pulsing in rhythm with the one that lay on the floor beside them.

Her gaze flew to Valin's. His mouth curled up in a broad grin. He leaned close, his words but a warm whisper across the side of her face. "Smile, Gabby. This is a happy moment, don't you think?"

Her lips curved upward, but stopped partway there. Something was different. Very much so. Practically hyperventilating, she rubbed her tongue over her front teeth. Her hand snapped over her mouth.

"Holy crap," she said, the exclamation muffled by her

hand. She felt her teeth, the evenness of them. "But I'm not…I didn't actually die, did I?"

He shook his head. "Technically, neither of us did."

"You didn't? Because, uh, you seemed pretty dead to me." No heartbeat. For what? Four? Five minutes?

"I *tried* to make a bargain, but He didn't much like it and kept me waiting while He sent Angeline to see if He had a better one…yours, to be precise."

"But I had nothing to give, nothing but my life."

"Oh Gabby, you're so wrong." He pushed a lock of hair back from her face, his bourbon eyes deepening with emotion as he looked into hers. "Luckily He's smarter than the both of us combined."

"So He took my life and made me a warrior?"

"You're still you, Gabby, warrior or not. But you'd bargained a life for mine. You just didn't specify which life, so He made an executive decision."

"Which life?"

"Your Paladin life, your life as a succubus, or your one as a vampire. Guess He picked to get rid of the life that had tainted you with the most darkness."

As if his words called to it, darkness edged in against the halo of light cast by the blades, memories both new and old tumbling through her mind.

"Oh, baby." Valin reached for her, his despair flooding her from across their bond. And wow, that was going to take some getting used to. This mate bond thing was far more intense than a simple blood bond.

"I'm sorry those couldn't be taken from you too," he said. "Sorry you ever had to go through that."

She wasn't. Not when those horrors had led to this moment. To them. She would not let those memories hurt him through their bond though, their *mate* bond. Ruthlessly she cut the streaming feed of horror off, wrangling them up into one ranging bonfire. But old habits, or in this case nightmares, died hard, and she needed something to smother all that hate and pain, to replace those emotions and shut those memories away for good.

She grabbed his shirt, pulling him close enough to smash her lips against his. He growled, his arms tightening around her back as he, too, sought to get closer. Yes, this is what she needed. His mouth on hers. His hands touching her. His mind caressing hers. And his soul... Light engulfed them, a great sense of peace taking over as their passion burned away the remaining darkness.

When they were both breathless, she pulled away, knowing now that she was going to be okay. No, better—she was finally free. This—a Paladin—was who she'd always been meant to be. And though the journey to now had frankly sucked, both dark and light had been needed to get her to this point.

Her smile faded, her gaze taking in the residual horror of the room. Darkness still lay like a blight here and would for so long as the man responsible lived. "Christos and his followers are still alive."

"Does it matter?" Valin asked. She could feel his concern and knew that he worried that what Christos had done to her still affected her, that she still might lose sight of the important things in life while searching for her revenge.

"No. Not in the way you mean." She shook her head, tipping it up to his. "Christos can't touch me anymore. Not when I'm with you."

He pushed back a tendril of hair, his dark eyes hot on hers. "You'll always be with me. Now that I've found you, there is no way I'm letting you go."

She raised her brow, wondering if she should sucker punch him again. "You sound kind of possessive, don't you?"

"I *am* possessive. You're mine, Gabby. My heart, my lover, and my partner."

And, all right then…she leaned against him, sighing. "I can live with that."

"Good." He pressed his lips to her forehead. "Now let's get out of here."

She smiled. "You ready to go kick some ass, partner?"

"After, but first…" He stood, scooping her up in the process, and carried her like some sort of helpless bride toward the doorway.

"Valin!" she yelped as he bumped her feet against the jagged doorframe and maneuvered them into the hall. "Put me down," she insisted, but oh, gee, it was strange she couldn't find an ounce of willpower to put up any sort of fight. And whoops, those were her arms wrapping around his neck, weren't they?

"Not on your life, cookie. You might run away."

She narrowed her eyes. "Why would I run away?"

"We have a honeymoon to go on."

"That doesn't sound so bad…"

"After we attend to the little detail of our formal bonding ceremony, that is."

"Hmmm…" She gnawed her lip. "I imagine that's not going to go over too well with your stuffy council."

"They're your stuffy council now too. And you think I care?"

"No." She tightened her arms around his neck, pecking his chin with a light kiss. "And that's what I love about you."

He stopped, his feet posed on the threshold of the mansion as he closed his eyes and drew in deep breath.

"Valin?" she asked, concern making her heart skip as she scanned the grounds. "Is ther—"

"Say that again."

She looked back at him. "What? That I love you?"

"Yes, that." He opened his eyes, his heart, no, his very soul burning into hers through his gaze. "You don't know how long I've waited to hear those words."

Her chest warmed, filling every dark corner and crevice she'd ever housed and burning away the last of the coldness that had touched her for so long. He loved her, and because she'd been brave enough to love him back, they had their whole lives to figure out just where their faith in each other would take them.

"I love you, Valin," she told him, letting him see all the way into her heart. "You're mine too. Heart, body, and soul."

"Ah, cookie, you were so worth the wait." And with that he carried her out into the falling twilight. Her black knight. Her beacon of strength in their dark and often crazy world. Her partner.

Epilogue

CHRISTOS FELL TO THE CAVE FLOOR, HIS KNEECAPS cracking against the blackened stone. Ignoring the pain, he lowered himself further, head against the rough surface, arms stretched out in supplication. There was no amount of too much in the groveling he was about to perform.

Lucifer stepped down from his thrown, paced around him, the dark caress of the shadows that enfolded him licking at Christos like ice-cold fire. Christos resisted the urge to plead, knowing that his failures would only be judged more harshly for such a weakness.

"Well, my son? Do you wish to try and tell me what went wrong?"

Christos clenched his teeth, his fury rekindled despite his precarious situation. What went wrong was that somehow the freak of a Paladin had overcome Christos and Gabby's blood bond. No, not overcome; somehow the Paladin had purged the blood Gabby had drunk from Christos's vein, making her his.

Shadows pulsed around Lucifer as he stared down at him, the oppressiveness of his lord's inaction setting every one of Christos's nerves on edge. The silence went on for so long that when his master finally spoke, Christos felt like he'd been severed.

"But your blood, you say it transformed her, obliterated her light."

"Not well enough, obviously." And didn't that burn. He'd thought, finally, that he'd found the one. The prophesied one, his queen. Born of light and dark; her Paladin heritage, his blood in her veins. It should have worked, for wasn't he, short of Lucifer himself, the epitome of dark? Beyond that other freak, Karissa, there had been no other who had come close to meeting the criteria. And since that experiment had backfired in all their faces, Christos had been born anew, sure in the knowledge that his original instincts that Gabby was the one had been correct. But no. He'd been wrong. Again. And now he'd be kowtowing to Lucifer and his general until he could live this failure down.

"Hmm…obviously you *are* correct."

Christos held his breath. Above him Lucifer rolled his shoulders, his wings unfurling to wrap around Christos's prone form. Black. Suffocating. The burning smell of smoke and charred flesh. Christos's ribs locked down, the putrid air trapped in his chest. A single thought was all it would take to end him.

The wings eased back and Christos worked hard not to gulp at the fresh air. A clawed finger stroked across his cheek, the action almost comforting if not for the indifference stamped in Lucifer's nightmarish face. "It did work though, for a while, yes?"

"My lord?" Christos asked, unsure whether to be hopeful or worried by his liege lord's question.

"Ah, my son…child of Lilith. How blind I have been."

Before Christos could fathom what he meant, Lucifer plucked a transparent blade out of nothingness and plunged it into Christos's gut. Christos screamed, his hand clenched over Lucifer's on the hilt as his lord and master began to chant. Christos watched in disbelief as his blood wicked up the blade, seeping into it and staining it black.

The blade was yanked free. Christos gasped, falling back to the floor. With his hands clutched over the wound, he watched Lucifer raise the black knife over his head, twisting it this way and that as he mounted the carved steps to his throne. Christos squinted, trying to see through the dimming fog of pain, but it was so hard to see, the light around the knife seeming to seep right into the hungry blade.

"Oh yes. How blind indeed." Lucifer reverently placed the black knife down on the arm of his throne before turning back and descending the stairs.

"Father?" Christos implored, his hand still clenched tight against the seeping wound. Surely his lord master would see to him now. Surely he would forgive him this simple mistake.

A flicker of annoyance crossed Lucifer's face, his steps faltering, but then he grumbled something under his breath, waving his hand negligently at his son as he stopped before him.

The pain eased, the skin knitting back together beneath Christos's hands. "Oh, thank you, thank you, my lord," he gasped, struggling back to his feet despite the dizziness that still swept over him.

"Come, my son," Lucifer said, stretching his right hand out to Christos. "There is much work to be done."

The significance of Lucifer offering his right hand was not lost on Christos. Elation rose in his blackened heart, giving him the strength to grasp the offering. It wasn't until Lucifer's hand closed over his own, dragging him to him, and a second knife drove into his newly healed wound that he thought, perhaps, he should have questioned such a gift.

"Fear not, my son," Lucifer attempted to soothe as he drew out the second blade and raised it over their heads. "I have finally discovered the purpose of your existence, don't you see?"

And as Christos lifted his eyes he did see... Unfortunately, what he saw made him weep. Five blades after that, he'd stopped, but only because his efforts had changed to something new: wishing he'd never been re-born.

Read on for an excerpt from book one
in the Paladin Warriors series

Deliver Me from Darkness

Shouldn't have opened the door. Roland instinctively knew the fragile-looking burden draped over Calhoun's arms was going to wreak all kinds of havoc on his well-ordered life.

To hell with the door; he shouldn't have answered the damn phone. Then he wouldn't have been swayed by the rare frantic tone in Calhoun's voice when he'd called begging for a favor. 'Course, even if Roland hadn't picked up the phone, Calhoun would have assumed Roland to be in at this time of the afternoon and come pounding anyway. And yeah, Roland could have ignored that too, but doing so went against every ingrained fabric of his being. At least the being he'd once been.

This is what I get for remembering my manners.

"Thanks for this." Calhoun brushed by Roland, twisting so as not to bump the head of his precious cargo on the master bedroom door.

Roland grunted and moved into the bathroom in search of a towel. Best to keep his opinion to himself. *Get that scrawny thing and your sorry ass out of here* would not go over well.

Mumbling a string of curses, Roland yanked on the faux-antique glass knob of the teak cabinet and searched the handcrafted shelving for a sacrifice. All his towels were new. Everything in his loft was new. He liked new. Crisp, clean.

Unsoiled.

The tension in his shoulders crept down his back. With senses as heightened as his, any tainting of his personal belongings made relaxing difficult. It was going to take him weeks of cleaning and nighttime airings to remove the urchin's scent: like a friggin' garden...fresh-bloomed lavender, dewy mornings, and dirt. The dirt would only ruin his sheets, but the other smells had him spiraling down toward crazy.

Eyeing his choices, he grabbed one of the pristine white towels that didn't still have a tag on it and headed back to the bedroom. His efforts were wasted. Calhoun had already pulled back the sleep-rumpled blankets and was laying the filthy jumble of scraped elbows and dirty denim on Roland's clean sheets. Roland sighed and tossed the towel on the nearby dresser.

The bed was officially ruined. He hoped the cost of his newfound kindness would be limited to the bed. He hadn't even been here a week and his new sanctuary was being unsanctified. It had taken him months to find a New York City loft without any stains of violence, another to have it remodeled to his exact specifications, and still another to purge it of the stink from the contractors who had redone it. He suspected the lingering presence of this...girl...would take far longer to expunge.

"How long are you going to be?" Roland asked, trying to keep his displeasure from sliding into his tone. Calhoun was right; Roland did owe him a favor—a big one too. Roland just wasn't sure if this qualified. This wasn't big; it was colossal, and not only because of the cost of his Stearns & Foster.

Calhoun glanced up at him absently from where he'd been carefully tucking Roland's new, unwanted guest into the vast California king bed.

Damn. I loved that bed.

Calhoun blinked as if he had to think about what Roland had asked, his concentration obviously still on the woman currently soiling Roland's new silk sheets.

"I hope to finish by dark. If not, soon after," Calhoun finally said when he got his head out of his ass—or maybe that was his head out of his dick.

"Make it dark," Roland said, his breath hissing through clenched teeth in an effort not to inhale anymore of *her* scent. Not that it mattered. All he succeeded in doing was altering the girl's heady pheromones into candied sugar on his tongue.

And this was why he didn't allow humans, especially females, into his home. The seductive scents, the gentle whoosh of blood pumping, and the soft murmurs she'd make as she tossed and turned in *his* sheets. Roland fisted his hands. The call to rut, to feed, was like a rabid animal clawing at his insides. He'd kept that animal carefully caged, would keep it caged. Yet something of his internal trauma must have shown in his eyes. Calhoun's gaze snapped from Roland to the skinny slip of a girl he'd so lovingly tucked in bed, and then back to Roland again, his expression becoming increasingly alarmed.

Calhoun stood to his full height, which at a towering six foot five put him nose to eyebrow with Roland. The air in the room began to tingle. Roland could feel the gathering of power. See the aura shimmering around his supposed friend. That faint light singed Roland's skin.

Roland hissed, hastily giving ground until he was across the room and practically pressed into the panel that hid his walk-in closet. Fury mounted within him and he had to work hard to suppress the vicious beast from awakening. He would never hurt Calhoun. His best friend, the only one who'd stood by him, the one Paladin who'd seen enough humanity left in Roland to take the chance to try and save him…to let him exist. But even Roland had his limits, and even for Calhoun he would not quiver like some cowed dog in a shadowy corner.

"You're teetering on the edge, Calhoun," he snarled, letting the fire spark in his eyes to emphasize his words. It might burn him, but he could have Calhoun's throat in his hand before the Paladin could draw enough heavenly light to turn him to ash.

Calhoun stopped glowing, but even so, Roland could sense the barely contained power bubbling beneath the surface.

"Is this going to be a problem for you?" Calhoun asked, his eyes flint gray.

"No." Roland rubbed his face. The skin was tender, but no real damage. "But it's been days."

Calhoun took a step forward, a lion ready to lunge into battle. "You won't touch her."

"I never said I would," Roland ground out from between clenched teeth. "She's safe from me."

Calhoun's eyes narrowed to slits.

"Jesus, Calhoun. I haven't taken an innocent since—"

"Since when?"

"Since you came after me," Roland finished. A flash

of memory: the red haze of the bloodlust, the loss of self. How many innocents had he taken? He didn't know.

"She's safe with me. Regardless of when you return," Roland said, then curled his lip in distaste. "I have some emergency supplies in the freezer."

Pig blood and Red Cross discards. Lucky for him he was immune to illness. Though sometimes he wondered if contracting some horrific disease would have been a better way to go than this interminable hell he lived.

The tension in Calhoun's body eased. He clamped a hand on Roland's shoulder. "Thank you. After this, I'll owe *you* one."

"Get back here by dark and we'll call it even," Roland told him, annoyance making his voice sound as if it were being dragged over gravel.

Calhoun chuckled. Turning back to the bed, he gave the slumbering girl one last long gaze. The softening in his eyes alarmed Roland. Calhoun was tough as nails. Hell, even his dry humor was rusty. What was she to him?

"She's special, Roland," Calhoun stated, his awed tone confirming Roland's fears. Calhoun was already half gone. "Take care of her."

"Special how?" Roland hoped Calhoun meant special in the gifted kind of way, not special in the till-death way. Humans and Paladin didn't mix. It was that whole mortality thing. "You said yourself that she passed out within seconds of showing up on your doorstep."

That's about all he'd gotten from Calhoun. Some woman had shown up at his door and passed out. Moments later the reason for her flight had become apparent as Calhoun's sensors all went off. Rather than face an army of Ganelon's underworld fiends, Calhoun had grabbed his new burden and abandoned ship. And come here.

Why here? Why not to Haven? And who was she that she'd attracted the attention of Ganelon's minions?

Acknowledgments

As always, I'd like to thank the hardworking team at Sourcebooks. Without them, this book wouldn't have been possible. Extra special thanks goes out to my BETA group and the awesome readers out there who've cheered me on and kept clamoring for more. And last but not least, I'd like to thank the great peeps on my Facebook page for their wonderful input, most especially Christina W. for the awesome villain name and Marlene R. for the inspiring sexy line.

About the Author

While growing up, Tes Hilaire always wanted to see a ghost. Or meet an angel. Or dine with a vampire. Despite her vivid imagination, none of these things ever happened…yet. In the meantime, she writes about them from her home in North Carolina where she lives with her hero, her cat, a son, and two daughters—one of whom claims to actually have *seen* a ghost (Tes is very jealous). She hates lima beans, loves spaghetti, and still believes in the impossible. For more about Tes and her books, visit TesHilaire.com or visit her on Facebook at www.facebook.com/TesHilaireAuthor.

Deliver Me from Temptation

Paladin Warriors

by Tes Hilaire

—◆◆◆—

He may look like an angel, but his touch is pure sin.

When things go bump in the night, Logan bumps back. Vampires, demons, succubi—you name it, he's fought it. His job as a Paladin angel warrior is to protect humans. Not fall for one.

Detective Jessica Waters protects humans too—with her Glock and a good set of handcuffs. She doesn't believe in fate. But if anyone looks like a gift from the gods, it's Logan. And he clearly knows more about her case than he's letting on…

—◆◆◆—

"Intriguing paranormal creatures and torment abound… The sex is great, and the ending is fun." —*Booklist*

"An enthralling, multilayered story…the passion and intensity of the story will sweep away series beginners and fans alike." —*RT Book Reviews*, 4 Stars

"Fast-paced…Fans of the first tale will be delighted to see more of their favorite characters." —*Publishers Weekly*

For more Tes Hilaire, visit:

www.sourcebooks.com

Deliver Me from Darkness

by Tes Hilaire

Angel to vampire is a long way to fall.

A stranger in the night...

He had once been a warrior of the Light, one of the revered Paladin. A protector. But now he lives in darkness, and the shadows are his sanctuary. Every day is a struggle to overcome the bloodlust. Especially the day Karissa shows up on his doorstep.

Comes knocking on the door

She is light and bright and everything beautiful—despite her scratches and torn clothes. Every creature of the night is after her. So is every male Paladin. Because Karissa is the last female of their kind. But she is *his*. Roland may not have a soul, but he can't deny his heart.

"Dark, sexy, and intense! Hilaire blazes a
new path in paranormal romance."
—Sophie Jordan, *New York Times* bestselling author

For more Tes Hilaire, visit:

www.sourcebooks.com

Tall, Dark, and Vampire

by Sara Humphreys

She always knew Fate was cruel...

The last person Olivia expected to turn up at her club was her one true love. It would normally be great to see him, *except he's been dead for centuries.* Olivia really thought she had moved on with her immortal life, but as soon as she sees Doug Paxton, she knows she'd rather die than lose him again. And that's a real problem...

But this is beyond the pale...

Doug is a no-nonsense cop by day, but his nights are tormented by dreams of a gorgeous redhead who's so much a part of him, she seems to be in his blood. When he meets Olivia face-to-face, long-buried memories begin to surface. She might be the answer to his prayers...or she might be the death of him.

Praise for Untamed:

"The characters are well-developed, the twists and turns of the plot are well-crafted, and the situations are alternately funny, action-packed, and sensual." —*Fresh Fiction*

"An excellent paranormal romance with awesome world-building and strong leads." —*The Romance Reviews*

For more Sara Humphreys, visit:

www.sourcebooks.com

Unclaimed

The Amoveo Legend

by Sara Humphreys

—⁓—

She brings out the beast in him…

She works hard to be normal…

Tatiana Winters loves the freedom of her life as a veterinarian in Oregon. It's only reluctantly that she agrees to help cure a mysterious illness among the horses on a Montana ranch—the ranch of the Amoveo Prince. Tatiana is no ordinary vet— she's a hybrid from the Timber Wolf Clan, but she wants nothing to do with the world of the Amoveo shifters.

But there's no escaping destiny

Dominic Trejada serves as a Guardian, one of the elite protectors of the Prince's Montana ranch. As a dedicated Amoveo warrior, he is desperate to find his mate, and time is running out. He knows Tatiana is the one—but if he can't convince her, he may not be able to protect her from the evil that's rapidly closing in…

—⁓—

Praise for Undone:

Spellbinding…This fast-paced, jam-packed thrill ride will delight paranormal romance fans." —*Publishers Weekly*

For more Sara Humphreys, visit:

www.sourcebooks.com

Prince of Power

by Elisabeth Staab

This fight is personal…

Wizards and vampires have been mortal enemies since the beginning. Now Anton, son of the Wizard Master, has one last chance to steal the unique powers of the vampire king's beautiful sister, Tyra…and then kill her. But when he meets Tyra face-to-face, everything changes…

Tyra will stop at nothing to defeat the wizards, until Anton saves her life and she suddenly sees an opportunity she never could have imagined.

As the sparks ignite between them, together they could bring an end to the war that's decimating their people, but only if they can find a way to trust each other…

"Staab's strong sophomore effort continues the dark fantasy romance series begun with King of Darkness." —*Publishers Weekly*

For more Elisabeth Staab, visit:

www.sourcebooks.com

A Spy to Die For

by Kris DeLake

—∿∿—

Two spies. A hundred secrets. And one true love.

On opposite sides of a high-stakes game, lust lures two spies together in a passionate encounter. Little do they know that the heat of the moment would bind them, turning their worlds upside down. Hunted by deadly assassins, can the pair and their love withstand the onslaught?

—∿∿—

"This lovely little read will leave you breathless as you turn each page, praying that Sky and Jack stay alive and in each other's arms." —*Book Loons*

"Inventive and charmingly funny…The emotional connection between the main characters is so heartfelt, and the witty repartee so engaging, that it's easy to get wrapped up in their story." —*RT Book Reviews*

For more Kris DeLake, visit:

www.sourcebooks.com

Lord of the Hunt

by Shona Husk

―᠁―

Raised in the mortal world, the fairy Taryn never planned on going back to Annwyn, much less to Court. But with the power shift imminent, she is her parents' only hope of securing a pardon from exile and avoiding certain death.

Verden, Lord of the Hunt, swore to serve the King. But as the magic of Annwyn fails and the Prince makes ready to take the throne, Verden knows his days as Hunter are numbered.

When Taryn and Verden meet, their attraction is instant and devastating. Their love could bring down a queen and change the mortal world forever.

―᠁―

Praise for **For the Love of a Goblin Warrior:**

"Ms. Husk outdid herself in this book…
Once I got into the story, I couldn't put it down."
—*Night Owl Romance* Reviewer Top Pick

"Husk has an amazing ability to weave a
mesmerizing story with a magical dark
fairy-tale feel." —*Love Romance Passion*

"An entertaining and unique read. Shona Husk
creates a dark yet delightful world where romance
and fantasy combine." —*Romance Reviews*

For more of the **Shadowlands** series, visit:

www.sourcebooks.com